JUDICIOUS MURDER

Val Bruech

Smoking Gun Publishing, LLC
St. Louis, MO

Cover and Interior Design by Smoking Gun Publishing, LLC

This is a work of fiction, and is produced from the author's imagination. People, places and things mentioned in this novel are used in a fictional manner.

ISBN: 978-1-940586-36-6

Library of Congress Control Number: 2016956220

Visit us on the web at www.smokinggunpublishing.com

Published by Smoking Gun Publishing, LLC
Printed in the United States of America

Acknowledgements

I wish to express my appreciation and gratitude to the following: my adult children, Sarah, Annie and Rob, for their encouragement and enthusiasm; to my ex, Brad Hayes, for putting dinner together from whatever he could find in the kitchen while I was writing; to good friend Dan Doody whose early review and thoughtful criticism moved this book forward; to the team at Smoking Gun Publishing: Claire Applewhite, Lois Mans, designer and Mary Ward Menke, editor, whose professionalism and patience are boundless.

A very special thank you to Myrna Daly and Joyce Lekas, my critique partners. Their countless hours of critical reading and wise suggestions made this book so much better.

Many thanks to Bob and Carla whose enthusiasm has kept me going.

My deepest gratitude to my friend of many years, Angela (Muffie) Zylka, who has a knack for bringing people together and introduced me to the wonderful people at Smoking Gun Publishing.

Dedication

For the criminal defense lawyers in Joliet, Illinois who taught me what it means to be a zealous advocate.

CHAPTER ONE

My client was clocked doing fifty in a thirty-mile-an-hour zone. Unfortunately, he was going the wrong way on a one-way street, but none of that mattered. The cocaine the arresting officer found in his car did. If we lost this trial, Ronald Perry would be spending his next several birthdays in the penitentiary.

It was my turn to cross-examine the arresting cop. I took a quick inventory, made sure my blouse was tucked into my skirt, and stood up.

"Officer." I tapped my pencil on counsel table so I had everyone's attention. "As you approached the car on foot, Mr. Perry rolled down his window without hesitation?"

"Well, he tried, but it was a manual window and the crank…well, it came off in his hand."

The jury's snickering faded with a stern look from Judge Denault.

"At that point, you grabbed the handle and yanked the driver's door open?"

"I pulled the door open, correct. Officer safety," he declared, and puffed his chest out a few inches.

Right. The ultimate justification for an intrusion into a place the cops want to go but have no right to be.

I stood and strode to the exhibit table, picked up a dark blue prescription bottle that had previously been admitted into evidence and held it up. The white powder inside it had tested positive for cocaine.

"This bottle was in plain view on the front passenger seat?"

"Plain view, yes."

"As you stood there outside the vehicle, you could not see inside the bottle, could you?"

"N…n…no." He shifted uneasily in the witness chair.

"And you had no reason to think there was an unlawful substance contained in that bottle, did you?"

The witness rubbed his chin. African-American male driving crazy in a high-crime neighborhood in a Chicago suburb *was* a reason, for a cop, but he knew he couldn't say that, and I knew he knew.

"Based on his driving behavior, I felt it was a legitimate request."

Zing. A flesh wound, not mortal. This guy was good.

I took a step toward the witness stand. "So let me get this straight, Officer. Mr. Perry made no attempt to push the bottle between the seat cushion and the seat back, no furtive gesture under the seat, didn't try to jam the bottle into his pocket?"

"Not that I recall." He glared at me. The jury couldn't miss it.

"The name on the prescription bottle was that of a Patricia McBroom?"

"Right."

"And Ms. McBroom is currently in long-term drug rehab, is that correct?"

"Objection!" Assistant state's attorney Roger Foster levitated out of his chair.

We argued over the relevancy of that question. The objection was sustained, so the cop didn't have to answer, but the jury was getting the picture.

"My client told you he had just dropped Patricia off at her home, correct?"

"Affirmative."

"And he told you he was driving fast because another car seemed to be chasing him?"

The officer chortled.

"He said that, yes."

"And he said he was not familiar with the neighborhood?"

"Yeah."

"And in fact it is a dangerous, high-crime area, isn't it?"

He fixed his gaze on a dust bunny scooting across the floor.

"Officer?"

"Only when clients like yours race through it."

"Your Honor, strike the last remark please."

"The witness will be responsive to the question. Answer stricken," the judge said.

I wrapped one hand around the other so I wouldn't be tempted to throw a pen at the witness.

"And when you asked him where the prescription bottle came from, he said it might have fallen out of his girlfriend's purse, is that right?"

"That's what he said."

"Isn't it true, officer, that when Mr. Perry first saw the bottle he picked it up and said, "What's that?"

"Yes." Lips pressed together in a grim line.

"And that reaction is consistent, is it not, with Mr. Perry's position that he was unaware of the bottle or its contents until you pointed it out to him?"

"It's consistent with a cover-up."

"Judge, will you please admonish the witness."

Reluctantly, like I had just asked him to remove his own molar, the judge told the cop to answer only the question posed and refrain from comment. Then, helpfully, he reminded the witness that the Assistant State's Attorney would have an opportunity to question him again on re-direct.

"Officer, Mr. Perry handed you the bottle immediately after you requested it, right?"

The cop glared. "Yeah."

"Hardly a cover-up." I sat down before the judge could chide me for the gratuitous observation.

"We've been working since eight forty-five. It is now ten o'clock." The judge was speaking for the benefit of the audio recorder which would be transcribed in the event of an appeal. "The jury deserves a coffee break. Fifteen minutes."

Judgespeak for weak kidneys. I warned my client not to make eye contact or speak to any of the jurors. As I swept through the wooden gate that separates the players from the spectators, my opponent, Roger Foster, got in my space.

"The jury never should have heard that bit about the girlfriend being in drug treatment," he fumed.

"Right. Juries should only hear what the State spoon-feeds them. Last time I checked the Bill of Rights, the defense gets to put on a case, too."

I opened the double doors into the main corridor. Usually by this time of morning the large volume calls like traffic were winding down and the halls were deserted except for a few folks who showed up at the wrong time or the wrong date or perhaps the wrong courthouse. But today attorneys and court personnel drifted by with expressions ranging from consternation to disbelief. I felt like I had just walked onto a movie set where everyone knew the script except me. I stopped short and Roger crashed into me.

"What are all these people doing here?" I asked.

His head swiveled around like a duckling searching for its mommy. "Dunno."

My good friend Kevin Lange materialized from a crowd disembarking from the elevators. His ruddy complexion was as gray as parchment paper.

"Susan. We need to talk." He grabbed my hand and led me around the corner to a quiet alcove near the jury commissioner's office. Behind rimless glasses his eyes were troubled. "Something's happened to Sam. I'm on my way to the hospital. I knew you'd want to come."

"Hospital? What do you mean? What's going on?"

"I heard he was attacked. Apparently it happened in his chambers."

This was not making sense, things like that don't happen, not here, not to Sam.

"You should come with me. Let's go." He pulled my hand and led me to the staircase.

"Kev, wait, I gotta tell Judge Denault. Be back in a minute."

I burst into Denault's office. He had been apprised of Sam's situation via e-mail when he arrived in his chambers. He was amenable to a recess until noon if my opponent would agree. I called Roger and he graciously acquiesced. He needed the time to shore up his case. I found my client, told him he was free for a while, then Kevin and I made a dash for his red BMW.

"Did someone break in? Have they arrested anybody?" My words tumbled out as our car doors slammed in unison.

"The courthouse called right before I came to get you. All I know is what they told me."

"What about Betty? Does she know? Where is she?"

Sam and his wife had the kind of marriage I wanted if I ever grew up and found the right guy. They thrived in their nine-to-five lives, and when they came together at the end of the day, they were like two teenagers in love for the first time. A cynic would call it a fairytale I called it damn lucky.

"I'm sure someone took care of that," Kevin responded. "They probably sent a car for her. She shouldn't drive."

The Beamer rumbled to life. We rocketed out of the lot and turned the corner on two wheels. White knuckles gripped the door handle. Mine.

"Maybe Betty's not the only one who shouldn't drive."

He shot me a glance, then lightened up on the gas. "Right. Sorry."

Minutes later we swerved into the hospital's circular drive. Kevin slammed on the brakes and we dashed in the emergency room entrance. The maternal-looking woman at the reception desk gave us a welcoming smile but it disappeared when Kevin asked her about Judge Kendall. She asked who we were, then told us to take a seat while she made a phone call. The weight of an entire law library settled on my chest.

We sank into two cushioned armchairs, deep in separate thoughts. Five years ago, when I had a chance to learn technique and share the passion of a master litigator like Sam Kendall, I didn't have to think twice. Since then he and I had tried dozens of cases together, always defending the unjustly accused. In the grubby world of toe-to-toe litigation he was my hero; in the real world he was my best friend. I leaned over, elbows on knees, my mind as scattered as the chips in the terrazzo floor. A minute, perhaps an hour later, gray slacks appeared above black tousled loafers. I looked up into a vaguely familiar face.

"Good of you to come." The voice was husky, deep.

"Griff," Kevin acknowledged.

That would be Griffen Bartley, Sam's nephew, and a newly-minted lawyer in Sam's former law firm.

The newcomer nodded at me, then sank to his haunches. We leaned toward each other till all three heads almost touched.

"He didn't make it." Bartley's voice broke. He took a ragged breath. "Sam's gone."

CHAPTER TWO

"I'm sorry, ma'am. No admittance."

One of Joliet's finest rookies folded his arms across a scrawny chest, blocking the entrance to a narrow hallway that was criss-crossed by a yellow banner that spelled "EVIDENCE" in bold letters.

"I'd like to see Ross, Chief of Homicide," I said.

"He's busy right now."

"Tell him Susan Marshfield is here."

"I can't leave my post."

"Use your radio."

He ran a tongue over pale, thin lips.

"The one on your shoulder." I tapped his transmitter helpfully.

The banner was thrust apart and a man whose size marked him as a regular customer at the Really Big and Tall Men's Store stepped through. He took in the scene with a brief glance.

"What's going on here, Jamison?"

"The lady wants to see Ross, Lieutenant. I told her he's busy."

"Can I help you." It was not a question. The giant's face was all hard planes. His buzz cut was just long enough to tell that his hair was bronze. The early-onset five o'clock shadow magnified the tough guy image.

"I'm Susan Marshfield. I'm a friend of Sam's…Judge Kendall and I…need to see Ross."

"Al Tite. Nice to meet you, Ms. Marshfield."

His gaze was no-holds-barred appraising, but his tone was a shade less curt than earlier. The name Tite didn't set off any alarms in my memory bank.

"I can take you to Ross."

He parted the ribbons of tape. I was still in battle gear: tailored blue business suit, nylons, and three-inch heels. There was no graceful way to navigate the yellow banners so I hiked up my skirt, bent my five-foot ten-inch frame at the waist and high-stepped through them. We followed the narrow corridor to a perimeter hallway and turned right.

A uniformed sergeant guarded the entry to a small anteroom. Tite nodded at her and we proceeded into Sam's tiny reception room which doubled as a court reporter's office. A second door, wide open now, led to Sam's chambers. A baseball-sized object stuck in my throat. Belatedly, I wondered if I really wanted to be here at this exact moment.

I crossed the threshold and stopped. Sam's massive "state occasion" desk dominated his chambers. If he had a net and paddles, he could play Ping-Pong on it. Behind the desk a floor-to-ceiling window framed a sky that grew darker as a spring thundercloud swept in. On the left wall, framed diplomas, tributes, and bar membership plaques hung above a leather couch. The other two walls held built-in bookshelves filled with monotonous rows of law volumes broken up by photographs of Sam and his family at various stages of their lives. A small chess table, pieces strategically deployed, waited in the center of the room for the players to resume the game. Sam's private bathroom was tucked away in the far rear corner: judges in Will County don't relieve themselves in the presence of the common folk.

A smaller desk rested near the bathroom. Briefs, books and legal pads were piled high concealing its chips and scars, but I knew most of them. This desk had come with Sam from his law office; he and I had toiled over this slab of wood, argued across it, pounded on it in frustration.

Constantine Ross had settled in comfortably behind the small desk and was examining the contents of each drawer. Anger surged at his invasion of Sam's private domain. On past occasions, when we had to deal with the police department and Ross was involved, he would go out of his way to make our task more difficult. Whenever I had had the pleasure of cross-examining him, the sneer in his voice conveyed his disdain for the defense.

I opened my mouth to protest, but my left brain quickly reminded me that venting at Ross wouldn't get me anywhere. He caught my non-cop scent, looked up and frowned.

"Ms. Marshfield has arrived. Glad you're here," Ross announced, without a trace of pleasure.

"That's my second shock of the day, chief. I can't remember when you've ever been happy to see me."

"I didn't say that. You've saved us the trouble of chasing you down." He glared at me like I was some scofflaw. "You're one of Kendall's closest friends and you know the drill—we're looking for anything unusual he did or said lately, changes in is routine, that kind of thing. Lieutenant Tite here's in charge. Al, when you wanna talk to Marshfield?"

"Now's a good time."

I mentally kicked myself for not suspecting why Tite had greased my way into Sam's chambers.

"Where did it happen?" I asked.

The half-dozen cops who were taking pictures or measurements stopped in their tracks. Ross scowled. Finally he waved a fat red marker in the direction of the big desk.

"We're still processing the scene. You wanna see, go over there." He pointed to the corner where the wall met the window.

I couldn't see behind the big desk from where Tite and I stood, so I picked my way to the corner for an unobstructed view of the area between the window and the desk. Blood spatter—some red, some speckled with bits of gray and brown—clung to the lower half of the window. More droplets appeared to be flung across the desktop in a perverse symmetry. A technician knelt on the floor and captured digital images of rusty brown stains that seeped into the carpet like a cancerous growth. Sam's leather chair was sprawled on its side. His case of golf clubs leaned against the wall in the opposite corner.

"Close enough," Ross commanded.

"Gunshot?" My voice cracked.

"Guess again."

I turned to face him. "Give it up, Sherlock. You know it'll be in the paper this afternoon."

The technicians suddenly busied themselves with their instruments. Ross exhaled, the noise resembling the sound of air swooshing from a tire. "Well then, I guess you'll find out along with the rest of the natives." Lips glued together, his mouth widened for a moment in what passed for a grin and he resumed rifling Sam's desk.

"Was the lock forced?" I pointed to the door I had just entered, the only way in or out of the room.

Ross pretended to study a document. I stared at him, not moving. Finally he looked up. "Marshfield, if you end up representing whoever did this, you'll get all the reports. Till then, just let us do our job and cooperate with Tite."

"If you can *find* the person who did this, I guarantee you I won't be representing them." I turned abruptly and brushed by Tite into the anteroom. He followed me and paused uncertainly.

"This way." I marched through narrow concrete hallways to an unmarked door on the other side of the building. It opened into a room that barely accommodated three straight-backed chairs and a table. Lawyers brought witnesses here to run them through their paces before show time in court.

"Do you feel up to this?"

"I'm ready, lieutenant."

"Please sit down, Ms. Marshfield. I'm sorry about what happened to your friend."

"Thanks. Good call."

His mouth twitched at the corners. He lowered himself onto a chair with surprising grace for someone of his bulk and sat, knees angled out from each other, feet directly underneath him, hands in repose on his thighs. "You and the judge were personal friends as well as business associates?"

Tite's tone was relaxed, conversational.

I ran my hand over the back of the empty chair and tried to find the right words, but not too many of them.

"I came to town five or six years ago. Sam and I hit it off right away. He was well known in legal circles — he had won a lot of high-profile trials, and I had heard him lecture. He was one of the founding partners of his law firm, Blane, Kendall and Montgomery. Sam had more cases than he or his firm could handle, and I needed cheap space, so he let me work on some of his files, with the clients' permission, of course. Eventually the firm gave me a sub-lease and secretarial support. I'm not an employee—I'm totally independent. My office is down the hall from the firm. Sam and I would discuss cases, we collaborated…something special happened, issues crystallized, answers fell from the sky…it was magical. Eventually we teamed up and tried cases together."

I paused. Tite now had the big-picture truth, and he didn't need to know the details.

"Where are you from?"

"I practiced in Springfield before I came here."

He studied my face the way people examine a canvas in a museum, curious but detached.

"The two of you were very successful."

"Some verdicts went our way. We were lucky."

"You and Sam just do criminal defense together?" He reached into his suit jacket and pulled out a notebook and plastic pen.

"For a few years. Then he started doing plaintiff's personal injury work. I stuck to the criminal. He was doing both when he was appointed to the bench."

"Other than your legal work, how often would you see the judge?"

"What the hell is that supposed to mean?"

"Don't take offense," he chided. "I mean did you go your separate ways after work or did you socialize?"

I sighed. "When you try a case, the judge and jurors go home at five. That's when the lawyers begin their second shift. Sam and I were pretty much inseparable when we were on trial."

"What did his wife think of that?" His tone implied he was wondering about the weather.

"Betty would joke that the only thing we didn't know about each other was what we wore to bed."

Tite nodded nonchalantly.

"She must have trusted both of you to an unusual degree."

"No reason not to trust, Lieutenant. Sam and Betty are like family to me."

Tite's eyes grabbed mine and didn't let go. They were gray, no, green.

Whatever. I returned his gaze, knowing I told the absolute truth. Then I started to wonder how Betty was feeling at this moment and looked away. He clicked the pen into action.

"Let's start with his criminal work. Think disgruntled defendants, pissed off witnesses, anyone with a motive."

"We run into a lot of whack-jobs in our work, Lieutenant," I warned.

The light-bulb thief. He broke into women's homes or apartments at night, unscrewed all the light bulbs and departed with them, leaving the occupant untouched. The jury found him insane, and some of his victims were upset that we got him committed to a mental facility instead of getting fifty years in the slammer.

Drug cases. The prosecutors were on a mission from God, the defendants couldn't communicate a narrative that made sense, and witnesses often had difficulty finding the courthouse.

"Remember Simmons and Dale?" I asked him.

"Sure. Undercover cops on a drug sting. You and Sam convinced the jury that the cops pressured the defendants to do the deal against their will."

"That's the entrapment defense — where the cops induce a person to commit a crime he wouldn't otherwise have committed. When the jury came back with its verdict, one of the cops, I forget which one, came up to us at counsel table. He said we should have our licenses yanked."

"That's a start." Tite made a note.

I studied him discreetly. Most cops would have rushed to the defense of a brother officer and condemned me and Sam for making them out to be liars.

"Who discovered Sam's body?"

Tite's head rose slowly from his notebook. He sat, inscrutable, then shrugged.

"The chief bailiff discovered Judge Kendall's body at eight thirty-five."

He tapped the notebook with his pen. "You said he took up civil work after a while. He ever nail someone for a big judgment?"

"Several, but there was always insurance. He never forced a defendant into bankruptcy."

"But he must have humiliated people on the stand?"

How had this guy made lieutenant? Did he have a clue? "Sometimes people do things they aren't proud of. When those things become public in a courtroom…" I shrugged. "If they're humiliated, it's their own fault."

The lines around his mouth deepened. "So is there anyone Sam exposed and coincidentally humiliated so badly they'd want to off him?"

The faces of rape victims, bitter prosecutors, and mistaken eyewitnesses flipped like Rolodex cards through my head.

"I'd have to give that question some thought, lieutenant, look at some old files." This seemed like a good time to go on the offensive. "Tite, just between us, what *was* the murder weapon?"

He rolled his eyes. "Ross can be difficult."

"There's a charitable word choice."

He reached in his pants pocket, pulled out a Tootsie Pop, unwrapped it and stuck it in his mouth. He worked it back and forth, up and down. If there was ever a picture of what a man in deep thought looks like, this was it.

"No harm in telling ya." He removed the sucker and held it in his left hand. "Someone tried out his three-wood on him. Very messy, very thorough."

A company of trapeze artists somersaulted in my gut.

"Righty or lefty?"

"Hard to say. The head was a mess, and the golf club's at the state lab. The handle was wrapped in some material that doesn't hold a print."

I don't know where the next few frames of my life went, but I do know my conscious mind left the building for a while.

"I'm sorry, Ms. Marsh. That's not a pleasant image."

"It hasn't been a pleasant day."

"Yeah." He examined his Tootsie Pop like it held the clue that would solve Sam's murder, then looked up as he pounced.

"Donna Gillespie."

"Who?"

"A client of Sam's who accused him of malpractice. Why didn't you tell me about her?"

"You didn't ask. Never crossed my mind. Pick one."

It was his turn to flash the skeptic look.

"You work fast, lieutenant. That case ended before I came to town— before I even knew Sam. So, it's not like right on the tip of my tongue, you know?"

Tite carefully rewrapped the sucker. "Tell me what you do know."

"O…kay." With a major effort I smothered my irritation. "Gillespie was charged with murder of her own kid. The child was less than a year old; it died of severe head trauma. Gillespie claimed the kid fell down the basement steps when she turned her back for a second. The state's experts said the injuries were caused by the child being struck with a blunt object. Sam's doctors testified that the injuries were consistent with what the mom said, so it was a battle of the experts. As I heard the story, Gillespie literally had a fit in the courtroom when the jury came back with a guilty verdict. She had to be restrained and carried out."

"What about her malpractice claim against Sam?"

"She claimed ineffective assistance of counsel on appeal," I corrected him. "The claim was dismissed as having no merit." I settled back in my chair. "When is she due out?"

I expected him to tell me to go scratch.

"We're checking with Corrections on that. How about Sam's personal life?"

"How about it?"

"Was he cheating on his wife, hurting for money, acting unusual?" Tite machine-gunned through the list, deadpan.

I burst out laughing. "No, no, and no. You gotta understand, lieutenant. Sam's whole life was the law. He was a zealot for every client. The idea of him cheating on Betty is ridiculous. He revered her. When they were together, he was so gentle and kind you'd never think it was the same guy who nailed folks to the wall in the courtroom. They were… a special couple."

"I see," he nodded. "Can you look at your old files today?"

"Umm. That'll be difficult. I'm on trial now and the court calls will be messed up for a few days with the funeral…"

In the defense business, the name of the game is postponement. Witnesses may disappear; more important matters may shove yours to the end of the line.

"I'll be at your office at one o'clock tomorrow, Ms. Marsh." He stood and the room shrunk around him.

"What?" I was sure I hadn't heard correctly.

"Have some names for me by then." His eyes were gray now, and hard in the fluorescent light. He slid a business card across the table and held on to it with two fingers.

"I'm sure tomorrow will be more productive."

He was at the door in two strides.

"It's Marshfield!" I crumpled up the card and threw it at him. It bounced harmlessly off his back.

He turned and stared at the wadded up card on the floor. I waited with interest for his reaction. Without raising his head he looked at me like a middle school teacher might regard a student he just caught throwing a spitball. He held up his right index finger, mouthed the word "one," and then pointed it directly at me.

CHAPTER THREE

Judge Denault told us the Perry case had to go to the jury Wednesday no matter how late we had to work. Sam's funeral would paralyze the courthouse for a few days, and Denault didn't want the jurors to come back to deliberate after a long break when the facts might not be fresh in their minds. When we reconvened, Roger had the cop back on the stand, but he couldn't show that my client knew the drugs were in his car. He rested his case. I called only one witness for the defense.

"Mrs. Witherspoon, you live on a one-way street?"

"Yes, I do. River Street is one-way southbound."

"In the early morning hours of last November 17, approximately 12:30 a.m., can you tell us where you were?"

"I was in my living room waiting for my daughter to come home."

"Where were you in your living room?"

"I was sitting by the window, looking for her. She's seventeen and she had a midnight curfew. I was getting worried."

"Did you notice anything unusual?"

"I shore did. That neighborhood ain't the greatest; you gotta be careful all the time. Well, two cars come a flyin' up my street, both goin' the wrong way, real fast. Looked like the one was chasin' the other. I ran out on the porch, and real soon a police car comes along, lights a flashin' like the Fourth of July and one of the speeders stopped right away, I think it was the first one. I dunno where the other car went."

My investigator had discovered Mrs. Witherspoon when we canvassed the vicinity of my client's arrest. If my client Perry testified, the prosecutor could inform the jury of his two previous convictions for possession of a controlled substance. Those twelve good citizens, no matter how well intentioned, assign enormous weight to previous convictions, and I might as well plead Perry guilty. If I didn't put him on the stand, they'd never know about his old run-ins with the law. McBroom, his girlfriend that evening, may have been able to explain the white powder and the prescription bottle, but she had disappeared from drug treatment and, unfortunately, from town.

Roger couldn't score any points on Witherspoon. The woman was as sure of what she saw that evening as she was of her own eye color, and she had no ax to grind either way. The perfect witness.

In my final argument, I hammered home the lack of any direct evidence that my client knew about the drugs. That, coupled with the independent verification of the car chasing Perry to explain his speeding, led to a "not guilty" in less than an hour.

My client wanted to hug me. I clutched my briefcase to my chest in self-defense and asked that he refer his friends, only the innocent ones.

Nothing matches the rush of beating the state; it even blocked out this morning's tragedy for a brief interlude.

I floated to the three-story office building kitty-corner from the courthouse that I call home during the workday. It was built in the middle of the last century. A recent remodel by a new owner resulted in attractive carpet, new paint and a serious rent increase. Sam's former law firm occupies the entire second floor. My suite is down the hall, tucked away from their imposing entrance. Our agreement lets me access their very competent staff and brainstorm with their twelve crackerjack lawyers. My clients check in at the firm's reception area and wait till I come for them. I'm totally independent, I don't stress over law firm politics, and I pay my rent on time.

As I jogged up the steps to the second floor, I reflected on the parts of my history with Sam that I hadn't shared with Tite. When I came home the summer after my first year in college, my brother Ryan, four years older than I, was arrested for rape. At the time he was one year away from completing a five-year engineering program and was on the Dean's List. He insisted he was innocent, but the case went to trial, he lost, and was sentenced to sixteen years in the penitentiary. My mom got a different lawyer, Sam Kendall, to take over Ryan's case on appeal, which at this juncture was a half-step above hopeless. Sam discovered a witness had lied about a key piece of evidence, the prosecutor knew about the lie and had encouraged the witness to testify falsely. By the time Sam got the conviction overturned, I was in law school. More importantly, my brother had been forced to join a gang in prison and, when released after serving three years of his sentence, chose the gang over the family. The engineering program welcomed him back but he refused to return. Ryan lives in Chicago now. He calls once in a while but he never tells me what he's doing, and I've learned not to ask.

I had met Sam a few times when he represented my brother. After I began practicing, we ran into each other at conferences, and though I contained my gratitude, I'm sure I overwhelmed him with admiration. He had saved my brother's life. What Ryan chose to do with that life was his issue, but Sam…he's my hero. *Was* my hero.

I opened the bottom drawer of my desk and rummaged around for the photo I knew was there. I had taken the picture a few days after Ryan's release from the pen. He and Sam were standing on the Michigan Avenue Bridge that spans the Chicago River, arms around each other's shoulders. Sam's energy was palpable, but Ryan appeared a little uncertain. At that point, no one knew the damage the prison experience had inflicted.

I turned on the computer, clicked on the client index and scrolled through the alphabetized list of gang-bangers, druggies, burglars and child molesters, Joliet's finest citizenry. I racked my brain as the names streamed by, hoping the murderer's face would pop up like a target in a shooting gallery.

By "L," I doubted the card was in the deck. I had practiced with Sam five or six years; he had co-counseled with me on maybe a third of my cases. His legal career spanned more than three decades. But I scrolled on.

"R." Righetti, Ellen. I paused. She was not a run-of-the-mill street defendant. Sam and I had been appointed to represent her long after she was convicted of murdering her next-door neighbor, Gordon Haskins. I struggled to remember the details of the case and went in search of my closed file. It was in the back of my tiny closet, wedged among discarded shoes and long-forgotten cleaning supplies. I wiped away a thin coat of dust and slid the elastic cord off. Pleadings, notes, and copies of cases we had used in argument were jammed into the folder in an unsightly mess. I grabbed a handful of paper and sifted through it in an attempt to jog my memory. In the middle of the stack I found the case summary and settled back to read.

A .22 caliber bullet abruptly ended Dr. Gordon Haskins' life one Saturday morning as he slept. His wife Brenda discovered the body and called the cops who arrived immediately. The coroner got there shortly after that and swore that Gordon had been a living, breathing specimen within the last hour.

The cops turned the Haskins home and surroundings upside out but failed to find a murder weapon. The cars in the garage were cold, and neighbors neither saw nor heard any vehicles leave the Haskins' house that morning. The freshly widowed Ms. Haskins told the cops the marriage was not burning as brightly as it once did, but she had no reason to snuff his candle. She had risen early, gone downstairs while the doc slept, made coffee, retrieved the paper and perused it, then brought a cup of java to her husband. Sadly, not even the caffeine could jolt him awake.

The widow was the original suspect, but without a gun it was just a nice theory. The police decided to bird-dog her till she made a wrong move.

Brenda didn't make wrong moves.

Our client, Ellen Righetti, was a recently divorced mother of two who lived next door to the Haskins. About a week after the murder, her baby-sitter, a fifteen-year-old named Cheryl Daniels, called the cops and told them she had discovered a gun in a linen closet in Ellen's home. Her concern was that Ellen's young children could get to it.

The cops were at the Righetti house faster than you could say "Gotcha." Ellen was giving the three-year-old a bath when they arrived, received her permission to search, and found the .22 handgun just as Cheryl had described, nestled next to a silencer. Ellen insisted she had never seen the weapon before and didn't allow guns in her house.

The coppers weren't buying what she was selling. Unfortunately for Ellen, in the time between the murder and the discovery of the .22, they learned that Ellen's oldest child, an eight-year-old boy named Keith, died while his appendix was being removed. The anesthesiologist in attendance was Dr. Gordon Haskins. Keith was buried about two months before Gordon.

Motive, opportunity, and weapon. It doesn't get much easier for the forces of righteousness.

Ballistics concluded that the gun in the linen closet was the same one that ended Gordon's medical career. Despite the best efforts of Ellen's experienced and respected defense attorney, Marty O'Toole, the trial jury fell into line. At the sentencing, Judge Parkinson told Ellen the better move would have been to sue Gordon Haskins for malpractice. Then he gave her a ticket to the slammer for fifty years. She could seek parole after twenty-five.

The case meandered through the appellate process without a ripple. Then Ellen filed a post-conviction petition from the penitentiary, a last-ditch effort to get a new trial or possibly a discharge. A proper p.c. petition must allege some serious Constitutional error like the authorities concealed evidence that was favorable to the defense. Ellen's pleading, which she prepared by herself, didn't meet the standard but it arrived on a day when the chief judge felt some empathy for his fellow mortals. Instead of dismissing it outright, he appointed Sam and yours truly to represent Ellen and gave us sixty days to file a proper petition, which meant our job was to find Constitutional error.

This work swallows up attorney time like a black hole. Ellen couldn't make office visits, so we had to go to the penitentiary, about an hour-and-a-half drive one way.

We met our new client in a prison interview room. She was in her mid-thirties, painfully thin, and her hair was totally gray. She seemed to suffer from shaken adult syndrome, like the world had slapped her around one too many times and now things were a bit blurry. She was able to follow our questions and described a cordial relationship with Gordon and Brenda Haskins. She knew Gordon was an anesthesiologist, and trusted him to safely put her son to sleep while his appendix was removed. She didn't seem to blame Haskins for the operating room death. In the months preceding her arrest for murder she had been divorced and her child had died. The only thing she remembered about the trial was that one of the jurors always wore a loud Hawaiian shirt.

The phone interrupted my reverie. It was Kelly Reed, Kevin's wife and my best friend, calling to console me about Sam and invite me to dinner. That was a no-brainer. I gave myself a quick inspection using the mirror on the back of the closet door. Hazel eyes took in a face that might be described as diamond-shaped; broadest at the cheekbones, narrowing to a small chin. My mouth is wide, made for stuffing with pasta. People say I look taller than I am but that's because I'm lanky. I need a rake in the morning to sort out the dark curls that explode out from my head. Once upon a time my face looked a lot more innocent than it does now.

I stuffed my briefcase with work I knew I wouldn't do and had the key in the lock when I remembered I had turned my phone off for Perry's trial this morning and forgotten to turn it back on. I did so and it hummed back to life. I groaned when I saw about thirty text messages. The first one came in at 7:58 this morning. An icy hand clamped around my heart when I saw it was from "Judgesam." My finger hesitated over the "open" button. I swallowed hard, then clicked, eyes locked on the monitor.

"Sooz, Got some trouble, need your help. Come now. Sam."

CHAPTER FOUR

Kevin and Kelly's two children exploded out the front door as I exited my vehicle. I swept three-year-old Travis up in my arms, while Caitlin bounced up and down with a first-grader's excitement.

"Suzie, why do vampires drink blood?"

"Let me think. Because they're thirsty?"

"No." She laughed so hard she could hardly get the words out. "Cause root beer makes them burp!"

"I knew that."

Kelly waited at the door attired in clingy black workout clothes. She was short and Hispanic and beautiful with large brown eyes that gave away her soul. Her long black hair was drawn back off her face. Despite being born and raised in the US, she still possessed the languid, fluid movements of people born nearer the equator. Her high definition arms were a testament to her hobby as a body builder. She had recently put her career with the state Department of Children and Family Services on hold when she found herself longing to be with her own kids when she was at work and worrying about other people's kids when she was at home. Her former employer was not my favorite government agency. If a child had an unexplained hangnail, CFS would go snooping in the parents' drawers, but the kid whose parents kept him in a dark closet or put cigarettes out on him seemed to go unnoticed.

She searched my face as we walked into the kitchen. "How are you?"

"Writhing in pain, twisting with anguish."

She rolled her eyes skyward. "I put up with this because...?"

I glanced skyward. "Today, I'm not really sure why you're putting up with me."

She understood right away and gave me a warm hug. I returned it but couldn't muster the energy to make it meaningful.

Kevin herded the kids in and we sat down. The Caesar salad, blue cheese burgers and apple pie disappeared as we discussed the challenges of first grade and the intricate plot of the latest Disney movie. After cleaning up and sending the kids to the playroom, we adjourned to "the cinema room" with some wine. Kevin turned on the enormous flat screen TV. Sam's murder was the lead story on the Chicago stations, but I didn't learn anything new.

"Kev told me about the hospital," Kelly said. "What happened after that?"

I highlighted the day's events: the scene in Sam's chambers, the interview with Tite, the successful verdict.

"The cops are looking at Sam's past to come up with possible motives. I told Tite I'd go through my old files."

"Good luck finding those," Kevin said.

I ignored him. "Tite's a strange one. He started out like Mr. Sensitive: 'So sorry about your friend,' then he switched to Mr. Inquisitor: 'tell me what I want to know.' Then, for no reason, he gave me information I never expected to get. He ended up demanding that I have answers for him by one o'clock tomorrow." I paused. "Maybe he's a psycho, or maybe I'm a suspect and he's got some agenda for snaring me."

"Sounds like the good cop/bad cop routine, but they're short-handed so they only sent one guy," Kevin said. "Do you know the cause of death?"

I told them about Sam's three-wood. Kelly's face turned the color of days-old cauliflower.

"Wouldn't Sam resist when his attacker grabbed the golf club? How did the person get in? And the killer doesn't have to be a male. A female swinging a golf club can be pretty lethal." Kevin got up, raised his arms and was about to demonstrate a violent overhead blow.

"Stop, Kev!" Kelly's voice was strained. "Maybe there were two people — Sam was talking to one and that's why he didn't see the golf club coming."

"Could be." Kevin leaned forward, elbows on his thighs. "But the real question is who wanted him dead and why."

"Remember Ellen Righetti?" I included them both in the question.

"Yeah," Kevin said slowly as his brain located the information. "She got big numbers for killing the anesthesiologist — Hawkins, Haskins? You and Sam did a post-conviction hearing for her. What about it?"

"Well, we lost the p.c., of course. I haven't really thought about the case since, bu…t ."

"But what?" Kelly asked.

I shook my head. "Something about that file bothers me but I can't put my finger on it."

"You lost, Susan; that's what bothers you," Kevin said. "I remember the hearing. It got a lot of press, but you guys had zip in terms of Constitutional error."

"Tell me more. What was it all about?" Kelly asked.

I recited from the case summary I had read earlier. As I did so, more facts came to mind. "Our client and the Haskins had keys to each other's houses, just being good neighbors. The state's theory was that Ellen used the Haskins' key to open the door, slipped upstairs, did the deed and exited the same way. Brenda Haskins was making coffee in the kitchen when this supposedly went down, but the kitchen was in the rear of the house and the stairs were right off the front entry. When the cops came to Ellen's house later, she cooperated and showed them her little cigar box where she kept keys and the Haskins' key was right there, labeled.

"Marty O'Toole was Ellen's trial attorney. His theory was that Brenda could have offed her husband, then used her key to Ellen's house to plant the gun there. Very creative, especially since his client didn't give him an alibi or much other help. But the state pre-empted him on that. When they put their case on, they actually asked Brenda whether she killed Gordon and planted the gun. Marty told us her denials were emphatic and totally believable."

"So what were your grounds for the post-conviction petition?"

"We were blowing smoke. We were desperate for any…" I snapped my fingers and bounced off the couch. "I got it! I remember why this case bothers me! The widow, Brenda Haskins! The way we split up the work, she was Sam's witness. He had her on the stand and from out of the blue, he asks if she was having an affair at the time of her husband's murder."

Kelly's jaw dropped. "Isn't that improper?"

"Extremely. Unless you have a damn good reason and it's relevant as hell. The prosecutor looked at Sam like he was speaking Russian."

"What did Brenda say?" Kelly asked.

"She didn't. The prosecutor flew out of his chair to object. The judge read Sam the riot act, and life as we know it went on."

"What possessed Sam to ask the 'affair' question?" Kevin inquired.

I shrugged. "Dunno. Ellen was just another client for me, but for Sam she was a cause. He was over the top, even for him. Research, tracking witnesses... he absolutely ate, drank and slept the case for a month. I figured the question about an affair was just his enthusiasm. He never mentioned anything to me about her having an affair."

"Did you put your client on the stand?" Kelly asked.

"You bet. She told the court, plain and simple, everything she saw and did the morning Haskins was shot. She was credible, the judge even said so, but as he pointed out, our burden at this juncture wasn't to prove who was lying and who wasn't. We had to prove error, and we didn't have the horses."

I drummed my fingers on the table.

"Are you thinking what I'm thinking?" Kevin's eyes slid to mine.

"Yeah. Can we get in now?"

"What *are* you two talking about?" Kelly demanded.

"The firm's closed files are in storage in the basement at the office," Kevin explained. "Sam's Righetti file should be there, and there might be notes that would give us an idea why he asked that question."

"I'm glad to see you guys getting into the spirit of the thing," I said. "But hang on a minute. I'm not sure I want to know the answers before I talk to Tite tomorrow."

"Tite's job is to chase down leads. *Your* job is to tell him what you know and go practice law." Kelly took a sip of wine. "What if she was having an affair? What would that have to do with Sam's being killed?"

"Brenda wouldn't want her infidelity to become public, and probably neither would her partner. If Sam found out, someone might want to make sure the news stopped there."

"Murder's a pretty drastic method of curtailing news." Kelly shivered.

"When someone's back is against a wall, they can get pretty desperate. In Brenda's social circle, I doubt they take out ads about things like that."

We decided that Kevin and I would retrieve Sam's file from storage the following day and bring it back to the house so the three of us could examine the contents together. It felt good to have a plan as opposed to aimlessly scrolling my client database.

As I drove away, my friends were backlit in the doorway, arms around each other's waists. I was happy to be going home, where the only person I had to take care of was a cat.

Fur was as happy to see me as a feline can be. She entwined herself around my legs, purring incessantly.

"My friend, I have some bad news. Sam isn't going to come tickle your chin anymore."

She stared at me, indignant, tail in hyper-drive. Unfortunately for her, Fur is a cuddle cat, and she's cursed with an owner who uses the house like a motel room. I work too many hours to give a pet what it deserves, but Fur never complains. She finds her pleasure chasing imaginary (hopefully) bugs and napping on my pillow. On the infrequent occasions when Sam visited, Fur would leap into his lap, he'd scratch her in all the right places, and she'd favor him with adoring, satiated gazes.

The day's events whirled in my brain. I shrugged out of my clothes and fell into bed, too tired to hang anything up.

I don't know if I was asleep or awake when an illusion swept into my head with the boldness and clarity of a big-screen movie. Sam and I were meeting Ellen Righetti for the first time in the attorney visiting room at the penitentiary. The walls might have been off-white a decade ago; they were dirty gray now. The steel table, more tarnished than stainless, was bolted to the floor. We were saying good-bye to our new client after an unproductive first meeting. She wore a baggy orange prison jump suit.

"This is hell," she said, gesturing toward to the bowels of the institution. "I never killed Gordon, I never even thought about killing him or anyone else. Please get me out of here, so I can be with my kids again." Tears welled in her eyes.

It wasn't a dream. It had happened exactly that way.

CHAPTER FIVE

"Lieutenant Al Tite is here," Darcy, the firm receptionist, announced into my phone.

I hiked down the hall. Tite's chair was dollhouse-size underneath him. His head was buried in *Golf Digest*. I waited a full minute before he became aware of my presence.

"Oh, hi!" He scrambled to his feet and tossed the magazine back on the table.

"Does your swing need some adjustment?"

"Nice to see you again too."

"Did the good cop or the bad cop come today?"

"Depends."

"On what?"

"On which lawyer shows up: the one who answers questions or the one who leads me in circles."

I threw up my hands in a 'what *are* you talking about?' gesture and led him back down the hall to my shop. I wanted a pipeline to the official investigation into Sam's death. Would he be willing to deal?

We passed through the outer conference room into my office.

"Have a seat." I gestured to the powder blue leather and chrome client chairs. Not one to accept an invitation, he took a slow, deliberate tour. Travel and nature photography, most of it mine, adorned the walls. He stared intently at the artwork, examined book titles.

"Colorado?" he asked in front of a picture of quaking aspens with the Rocky Mountains in the background.

"Um-hum." A crisp blue shirt and well-tailored windowpane suit did wonders for his appearance. I pretended to read a recent Supreme

Court opinion while covertly observing him. He wasn't overweight, just huge in the way that an oak tree is huge: massive and solid.

Finally he sat down. "You do well, Ms. Marshfield."

The lyrics of *"She Works Hard for the Money"* crossed my mind. "Good defense has a price."

We fell silent. Today's interview technique was to stare his subject into submission. An Omaha minute passed.

"This is more fun than getting busted for speeding, lieutenant, but can we move along? I have another appointment at two-thirty."

He nodded, reached into his briefcase, pulled out a photo of a middle-aged white woman and placed it on my desk.

"Recognize her?"

I looked at the picture, not touching it.

"I've never seen this person."

"That's Donna Gillespie, the woman Sam represented when she was convicted of murdering her seven-month-old baby."

My mouth formed an "O" shape. The woman in the photo was wide-eyed, as if the photographer had surprised her. Wire-rim glasses gave her a stern look. Her lips were set in a grim line. "Humorless" was how to best describe her.

"Is she still in?"

"She caught an eighteen, and she was convicted nine years ago."

Illinois' sentencing scheme features day-for-day good time. For every day of good behavior served, a prisoner gets a day knocked off his sentence, so a model inmate would serve half the announced sentence.

"Let me guess. She's due out today."

"Close. That's her release photo from two months ago."

"Where is she now?"

After inmates are released, they're on parole, a long leash that keeps them in a gray area between the total freedom that most of us enjoy and the friendly confines of the eight-by-twelve cell they've recently vacated. For murder, the leash is five years.

Al referred to his notebook. "She gave them her mother's address in Chicago. Her parole officer verified she's living there."

"Is she on your list?"

His look said 'What do *you* think?'

"How high on your list?"

His hand reached out between us and dipped and rose. "It's a long shot for a defendant to physically assault her attorney. Judges get hate mail, prosecutors get threats, but defense attorneys just get more cases."

Amen to that.

"Some defendants truly believe they're innocent, in which case it's the attorney's fault they lost."

Al's eyes narrowed. "Are you saying Sam should have won her case?"

I fingered the smooth black stone that sits on my desk. The words *Never Quit* were etched on it. Sam had given me the rock a few years ago in the middle of a trial I was sure I was losing.

"He felt that way," I answered slowly. "Personally, I don't have a clue; it was before my time, like I said yesterday."

"What else did he say about Gillespie?" Tite's eyes were vigilant, evaluating.

I nodded to myself. I had something Tite wanted, lots of stories and tidbits about Sam he'd find helpful in his investigation. I had to play this right.

I leaned back and tuned Tite out, trying to recall the incident clearly.

Sam and I were in his chambers together. He pointed to the newspaper lying open on his working desk.

"Jack Gillespie's tying the knot."

"Related to Donna?" I inquired.

"Former husband. He divorced her after the trial." Sam's fingers tap-danced on the desk.

"So?" I asked.

"Just thinking. Case still haunts me, Susan."

"I can see that. What about Jack Gillespie?"

He stopped tapping. "He didn't come across as the most enthusiastic believer in his wife's innocence. It was his demeanor, the way he answered questions, the intangibles that give a message to the jury but don't show up in the transcript."

"Maybe he did doubt her innocence," I said.

"Fine." Sam's hand crashed down on the desk. "But don't torpedo the defense when we're counting on you. The medical experts were so evenly divided in that case, the jury was scrutinizing every little thing...." He shoved the newspaper to the floor in disgust.

My mental movie ended.

"I can help you, lieutenant, but I want this to be a two-way street. I can tell you exactly what Sam said about Gillespie. And after your... encouragement yesterday, I have some other interesting characters you may want to think about too. But I need to know what your investigation finds out. I want to be a silent partner in this."

Tite fished around in his pocket, produced a Tootsie Pop, unwrapped it and popped it into his mouth. He placed the wrapper on my desk and carefully smoothed it out.

"We don't 'partner' with civilians, Ms. Marsh. You wanna find out who did your friend, start by telling me *everything* and I promise you, we'll do our best to find the killer."

Maybe if I told him what Sam had done for Ryan, he'd understand the miracle that had happened in my family and see it my way. No, it was a story few people knew, and I doubted Tite should be one of them. I'd wait for the next opportunity.

"Okay, lieutenant, we'll do it your way." I made no effort to hide my irritation, but recounted the conversation with Sam about Jack Gillespie.

"Sam was bitter," Tite commented.

"He lost a case he thought he should've won," I disagreed. "But if Gillespie *did* murder her kid, she's capable of the kind of violence that killed Sam."

The Tootsie Pop journeyed from one side of his mouth to the other. "Interesting thought. Tell me what else you came up with."

"This one-way street never ends, does it?"

I thought I saw a satisfied smirk flit across his face. I hoped I was mistaken.

Sam had sued Roy Stevens, a local obstetrical gynecologist who failed to detect signs of fetal distress during labor. The sad result was a stillborn infant whose parents had been trying to have a baby for years. Sam got a half million-dollar verdict against Stevens and in a town the size of Joliet, that's a career-buster. The doc's business dried up before you could say "malpractice."

Mark Wheaton. A probate lawyer who had liquidated a substantial estate for his client, a ditsy woman with no talent for money other than spending it. Sam represented a niece of the deceased and became suspicious of Wheaton's valuation of the holdings. An appraiser confirmed that the assets had been undervalued some $80,000 and the subsequent investigation revealed Wheaton was siphoning cash from the estate, hoping to make up the difference when the assets were sold. After Sam unearthed the fraud, the Attorney Disciplinary Commission jumped all over it. Wheaton lost his law license as well as a year of his liberty.

I had played a minor role in these cases as a favor to Sam, learning just enough about the civil side of the law to realize that my heart would always be with my felony clients.

I related the Roy Stevens and Mark Wheaton stories. When I finished, Tite tapped his note pad in a measured cadence.

"The courthouse was invented for disputes like this. What makes these two cases so special?"

"Lieutenant, you asked for my good faith assistance, and I'm doing my best. *You're* the investigator. *You* figure it out. This is *not* a partnership."

Tite rotated his neck in a slow circle causing small popping noises.

"People don't kill each over professional licenses." He leaned forward, crossing his arms on top of my desk. "I need solid leads, not ancient crap-o-la." He pronounced the last word like some Italian pasta dish.

"Maybe this case won't be solved by talking to Susan Marshfield," I snapped. "Maybe you're going to have to get your butt out of my client chair and burn some shoe leather."

Tite leaned back and braced his hands behind his head as if we were sipping drinks at an outdoor cafe. His eyes behind half-closed lids never left my face.

"Tell me about Sam's last text."

Years of litigation had honed an ability to maintain a poker face even when cases took a disastrous turn. "You're smooth, lieutenant."

"Ditto," he replied. "What did he mean when he said he had some trouble? What did he think you could do?"

The same question had kept me tossing and turning the previous night.

"I wish I knew." I sighed. "The truth is, since Sam went on the bench, we haven't been as close as we used to be. Lawyers and judges have to keep a certain distance from each other and we...drifted apart."

Tite frowned, perhaps in empathy, more likely in disappointment. "Other than the text, what else haven't you mentioned?" The dark eyes bored into mine.

"Nothing." If Righetti became more than just a bad feeling, I'd be sure to let him know. "And by the way, how'd you find the text?"

"We didn't go near your phone. We got it off Sam's 'sent' texts. Simple." He stood, towering over me. "I'm sure you're familiar with the offense of obstructing justice, Ms. Marsh. If I can prove you're holding something back, I'll have a warrant the next time we meet."

I threw my shoulders back in anger. "Are you familiar with the crime of harassment, lieutenant? You're just about there." I distinctly enunciated each word of the last sentence.

He stiffened, every muscle in his face knotted.

"Marshland, this isn't about who's tougher or can make the bigger threats. It's about catching a killer. I don't want to fight you for information."

"Good, 'cause you'll never win that battle."

Tite crossed his arms tightly across his chest. His gaze circled the office while the Tootsie Pop roiled back and forth.

"And my name is Marsh*field*."

"Right." He turned and lumbered to the door. It closed with a quiet click.

Guess I charmed him.

***

I ordered a BLT delivered to the office. It arrived with a young man who resembled my drug clients on a bad day. The sandwich was seven dollars. I gave him eight and he wandered off without acknowledgment.

The afternoon calendar was stacked with pretrials, a moment in time when the opposing lawyers eyeball each other, cut to the chase on the real strengths and weaknesses of their case and try to resolve it, all in roughly two or three minutes. I got the same message on all eight pretrials: no deals, no settlements; all my cases were going to trial. This was the state's attorney's office revenge play for yesterday's Perry verdict. Two can play that game.

CHAPTER SIX

Kevin and I met at the elevators at three-thirty, a time when most people hunkered down to finish the day's work, and vertical travel in our three-story office building was limited. We rode down to the lobby, then transferred to the other elevator, the only one that went to the basement.

"You have the key?"

Kevin looked at me like he was Tiger Woods and I had asked if he could sink a six-inch putt.

The elevator descended hesitantly, like an elderly woman going down unfamiliar steps. Finally the doors parted and we stepped out into inky blackness.

"There's a switch here somewhere," Kevin mumbled as he disappeared.

"Got it!" I heard a click and a dozen hundred-watt eyes suddenly burst out of the darkness.

The cavern was divided into four aisles bordered by storage spaces marked by a floor-to-ceiling vinyl-coated chain link fence. I followed Kevin to the firm's enclosure. He pulled out a large key with a tag attached and worked it into the padlock that secured the gate. A dank, musty smell came from everywhere and went nowhere. The basement was a tomb for files.

He pulled the padlock open and we stepped inside the cage. "Every closed file is assigned a number. The first two digits are the year it's closed, then a chronological number starting with one for the first closed file of the year. Righetti's file was…" He fished a piece of paper from his pocket. "Fourteen sixty-seven which means…"

"I get it. Very high-tech."

He grunted. "I didn't want to ask any staff for help. I figured you'd want to keep this quiet."

"Good call. A certain senior partner might not be too pleased that I'm mucking around down here." Theodore Iverson was the managing partner of the firm, and nobody called him Ted. Though he recognized the necessity of the firm's litigation work, he regarded it as unsavory at best. His specialty was tax and estate planning, where the profits are astronomical and the clients are upper-crust.

Rows of black metal racks were crammed full of files. Kevin squeezed down one aisle and I navigated down the next. Fortunately, the closed numbers were written in bold marker on the side of each file.

"Seven!" I shouted.

We turned the corner and started on the opposite side.

"Eleven…"

"Here's fourteen sixty-seven! Bingo!"

I hurried over and we wrestled three large brown accordion files from their nesting place, leaving a foot of empty shelf space.

"Thirty pounds, easy," Kevin estimated.

"How do we get them out of here…

"Without being seen?" He finished my thought.

"They're your files. You're a partner. I, on the other hand, am a mere thief."

"Yeah, but if anyone sees me with three huge files, they'll be more than curious."

"Let's take them out one at a time. You take one, dump it in my trunk, I'll follow a minute or two later with another one, then you come back for the last one."

"That'll work, especially if we go now before anyone leaves for the day."

"Let's take a quick look."

We knelt and riffled through the paper. The first file was devoted solely to research: copies of appellate court cases that were littered with Sam's familiar scrawl. The other two contained interviews, police reports and areas of questioning for various witnesses. Each manila file was labeled, the papers neatly stacked inside.

"Sam was never this neat," I said.

"The firm's changed the policy on closed files," Kevin answered. "The staff member who's most familiar with the file closes it, and they have to make sure it's complete and ship-shape before it comes down here. It costs secretarial time, but it's worth it in the long run."

"Where would the trial transcript be?" This is the court reporter's product, bound volumes of transcribed testimony.

Kevin's eyes searched the empty shelf space. "It should be stored with the file."

"It was huge, Kev. The original trial was a week long. I remember studying the transcript with Sam."

"Hmm. I'll try to track it down."

"Do that." I made a mental note. I balanced one file on my hip and inched my way back to the door of the cage where I noticed a clipboard hanging inside the fence with a sheaf of printout paper attached. I pointed at it with my free hand.

"What's that?

Kevin almost crashed into me with his two files. He grunted as he lowered them to the floor and grabbed the clipboard.

"Duplicate of the record we keep upstairs, listing the closed files alpha and chrono." He leafed through it.

"Where's the list kept upstairs?" I asked.

"The physical list is in the supply room. The up-to-date one is on the computer."

"Do you have to sign the files out when you look at them?"

His forehead wrinkled. "We're not that paranoid."

"Where's the key to the padlock kept?"

"In the drawer with the index," he responded impatiently.

"So…" I said, thinking aloud. ". . . if someone got hold of the key, they could come in at street level, catch the elevator down, find any file with the index here, and take whatever they wanted."

He looked at me like I was a noxious visitor from another galaxy.

"I suppose. But who'd be interested in these things? And how would they know where we store them, and how could they get the key?"

"That key is not secure. The supply room's open to any employee.

I've been in there a dozen times myself. Someone could 'borrow' the key, take it home for the night, duplicate it and return it the next day with no one being the wiser."

He frowned. "Yeah, you got a point."

I leaned against one of the racks and shoved my brain into the next gear. "Some of these files have sensitive information in them. Let's say one of Iverson's tax files shows that a business underreported its income. Iverson might not realize it, since he just gets what the client gives him. But in the wrong hands, that information could hurt someone. Or in litigation, maybe you dig up an old felony conviction on a witness or evidence that they're lying. We dutifully write it all down and file it away."

"Okay, okay. Listen, I've got an appointment, and I can't keep this client waiting."

We stepped outside the chain-link door. Kevin put his files down and bent over to lock the padlock. At that moment the elevator door started to slide open. We were right in the main aisle, as exposed as two convicts in an otherwise empty prison yard.

"Kev, back inside!" I whispered urgently.

He gave me an amused look but shoved the door back open and swept up the files. He pushed the gate closed and we plastered ourselves against the wall of paper.

"Kevin, are you here?" The strident voice of Janice Curtis, Theodore Iverson's administrative assistant and the office slave-driver was unmistakable.

"Yeah, coming!" Kevin yelled back. Her stiletto heels punished the concrete floor as she headed our way. I grabbed a random file from the shelf, thrust it at Kevin and motioned for him to intercept her. He rushed from the enclosure to meet her. "What's up?"

"Mr. Iverson needs you *now*."

"Sure. Let's go."

"The door?"

The gate was at half-mast, key dangling from the lock. I was hidden six feet back inside, the Righetti files at my feet, invisible to them now but I'd be the star of the show for whichever of them closed the gate.

"Right. Let me get that." Kevin hurried back, shut the door and snapped the padlock. He didn't give me a glance. "Done!"

"Why didn't you send Becky to fetch this?" Janine asked, irritated. "I really don't appreciate having to track you down."

"Uh, I need some special language for a trust I'm drafting. There were three or four files I had to look at—I didn't want her to drag them all upstairs." Kevin lied easily. "We better go. I don't need Theodore upset with me."

They hurried off together. One of them dutifully turned off the lights just before they got back on the elevator. I was left in total darkness, locked in the cage.

CHAPTER SEVEN

Kevin would return as soon as he could, but it might be hours. Kelly was the only other person who knew what we were doing, but it was almost four o'clock, and the kids were home. It would be a huge imposition to ask her to come downtown, somehow procure the key and rescue me. Maybe I could find someone to call in my contact list. I tapped my phone.

No Service. Of course: basement of an old reinforced steel and concrete building. I growled deep in my throat and settled back to wait. The storage room was drenched in darkness.

I lowered myself gingerly to the cement floor and stretched my legs down the narrow aisle. In the thick blackness, I could discern nothing. My hearing went on hyper-alert but there was no sound to pick up: no electric hum, no old building creaks. This must be what life was like for the pharaohs buried in the pyramids. I twisted and turned, trying to make myself as comfortable as possible, but in lawyer duds on a concrete floor, comfort was not a viable option. I could deal with the darkness, the silence was manageable, but the deal-breaker was the absolute certainty that I couldn't leave. I was hemmed in by antiquated, long forgotten cases that, let's face it, no one cared about anymore. I wondered if there were rats or mice down here and propelled hurriedly off the floor. Maybe Kevin had been clever enough to fake locking the padlock, and I could maneuver the wire gate sufficiently to escape. I felt my way to the gate but it gave only a half-inch and I couldn't fit my hand through the gap. Frustrated, I grabbed the fencing with both hands and shook it as hard as I could. No give. I kicked it for good measure. How much longer before Kevin would appear? Would he call someone to get me? For a second, I thought he might call Sam. He'd be here in a heartbeat. Then I remembered.

I sank to the floor and buried my face in hands I couldn't see. "Get me out of here!" I shouted.

As if on cue, I heard a loud thud and the elevator door labored open. I sprang to my feet, opened my mouth to scream for Kevin, then sank back, remembering it could be any one of the other tenants who had more right to be in this room than I did. Whoever the newcomer was, he or she was in no hurry. The elevator closed, but no lights came on. I waited, perfectly still, listening attentively. Uneven footfalls, one normal, the other long and dragging, toiled down the middle aisle directly toward me. I knew all the tenants and none of them limped. Why didn't he turn on the lights? As the footsteps drew closer, the air grew foul with the stench of something like raw meat left out too long in the hot sun. The visitor drew up even with the entrance of the firm's area and I shrank back. Even in the absolute dark I was conscious of a looming presence, a shapeless bulkiness. I fought an impulse to gag.

The visitor lumbered past to the back wall, turned left and trudged on. There must be an aisle between the last storage space and the wall. The rotten smell started to recede. There were long, drawn-out rustling sounds followed by a soft moan. Then a tiny click and suddenly classical music filled the basement.

Puzzle solved. It had to be Moses, a street person whom some of us downtowners named after the biblical character because of his flowing white mane and beard. His territory was the southeast corner of Chicago and Van Buren Streets. We'd usually see him on a camp chair with his transistor radio set to WFMT, a Chicago classical station. Once in a while he'd wield an imaginary baton and direct the piece. I'd occasionally toss loose change into his cardboard box, but I don't think he took in more than ten dollars on his best day. I never gave a thought to where he slept, but now I knew. He probably waited till the lobby of the building was deserted, then caught a free ride down here.

The elevator balked open again. "Sooz!" Kevin shouted.

"Yo! Here I am, right where you left me!"

The music ceased and the lights burst on. Kevin hurried to the cage door, jammed the key in the lock. "You okay?"

"Just peachy," I lied.

"I told 'em I needed a bathroom break, so I gotta get back quick."

"Yeah, no problem. I'll take the files out one at a time and stash them in my trunk."

He half nodded then wrinkled his nose. "What's that smell?"

"I don't smell anything."

He shrugged and turned back toward the elevator.

"Don't forget to check on the trial transcript," I reminded him.

"I'll figure it out. What about the key?" It was dangling from the lock.

"I'll bring it to you after I load the car. You can put it back."

"That's a plan. Leave it on my desk if I'm still tied up."

"Right. Dazzle them with your brilliance."

"More like baffle them with my b.s." He gave me a thumbs-up and was gone.

I balanced the first file in my arms and rode the elevator up to daylight. I filled my lungs with the chilly spring air and noticed the city had planted flowers in the little plaza between the office and the parking deck. Pink and white geraniums. They were brilliant. Even the dull office buildings seemed to take on different hues at this moment.

It took twenty minutes to transport the three files out of the basement, over to the parking structure, up a flight of stairs and into my trunk. On the final trip, I locked up the storage area and pocketed the key.

"Moses?" I called out.

No answer. I could sense his presence, and my nose knew he was here.

"You can turn your radio back on. I'm leaving now. I won't tell anybody you're here."

I waited a silent minute, wondering—well, hoping—that he would turn the radio on again. I turned to leave when the quiet strains of a Mozart concerto filled the basement. Why did I feel a connection to this street person? Perhaps because Moses, whom we all thought of as somewhat unhinged, and myself, recently cowering in a metal cage, were not quite as different as I thought.

CHAPTER EIGHT

Every parking space, legal and illegal, within a half mile of Mohan's Funeral Home was taken. I spied someone pulling out a block ahead, pushed the Acura into rocket gear, and grabbed the spot. Part of me wanted to get this over with; the rest of me dreaded saying good-bye to Sam.

The doors of the funeral home were out of the Middle Ages, made of carved wood twelve feet high and four inches thick with vertical handles as long as my leg. I tugged at one till it swung open and a wall of humanity greeted me, a giant cocktail party without the alcohol. The crowd was mostly business-attired professional types, but I recognized a few of Sam's clients. A trio of convicted burglars chatted up a female shoplifter. A fellow on probation for credit card fraud consoled a child molester. I nodded to them, saving my limited social skills for the judges and politicians and squeezed through the throng toward the "parlor" where Sam euphemistically rested. This room was noticeably quieter: perhaps the specter of death had a chilling effect.

Harry and Gina, Sam's two adult children, dutifully greeted guests near the closed casket. Gina was matchstick thin, with the kind of cheekbones that graced fashion magazine covers. She welcomed each visitor with warm cordiality while her brother shook hands solemnly. During college, Harry had gone to a fraternity party and decided to stay for several years. His underage drinking adventures, excessive speeding tickets, and prodigious stupidity gave his parents endless worry. He was invited to leave two colleges but graduated from a third and finally seemed to settle down when he landed a job in Chicago. He would be about twenty-four now. Gina was a few years older.

"Hi ya, Toots," a familiar voice whispered in my ear.

I tried a smile but couldn't quite pull it off. I sang in a low voice "Big Girls Don't Cry."

"The Four Seasons, nineteen sixty-two," Kelly retorted. A game we often play after a glass or two of wine. One player sings the first line of a song, the other guesses the title, artist, and year. My radio dial rarely moves from the oldies station.

We queued up for our audience with the siblings. Unbidden memories shoved each other around my psyche: Sam the strategist, tie loosened, collar open, all lit up about a new case or theory of defense; Samuel Kendall, leaning casually on the courtroom podium, leading a witness by seemingly innocuous questions till the trap was sprung and the witness went wide-eyed with panic, as he realized that the one thing he least wanted to admit was being inexorably extracted from him. Another memory, much deeper but as vivid as if it occurred this morning, crowded out the others: in my mind's eye Sam was arguing to overturn my brother's conviction on the grounds of the prosecution's intentional subornation of perjury. He started out controlled and steady, but as he got more into the facts and the argument, he was flooded with rage and became so impassioned, even the jaded three-judge panel was spellbound.

It was our turn. I mumbled my condolences.

"Thanks, Susan," Gina looked at me like *I* was the one who needed sympathy. "Dad thought you were the best partner he ever had. I hope he told you so."

"More like the best student. He was in a whole different league than the rest of us."

I turned to Harry. "You've grown up since I saw you last."

His freckled face went crimson. "Ran out of wild oats to sow. It was time."

"How's your mom doing?"

They exchanged glances.

"Okay. It's been so hectic, I don't think the reality has sunk in yet."

Harry squeezed his sister's shoulder. "We'll be here when it does," he assured her.

"She'll need you both."

Harry nodded solemnly.

"Mom's been asking about you," Gina said.

I nodded. "I'll do what I can do help her get through this," I responded, trying to sound reassuring. The crowd pressed from behind.

I moved on to the rectangular cherry wood box. The cover was closed but a portrait of Sam graced the top of the coffin. He leaned toward the camera with an open, confident smile. I clasped my hands together and silently asked the heavenly tribunal to allow him in as a member of the bar.

Kelly knelt briefly, then rose. Her eyes were brimming. "I'll miss him," she lamented.

I was mesmerized by the picture.

"You all right?" she asked.

"Wakes are macabre."

"People need to celebrate the deceased's life and grieve together at his passing." She dabbed at her eyes with a Kleenex. "It's a process."

"One I can do without."

"Feelings have to be acknowledged and dealt with."

"Psycho-babble."

She sighed and gave my shoulder a hard squeeze.

Betty sat to the left of the casket, a venerable queen surrounded by fawning attendants. Snowy-white hair curled softly around her cherubic face. She took my hand in both of hers and grasped it tightly.

"This is awful." I said the first thing that popped into my head.

She let go of my hand and wrapped me in a big hug. "It's…more than I can grasp right now," she whispered.

I remembered the last victory dinner we celebrated at their house, probably a year and a half ago. We lingered over dessert, just the three of us, recreated the justice system and did it right. I was awed by their commitment to each other and to leave the world a better place than they found it.

"He was so proud of you, Susan." She released me and leaned back. "When you started winning the big cases all on your own, he was like a proud papa." She glanced around the rapidly filling room. "I've met clients tonight who say he saved their lives…other lawyers who tell me he was an inspiration. It's overwhelming."

"He was all of that…and so much more."

Betty's eyes searched mine and for a brief time we were the only two people in that crowded room. "I know."

A diminutive but energetic woman approached and slipped an arm fondly through Betty's.

"I'm sorry to interrupt, but the restaurant wants to know how many will attend the luncheon after the funeral tomorrow."

Betty shrugged helplessly.

"The entire bar association, every courthouse employee, and friends you never knew you had. Three hundred, easy," I responded.

The new arrival clutched her necklace, alarmed.

"Could you tell him that, please, Aggie?"

"Of course."

"Susan, have you met my good friend Agnes Hart?"

We nodded at each other. Agnes appeared a few years younger than Betty, with bright eyes that didn't miss much.

"Aggie is a treasure. She's taking care of all the details that I just can't deal with right now."

"It's nothing." Agnes gave her friend an affectionate hug.

"I just wish he could be here to enjoy this," Betty said.

Agnes and I exchanged a quick glance.

Chief Judge Cardona bore down upon us. I bid farewell to Betty and Agnes and slipped into the crowd, hoping my social obligations were at an end.

The face that had stared at me from Tite's photograph only a few hours ago was suddenly in my path. Donna Gillespie stood to the side of the crowded room, staring coldly at the coffin. Al Tite was behind her, doing a lousy job of fading into the woodwork. I wound my way over to the woman, extended my hand and gave her what I hoped was a warm smile.

"Ms. Gillespie? I'm Susan Marshfield. I used to work with Sam."

She inspected my hand like it was a smelly old rag.

"He felt terrible about your case."

She returned her gaze to the front of the room.

"The verdict haunted him."

She speared me with a look. "You're haunting *me*, bitch, and you better stop right now. I didn't come here to talk to you or nobody else." She brushed past me to a vacant chair, sat down and crossed her arms balefully.

Kevin appeared from nowhere. "Are we having fun yet?"

I looked at him, puzzling over Gillespie's response.

"Kelly wants pizza. Whaddya say?"

"Pepperoni and anchovies."

Kevin and I wove our way back to the entrance, collecting Kelly on the way. The funeral home was now a fire marshal's nightmare.

As Kevin reached for the main door it swung open from the other side, and a striking-looking woman in a gleaming, black fur coat entered with a regal air. We stared at each other for several seconds.

"Nice to see you, Mrs. Haskins," I said.

She hesitated, then the corners of her mouth turned microscopically upward. "Nice to see you, too…um…"

"Susan Marshfield," I volunteered. "Sam and I represented Ellen Righetti on her post-conviction case."

She smiled condescendingly. "I remember *what* you were. I just didn't remember *who* you were. Forgive me. It's been a long time."

Long enough for Brenda's hair to change from something vaguely reddish to a brilliant silver blonde, from a bob to a series of elegant swirls. Not a style for someone like me, whose daily wardrobe includes a swim cap. The large silver balls that dangled from her ears made me wonder how she adorned herself for a real dress-up occasion like New Year's Eve. Her image was so radically different from that of the bereaved widow who had testified in our case that I would not have recognized her but for the fact that she had been on my mind recently.

I introduced Kevin and Kelly, hoping Brenda would reciprocate and introduce her escort, a long, sinewy gentleman in a pinstripe gray suit that probably cost as much as I charged for my last felony case. He towered over everyone else in the vestibule. She hesitated, then touched his arm.

"This is Eric Benton," she said, making it clear that the effort to introduce him was an imposition.

The two couples made the necessary noises at each other, and then Benton inclined his head in my direction. Pale blue eyes twinkled at me from under eyebrows that resembled twin bird nests. His face was thin, with a ruddy complexion. A half-smile, urbane but not kind, sat above a well-trimmed goatee.

"So very nice to meet you, Ms. Marshfield." He bowed slightly and proffered a well-manicured hand. "You worked with Judge Kendall? Are you a lawyer also?"

He pumped my hand once and held onto it several seconds longer than necessary.

"Yes. Sam and I worked together many times."

"Then I'm sorry for the loss of your friend. I too lost a friend to a violent death, and I remember the huge gap in my life when he wasn't there anymore."

"Thank you. Once the shock dissipates, there'll be a gap in a lot of people's lives."

We were hemmed in near the entrance. "What friend did you lose, Mr. Benton?"

His smile widened, a disarming movement of the lips that divulged perfect teeth. "Actually, it's Doctor Benton." He didn't give me time to bow and scrape. "Brenda's husband, Gordon, was my good friend and partner."

"Oh."

"And if you helped Sam Kendall represent that Righetti woman, you know a lot more about why he was killed than I ever will."

His tone was without the contempt many reserve for us scum-of-the-earth defense attorneys.

"Sometimes it's easy to figure out the 'why' but difficult to come up with the 'who' in murder cases. In your partner's case, both questions were perplexing."

"Apparently not for the jury, or the judge that heard her case later," he said crisply. "I know you and Judge Kendall had a job to do, and I respect the dedication you must have, but where it's so clear cut, where the jury has already spoken, that should be the end. The retrial was incredibly difficult for Brenda. She had to relive the whole thing again, for what? So the murderess could get her face into court one more time? Ridiculous, I think."

Benton was fervent but not disagreeable. I started to launch into my standard refrain citing the times that juries are proven wrong when the real murderer later confesses or when DNA testing reveals a wrongly convicted defendant, but Brenda nudged him.

"Let's go, Eric. I have to be home early for that phone call from the coast."

"Of course." He turned back to me. "Don't misunderstand me, Ms. Marshfield. The criminal justice system is a necessary evil. But when you get personally involved in it, like Brenda was, it's a lot different from reading about it in the paper."

I borrowed a page from Kelly's empathy textbook. "Brenda's feelings are certainly valid."

He nodded and started to turn away.

"Given that, why would you bother coming to Sam's wake?" I asked.

"Of course," he said, brought up short. "After my ramblings, that's a good question."

He looked at me, head cocked as if studying a specimen. "For whatever reason, Brenda has a soft spot for Judge Kendall."

He raised those bird's nest eyebrows at her, as if inviting an explanation. Her eyes were black, her expression ice. She turned away, tugging at his hand with more force than was necessary and started snaking through the mob.

"Very nice to meet you, Ms. Marshfield." He shrugged as if to say "I just go where she takes me," then followed her.

Kevin, Kelly, and I finally extricated ourselves, piled into Kevin's BMW, and pointed it toward dinner.

CHAPTER NINE

The rows of Sam's church were packed as tight as containers on ocean-going vessels. I hoped every person was here because Sam had touched them in some way, but I suspected a percentage attended out of curiosity and a few due to fascination with violent, sudden death.

The priest's eulogy recalled Sam's passionate advocacy for those who didn't draw great seats at the table of life. Harry, his son, took the podium and told of being wrongly accused of cheating while in college and how upset he was when his dad didn't leap ferociously to his defense like he did for his clients. Choking back tears, Harry repeated Sam's words to him at that time: a defense attorney takes over the reins of the defense, plotting every last detail, calling all the shots; a parent needs to let go the reins as the child matures, allowing him to earn his own respect and dignity.

No one mentioned Sam's abject refusal to lose: perhaps that was unseemly. The soloist's clear mezzo-soprano was a showstopper. A number of guests fumbled for handkerchiefs.

At the conclusion of the service, the casket was guided down the aisle and loaded carefully into the hearse. Constantine Ross and Al Tite had staked out positions at the rear of the church, one on each side. They could have been undertakers, except for the eyes that scrutinized every face. When he got to me, Tite's gaze lingered at certain strategic locations. I gave him a pitying shake of the head to let him know I'd caught him. He shrugged in a "just looking" response, and his attention shifted to those who filed out behind me.

I rode to the cemetery with Kevin and Sarah. The canopy at the gravesite could shelter only about fifty people; the rest of us huddled into our coats against a fine mist. We were handed a sheet of paper with the graveside program and the words of a final song. When the priest got to the part about Sam returning to dust, I bit my lip. More likely he'd be reincarnated as a samurai warrior, fighting the forces of evil. The mourners struggled through the closing hymn. Soggy handouts were shoved into pockets as individuals filed past the casket for a final farewell. The crowd thinned, and the cars departed in a somber procession.

Kevin and Kelly started back to their vehicle, arms wrapped around each other. A big Caterpillar machine lurked back in the trees surrounded by four guys with shovels. I threw the hood of my coat back and let the drizzle permeate my hair and scalp until I was chilled. Then I turned to follow my friends with new respect for the term "a heavy heart," when I noticed an elderly black man materialize out of the gloom. A nylon windbreaker flapped against his thin, bent frame, a misshapen woolen hat hugged his head. He relied on a cane for balance, causing his gait to be jerky and uneven. I continued to glance at him as I picked my way to the car. He came to a halt just inside the protection of the canopy, hands clasped on the cane in front of him. His shoulders rose and fell in a gigantic shrug that was obvious even from a distance. He bowed his head as if in prayer. The next time I checked he was limping away, and the Caterpillar was closing in.

I asked Kelly and Kevin if they recognized the visitor. Kevin peered at his retreating back. "I don't think so. But I never saw half the people who were here today."

We watched the curious fellow get into a vintage Chevy from the late 60s. I made a mental note of the number on his license plate.

Antonelli's, a restaurant renowned for their smorgasbord buffet, was the post-mortem reception/luncheon destination. I left the coat check room and almost slammed into Ross, who had planted himself squarely in my path. He's my height, built like a can of tomato sauce, and proudly carries an extra twenty-five pounds or so around his middle.

"I hear we're not getting total cooperation," he said.

"Good to see you, too."

"Al's certain you're holding something back. I want to get this case behind us just as much as you do, Marshfield. It's time for you to tell us what you know, so no one has to get nasty."

I counted to ten. That enabled me to start with something other than, "Look, dick-head…"

"Al's wrong," I said heatedly. "I spent the better part of a day reviewing all the work Sam and I did together, trying to come up with anyone who'd have a motive. I gave him some possibilities, and all he does is flagellate me. I'm still working on it. If I think of something, I'll call him. But I can't solve his damn case for him."

He took a wide stance, hands on hips, head thrust forward. "No one's asking you to solve anything, Marshfield. You just be a good citizen and stop trying to snow Al with a bunch of b.s."

"Tite apparently doesn't think that people murder each other over professional livelihoods and licenses. Did he tell you the facts on the Wheaton and Stevens' cases?"

The chief looked at me stonily, but I sensed an advantage. "I thought so. You make him tell you and *you* decide if it's b.s. or not."

We had a little staring contest. "Awright," he said. "Stay in touch."

I glided away, smugly certain that I had planted a seed of doubt about Tite's assessment of me with the homicide chief.

There was a long line for the buffet, and the early arrivals were already feasting on fried chicken, their appetites whetted by a half day of mourning. I scanned the room for Brenda Haskins, Donna Gillespie, or the man in the windbreaker, all in vain. Marlene Edwards, an assistant circuit court clerk and notorious courthouse gossip, chatted with a group from her office on an outside patio, where smoking was allowed. I pushed through the door, approached her, and said hello.

"Such an awful tragedy! Who could ever do such a thing?" She drew on a cigarette, blowing the smoke away from me. Was she referring to Sam's demise or her nicotine habit?

"I'm sure the police will figure that out," I said and winced.

"Oh, you don't like my cigarette. Let me put it out." She snuffed it, carefully saving the butt.

"Marlene, can we talk in private?" I gestured to an empty table in the corner of the deck.

She bounced ahead of me eagerly. The chief clerk insisted that her staff look professional and Marlene complied, dignified in a rose-colored blouse and gray skirt. Her hair, more bleached than blond, perched in an old-fashioned beehive atop her head. Saying "Good morning" to Marlene was like putting a quarter in a merry-go-round: she started talking and didn't stop till you walked away, sometimes not even then.

We settled ourselves at the table, and she looked at me expectantly.

"You know Sam and I were close."

"Oh, yes. Everyone knows that." She nodded enthusiastically. "Always on the up and up. No one ever thought you and Sam...uh..." She ran out of words, an unusual occurrence.

"Of course not, Marlene." I leaned toward her like we were co-conspirators. "What are people saying about him?"

"Oh, he was such a lovely man! So considerate to us clerks—he'd spell out those long legal words, and he'd never yell if we made a mistake."

"Yes, I know. I mean, what are people saying about why he was killed? There must be rumors floating around."

Her eyes searched all points of the compass, avoiding mine.

"C'mon, Marlene. Good, bad, or indifferent, I don't care."

She rubbed her chin nervously. "Well, there is a *bit* of gossip."

"And...?"

Her face lit up like a homeless person invited to a Thanksgiving feast. "Mmm...other women...gambling debts...a client or witness who hated him...someone said he had an incurable disease and paid to have it done."

"Oh, brother," I muttered.

"What?"

"Nothing. What do you know about other women, Marlene?"

"Let's see." Her face screwed up in concentration. "I only know about two times."

"Tell me."

"He had a woman in his chambers. I walked in on them."

"What were they doing?" An impossible vision of desktop sex flitted across my mental movie screen.

"Talking. He was in his big chair and she was across the desk from him."

"Was anything inappropriate going on?"

Her tongue massaged her gums as she wavered between truth and trash. "I guess not."

"When was this woman in his chambers?"

"Today's Friday, right? Judge Kendall was killed Wednesday. Yes, it was the beginning of the week. Monday, I'm sure it was Monday."

"What did she look like?"

"She's here," Marlene said.

"Here? Where?"

Marlene got up, walked to the door leading inside and pointed triumphantly to the tables where Betty's friends had gathered: the bridge club group, the cause people, the social friends.

"That's her!"

"Which one?"

"The one with the blue hat."

I sighed aloud. Agnes Hart. The dark blue hat perched on top of her head contrasted nicely with her pearl white hair. Betty's best friend, and certainly a close acquaintance of Sam.

"She was wearing the same hat," Marlene added.

"You said two times. Was it the same woman the other time?"

"Oh, no. The other time it was a black lady, young, well-dressed, with lots of jewelry. I'd remember her, too."

"Is she here?"

Marlene searched the room. There were maybe fifteen or twenty African Americans, mostly men.

"Uh-uh."

"When did you see Sam with the black woman?"

"A couple of weeks ago. We were taking Sally out to Majors for her birthday. They were in a booth in the back."

Major's was a carriage trade restaurant specializing in tax-deductible business lunches and expensive dinners. Patrons can choose a secluded, intimate booth or a spotlit table.

"Go on."

"They had papers spread out in front of them."

"Did the judge see you?"

"I don't think so. I noticed them when I went to the ladies'. I couldn't see them while we ate or anything."

"Now, Marlene, this is really important." I held her gaze. "Is there anything about these two women that made you suspect that everything wasn't on the up and up? Anything at all?"

She traced an eyebrow with a fingertip.

"Well?"

"Nn...ot really."

"What have you been telling people?"

Marlene focused on a point behind my left ear.

"I...never say anything. If someone asks I might mention that Sam...was with another woman...Her voice trailed off. "I can't help it if people think the worst."

I slammed my fist on the table. "You know damn well what people think when they hear that. If I catch you talking out of school any more, Diane will definitely know about it!" Meaning Diane Campbell, the circuit clerk and Marlene's boss. "And I'll sue you for defamation." Never mind that a third-year law student could get that lawsuit tossed out.

She examined her cigarette butt with the hangdog look of a reprimanded child. "I won't say...anything more."

"Don't." I wanted to drop-kick Marlene all the way downtown.

She hurried into the restaurant, cheeks aflame. Her fellow clerks stared at her in puzzlement, then their collective gaze swept back to me. I vaulted off the deck and stomped down a narrow walkway to the rear parking lot, throbbing with anger. Why wasn't gossip-mongering a felony?

I paced up and down the rows of cars until my wrath abated, and I thought I could behave in a socially acceptable manner. I returned to the restaurant, loaded a plate at the buffet, and searched for a vacant chair.

My opponent for Monday's drug trial, Dave Roberts, waved me

over. He was not one of the evil cabal of assistants looking to put me in my place after Wednesday's jury verdict, and by the time we finished lunch he had reduced his offer to settle from a seven-year sentence to four. I thought I might be able to sell my client, and we promised to talk again.

Agnes Hart's blue hat wasn't difficult to locate. The multi-colored scarf tied loosely around her neck complemented both the hat and her soft, translucent complexion. Even the fashion-challenged like myself recognized that the woman, while no longer young, had style.

I borrowed a chair from the next table and slid in beside her. "Lunch was good. What was the final count?"

She looked baffled, then smiled in acknowledgment. "Sam had a lot of friends."

"Were you were a friend of his, Agnes?"

"I've known Sam for years, through Betty, of course. He was my lawyer when he was a...lawyer."

"I'm chasing down some loose ends," I said carefully. "Did you ever visit him in the courthouse?"

She gave me a puzzled look but answered without hesitation.

"Certainly. After he became a judge he continued to advise me. Of course, he couldn't take any money then," she assured me. "He gave me *carte blanche* to see him about insurance, or real estate, or whatever I needed. He was more than kind."

Agnes smiled. "I guess I've lost my counselor. But they're easy to replace." She picked up on the look that crossed my face. "No offense, dear. Sam's irreplaceable, especially in Betty's life."

"Did you see him last Monday?"

"Let me think. This whole week has been so discombobulated..." The crow's feet deepened around her eyes.

"One of my tenants hasn't paid rent for two months. I gave him the notice Sam had always prepared, but I filled it in myself, and slipped it under his door, and he still didn't pay. I didn't know what to do, so I called Sam and met him." She nodded. "It had to be Monday."

Her eyes widened. "Why are you asking all these questions? Is something wrong?"

I smiled reassuringly. "No. I'm just wondering about Sam's last days."

"Betty told me how close you and he were." She perched a pair of wire-rim glasses on her nose and regarded me shrewdly. "She thinks you walk on water."

"I prefer to swim in water, but thanks for the compliment," I said.

"Agnes, you saw Sam just two days before he died. Tell me, did he seem distraught or upset?"

She nudged her chair back, reflecting. "No...he was in good spirits. He could be a tad moody now and then, you know. I saw him mid-morning and he seemed almost jovial."

"As you look back now, does anything seem a bit strange?"

She blinked thoughtfully, mouth puckered. "We chatted about family a bit, and then we got down to business. I got the impression his time was limited, and he wanted to hear my little problem out as quickly as he could."

"I see. Agnes, if I need to talk to you again, can I get your number?"

"I'll give it to you now. Do you have a paper and pencil?"

Usually I'd enter a new number into my phone but I wanted to observe her dexterity. I found the necessary implements in my purse. She wrote her name and number easily, without arthritis or other difficulty. I wondered at her age, and made a mental note to ask Betty. Just then two or three others of the widow's entourage came to keep Agnes company, affording me a graceful exit.

Many of the guests had departed, but the dessert table was still full of cake, chocolate candies, and other delights. The person in line ahead of me offered a plate from the stack. I accepted it with mumbled thanks. When he wouldn't let go of the plate, I tugged at it. Griffen Bartley grinned back at me. His copper red hair wanted to jut out in every direction but had been disabled by a stylist. "Howzit goin', counselor?"

"I haven't had a chance to pass on my condolences. I'm sorry about your uncle, Griffen."

"My friends call me Griff." His breeziness faded. "From what I hear you two were quite a team. Condolences back at you."

His eyes were an amazing shade of blue flecked with green. I nodded, mesmerized.

"Will you miss him?"

He ran a strong looking hand through his barely-tamed hair. "Sam's the reason I went to law school. Harry…do you know his son Harry?"

"Sure."

"He's my cousin. We're only eight months apart. When we were small, Sam would talk about how the law was this great tool for righting wrongs and exposing liars."

"You make that sound vaguely ridiculous."

"Let's just say Sam had a talent for exaggeration."

Using a cake knife, I served a walnut brownie onto the plate and gave it back to him. "Maybe what you call 'exaggeration' others call 'advocacy.' Did you ever catch one of his final arguments? He'd take the facts we wanted the jury to believe and connect the dots until it was seamless. The jury would follow him anywhere, like he was the Pied Piper."

"Yeah, but where was he leading them? I don't mean any disrespect, but Sam was all about winning, forget the victim." He picked up a fork, cut off a corner of the brownie, and offered it to me. "How about something sweet?"

Kelly shrugged into her coat near the entrance. I wanted to continue the conversation with Griffen, but Kelly and Kevin and I had planned to return to their house after the luncheon and go through Sam's file.

"Some other time, Griff. My ride's leaving."

I took two steps, then turned back. "By the way, it *is* all about winning."

I hurried to meet Kelly at the door. Once there I gave the room a final survey. Al Tite was leaning against a far wall, his gaze sliding between Bartley and me, a thoughtful look on his face. I could see, even at this distance, the stick of a Tootsie Pop protruding from his mouth, gyrating like a cha-cha dancer.

CHAPTER TEN

Sam's huge Righetti file listed like a wrecked ship on the floor of Kelly and Kevin's den. "So, we're looking for any hint that Brenda was unfaithful."

"And any information that would make Sam a target." My glance shifted from the file to Kevin.

"You really know how to have fun."

We each grabbed a brown accordion file and settled down in silence. Kelly was picking up the kids and would be back in a while.

I examined witness folders: Cheryl Daniels, the baby-sitter who discovered the gun at Righetti's house; friends of our client who testified that she never bore a grudge against Gordon Haskins after her child died on the operating table. Others testified about her abhorrence of guns: though she had little money to spare, Ellen regularly contributed to handgun control organizations.

Paging through the police reports and summaries of testimony brought back the synergy, the magic, of working with Sam. So often one of us would dream up a "what if" scenario; we'd spin it back and forth and build on the provable facts till we came up with a plausible explanation or ingenious justification that might exculpate our client. The process was too much fun to be called work.

"What are you smiling about?" Kevin asked.

"Memories."

"Must be good ones." Kevin tossed a United Airlines ticket folder in my direction. A boarding pass and baggage receipt for a flight from Chicago to St. Louis snuggled together inside the pocket.

"I remember once we pulled one of Sam's old files to look for some billing information. There was a striped tie buried in the bottom of it.

His birthday was coming up, so we had it cleaned, gift-wrapped it and gave it to him. He really liked it—wore it all the time. We never told him he already owned it."

I felt behind the receipts and boarding pass and pulled out a sheet of legal paper folded carefully in half and then in half again. I unfolded it eagerly.

Two handwritten columns of numbers appeared on the sheet:

2012   25
2013   60

The handwriting resembled Sam's, but I wasn't positive.

"Sooz, what's up? You look like you're reading Chinese."

"What do you make of this?" I handed him the yellow sheet.

"The first column is years and the other…uh, how many cases he tried that year, how many books he read, maybe a good stock that went up?"

Kevin held the paper up to the light.

"Did this come from your file, Susan?"

"No, it was in the airline ticket folder."

"Did Sam ever travel on Righetti?"

"We drove downstate to see the client, but I don't think he went anywhere else. Maybe this is about a personal injury matter. The numbers on the right are out-of-pocket medical expenses or lost wages."

We frowned at each other. "Let's keep digging," I said.

The only sound for the next half-hour was of rustling paper. Everything in my file was straightforward Righetti material, nothing sinister. I saw no possible threat to Sam.

I stretched. Trying a case in court is exciting. Looking at it again years later is depressing, especially when the other side won.

As a last resort, I dumped the file upside down. The last thing to tumble out, crumbled and crushed under all the weight, was a small piece of paper. I smoothed it out on the desk.

The white phone message memo was dated January 26, no year. The number was written boldly, the "please call back" box was checked, the caller was Lisa Navarro.

Who?

I gave it to Kevin. "Ring any bells?"

He studied the message. "Nope. Was she a witness?"

"I don't think so."

I grabbed the phone, read the number over his shoulder and dialed. Twenty rings later I hung up.

"How can anyone survive without an answering machine in this day and age?"

"Those who don't care about who calls them."

"Bingo. We'll try Lisa some other time."

Kevin handed me a large envelope. "Take a look at this."

I pulled out a sheaf of black and white photographs. They captured the interior of a house: kitchen, living room, stairs, and a bedroom. None were labeled or identified in any way.

"I know the firm is diligent about its closed files, Kev. But look at what's going on here. The transcript is missing, there's an airline ticket with an unexplained doodle, photographs that aren't labeled or identified, and a phone message that may or may not have anything to do with the case. And it's like Brenda Haskins was never involved—her entire file is gone."

Chin in hand, I stared at the scattered debris of Righetti v. State.

"I found the paralegal who closed the file and asked about the transcript. She thought it was filed away with all this," Kevin said.

"Does any of this really matter?" I banged the file on the coffee table. "There's nothing concrete that connects this case with what happened to Sam."

Kevin leaned forward and wrapped his hands around his forehead. I'd seen this pose before: he was intently focused, blocking out everything but the train of his thought.

"Did you know Eric Benton was voted chief of staff at the hospital, twice?"

"Is he married?" I inquired.

"Not your type, Sooz." Kevin shook his head.

"Aw, shucks," I pouted. "He told me last night he and Gordon Haskins were partners. Kev, are you thinking Benton might be the one Brenda was having an affair with, *if* she was?"

We looked at each other blankly.

Caitlin stormed into the room just then. "Daddy! Susie!" She vaulted into Kevin's lap.

"Hi, princess, how are you?"

"I'm good, Daddy. Did Sam go to Jesus today?"

Her father bent his bespectacled blond head over hers. "Yes, Sam is in heaven with Jesus."

"Good." Caitlin smiled.

Kelly hurried into the room, Travis riding on one hip.

"What did I miss?"

"Not a thing. We're getting nowhere," I said glumly.

Kevin gestured to the remaining file we hadn't yet examined. "We didn't want to leave you out of the party."

Kevin and his daughter went out to practice riding a bicycle without training wheels. Kelly went to put her son down for a nap and I started in on the last file. This was the "law" file, which contained motions, briefs and copies of cases for the points we needed to argue. I combed through it quickly, since it wasn't focused on facts or witnesses. Kelly returned as I was finishing up.

"What can I do?"

"Make this file talk."

"Are you going to tell Tite about Haskins?"

"What's to tell? Sam asks a crazy question on cross in a forgotten case, the file's a bit disorganized, and I've wasted your time and mine."

"And Brenda Haskins shows up out of the blue at Sam's wake."

"There's that."

"Tell Tite what's going on."

"He's an idiot!" I protested, then burst out laughing.

Kelly looked at me with concern.

"It's okay." I couldn't stop giggling.

"It won't be okay for a while." Kelly put an arm around my shoulder. "You've had a rough day."

"I need a chlorine fix. I have to swim."

She shook her head. "You need to sit down and get emotionally reacquainted with yourself. Your feelings are buried so deep you need a backhoe to dig them out."

The usual cynical retort was primed and ready, but it caught in my throat. Kelly's words opened up a new door in my brain. Ever since the real Ryan had gone away, I had locked up my emotions and lost the key. Maybe it was time to find it.

CHAPTER ELEVEN

Members joke that the downtown "Y" is held together by baling wire and spit. It's a three-story building, about eighty years old, and takes up an entire city block. Much of it is closed off due to lack of use and safety issues, but the pool and the gyms get a lot of traffic from downtown office workers. I like it because I can walk there from the office, the pool's clean, and I usually get a lap lane to myself. A row of horizontal windows near the top an outside wall allow the natural light to penetrate. Today there were only two other lappers and no lifeguard during adult swim time.

Five laps to warm up, then a series of three: one all-out speed, the second recovery and stretch; third, pull as hard as possible. Then start over again. I always do a mile, which is thirty-two minutes, give or take. Usually, the rhythmic strokes and deep breathing induce a pleasant mindlessness, and the day's stress ebbs away into the outflow of the pool.

Not today. I couldn't shake the graveside farewell; the conversation yesterday with Dr. Benton popped into my head and wouldn't leave. I super-charged my workout, cutting through the water like a barracuda till I could barely swim straight, then I did an extra five laps. Exhausted, I turned and floated on my back. The Haskins' case had too many questions and no answers.

Success, they say, is ninety-nine per cent perspiration and one per cent inspiration. My one per cent usually occurs in the shower. As the scalding water pulverized my body, I suddenly knew how I'd find Lisa Navarro. Several cases ago, a private investigator told me about a website where one can obtain the billing address of any listed phone number. I had made a note of it for future reference. But I needed the number in Sam's file to be a landline and not a cell phone. I dressed and drove home. Fur roiled around my legs, purring like a gas mower on a summer day. I flattered myself that she was delighted to see me, but deep down I knew she was starved, and I was her waitress. I gave her a generous dinner, then went right to the computer. I had Navarro's address in a cyber minute: 1004 Spring Street. A consultation with the local map indicated Spring was in a financially-challenged neighborhood near the Broadway section of town where cheap bars and tattoo parlors vied for customers. Tomorrow was the weekend, so Lisa Navarro might be home.

I went to bed hoping that she would provide the thread that would start to unravel the Haskins' puzzle.

CHAPTER TWELVE

I strode down the ramp to the jail entrance at the rear of the courthouse, pressed the buzzer for the civilian entrance and saluted the closed circuit TV camera that was trained on me. Thirty seconds later, the thick steel door screeched open, and I proceeded into it, suddenly chilled. Behind me, the door grated closed like a hundred fingernails scraping cross a blackboard. Fluorescent lights enclosed in heavy wire cages cast an eerie glow down the passageway. Time, if it existed here, was of no consequence. The tunnel ended at a triple-thick, bulletproof glass door, also electronically controlled.

On the other side of the door, Deputy Yolanda Russell reigned from a large wraparound desk similar to the command deck of the starship Enterprise. She buzzed me into the jail's public reception area, resplendent with cheap plastic chairs that looked like they had been bounced off the wall numerous times. The smell of disinfectant was a small improvement over the nasty odors it conquered. The bank of monitors facing the deputy displayed live closed-circuit coverage of the cells, common areas and jail kitchen, all of which were sealed off behind her. An elevator in the corner of the reception area delivered visitors to and from the courthouse above. A second elevator, much more secure, was located back in the bowels of the jail and was used to transport the inmates to and from court, under guard.

The deputy continued typing just long enough to establish which of us was in charge of the situation, then nodded in my direction.

"Who do you want this morning?"

"Nobody. I need to do some research."

She pulled an oversize black ledger from a lower shelf, handed it to me with a mechanical smile, and went back to her typing.

The only public entrance into the courthouse between five p.m. when the building is closed to the public and 8:30 a.m. when it opens again is through the county jail, the way I had just come in. It's manned 24/7 so family and friends can bail prisoners out. After hours, the cops access the building down a ramp in their cars. Special sensors recognize their vehicles, open a bay door and allow them in. The inmate population should top out at 160, but it's much higher on the weekends. Lawyers can visit their incarcerated clients or do research in the law library on the fourth floor at any hour. The State's Attorney's office is in the courthouse, and those folks work long hours. But for "security reasons" anyone who enters the building when it's closed must record his or her name and the date and time of entry in the book Yolanda handed me. I doubted if the chief warden himself would swear to the accuracy of this record, but it was a place to start.

Sam's text to me was sent at 7:58 a.m. Wednesday. The courthouse officially opened for business at 8:30 a.m. His body was discovered at 8:35 a.m. It would be impossible for someone to get through the mandatory security check and metal detector at the public entrance, go up four floors to Sam's chambers and trash him between 8:30 and 8:35, so I was sure the killer was inside the building before it opened to the public.

The book fell open at the stark line between shopworn gray pages and clean, white ones. The last entry was yesterday, Friday. I recognized the scrawls of two experienced assistant state's attorneys who were putting on an aggravated rape case. They were in at 6:45 a.m. even though the courthouse was closed for Sam's funeral. Hope their boss was impressed.

Thursday had been a busy day: three attorneys and a clerk early in the morning and another attorney who signed in at nine that night. Wednesday, the day of Sam's death, four names, all in the morning: Judge Frederick at 7:40, Sam at 7:55, Griffen Bartley at 8:07, and Judge Krychewski at 8:15. I stared at the third name. What was he doing at the courthouse at that hour?

"Earth calling Susan."

I was jolted to the present.

"Cops already checked our little book."

"Am I that transparent, or are you just that smart?"

"They interviewed our desk people for Wednesday, too."

"You're telling me all this because…?"

"Al Tite said you might be down to look at the journal."

I frowned. "What else did he say?"

"He said you should call him if you want to know what he found out." Yolanda leaned back in her chair and gave me a look that said "Honey, what *are* you up to?"

"Are the desk people here today?" I asked hopefully.

"No way. They're all nine-to-fivers." Meaning Monday to Friday.

I resumed paging through the book. On Tuesday, a couple of insurance defense lawyers signed in at six p.m. and out at eight. If a visitor leaves after hours through the jail, they should sign out, but that rule is ignored for the most part. It's possible to exit from the first floor doors at any time because the fire code requires that people have an escape. A civilian watchman pads around the courthouse after hours, and a cleaning crew starts at six p.m. and finishes up about ten.

"Employees and judges and lawyers have to sign in when they come early or late. What if one of them brings someone who doesn't work at the courthouse?"

Yolanda scratched her neck. "That happens sometimes," she said slowly. "I don't know that there's a rule about it. I just ask the person for photo I.D. and let 'em go in, as long as they're with someone I know. Prosecutors sneak witnesses in sometimes and we just wave them through."

The phone rang. "Cunjil," she answered, unintentionally butchering the name of her workplace. Yolanda then attempted to explain visiting hours to someone who was having difficulty with the concept.

"Gotta go." I rose abruptly.

She covered the receiver with a hand. "I thought you was gonna use the library." She smiled sweetly.

"Press the button."

She raised her hands in an "I don't know what you're talking about" gesture. I reached over her desk and jabbed the control on her console. The door rumbled open.

"Thanks," I yelled, stepping into the time warp again. Al had beaten me to the jail list, but he wouldn't beat me to Lisa Navarro.

***

The neighborhood was a dismal copy of dozens of others I had trudged through while trolling for witnesses on public defender cases in Springfield. Not all the houses bore numbers, but a process of addition and subtraction led me to 1004 Spring, a small one-story wood frame dwelling. The paint, or what was left of it, was the color of baby spit-up. No white picket fence, no welcome mat, no friendly ding-dong when I leaned on the cracked plastic bell. The lower half of the aluminum door had held a screen in a former life: now the mesh was ripped and hanging. The sound of sticky surfaces being peeled apart ripped the air and I was suddenly eye-to-collarbone with a woman who made me feel like a sapling in a redwood forest. I craned my neck northward.

"Whachawant?"

The ring in her nose was fascinating. Her red hair was about three inches long and blown back as if she had just emerged from a wind tunnel. It matched the red heart tattoo on the side of her neck.

I took a second to regroup. "Lisa Navarro?"

She tapped her cigarette. Ash fell close enough to get my attention but far enough away so I wouldn't be singed.

"Who exactly wants to know?"

"Susan Marshfield. I was a friend of Sam Kendall. He was killed this week, and I'd like to talk to you about him, if you have five minutes."

Her eyes were deep black, set off by gold eye shadow. "You got a subpoena?" This woman would not have blinked if Al Capone and his machine-gun-toting thugs were on her doorstep.

"No, nothing like that. I'm not official, and I'm not the police." I gestured to my jeans and a turtleneck. "I'm just a friend who's looking for answers."

"Well then, honey, why exactly do you think you'll find any answers *here*?" She gestured grandly, almost knocking me off the stoop.

"It's chilly out here." I pretended to shiver. "Can I come in?"

She stared hard, peered down the street to the left, then swung her head to the right. "Oh, shit, c'mon in then, but I only got a minute."

The biggest flat screen TV I'd ever seen dominated the room. At the moment, a gigantic roadrunner bounded across it. A sofa, patterned in flowers, faced the TV, covered in clear plastic and food stains,

"Siddown." The Amazon muted the cartoon with the remote. "You were just going to tell me why you came." She captured my undivided attention by picking up a sagging armchair with one hand and toting it across the room to the sofa. The chair must've weighed a hundred pounds. Her tee shirt proclaimed 'Women Rule, Men Drool' and could not conceal the fact that she outweighed me by a lot.

"Sam was a county judge. He was killed this week in his office at the courthouse."

My hostess lowered herself into the chair and looked at me like I had just informed her the mail would arrive a bit late today.

"I was going through a file we had worked on and found a phone message that a Lisa Navarro had called, and left this number here."

"Well, judges talk to lots of people. Lots. They have to get elected and everything, so why should one little message concern you?"

"Sam wasn't elected. He was appointed," I said. "And the message concerns me because it was in a file he cared very much about. It may have something to do with why he was killed."

"No fooling." She hoisted her feet up on a coffee table that was supported by three legs and a stack of comic books.

I sat on the sofa and rubbed the plastic covering. "You know, my mom had this stuff on all the furniture in her house."

"Mine too." She broke into a smile revealing teeth the color of daisies. "I asked her one day why we had a sofa, and she said, 'so we have a place to put the plastic.'" Navarro convulsed with laughter, slapping her thighs so hard the cigarette ash cascaded to the floor.

"Lisa, I'll level with you."

She didn't blink when I said the name, though she had not yet identified herself. "The file, the one your number was in, concerned a young mother who was accused of killing her neighbor. Sam and I lost the hearing. The mother is still in the pen, and her kids are God-knows-where. I'm trying to track every possible lead."

She gave me a long, penetrating stare. A clock boldly ticked off the passing seconds. With no warning, Lisa heaved herself up and clumped to the back of the room. She closed a door which presumably led to the kitchen, then returned and settled next to me on the sofa, so close that our knees touched.

"I'm Lisa," she admitted. "Ain't no big secret. You could have checked at the post office or with the neighbors. But I don't like welfare folks and the police coming around bothering me. I got more'n enough to worry about, just paying the rent and taking care of my kid." She wiped her brow with the back of her hand, exhausted by the thought of her responsibilities.

"I got my rights." She sat up straight and jabbed my arm with a stubby forefinger for emphasis. "The cops know I know my rights. I had Sam dress 'em down once after they hassled me."

Pay dirt, I thought.

"Were you a client of his?" I tried to keep the elation out of my voice.

"Not exactly. When he came to see me he left his card and told me to call him when I needed some help." She leaned toward me. The scent of garlic was unmistakable. "You a lawyer?"

I nodded. At that moment, a young girl in short shorts and a sweatshirt burst in through the door Lisa had just closed. "Ma, where's my big heels?" she hollered.

"Top shelf in your closet, honey," Lisa yelled back. "That's my daughter, Cheryl."

I stared at the doorway through which the girl disappeared, dumbfounded. Cheryl had been a witness in the Righetti case, the baby-sitter who tipped off the police about the gun in Ellen's linen closet.

"Cheryl Daniels."

"I never married her dad." Lisa shrugged by way of explanation.

"Cheryl found the gun…"

"Yeah, yeah." She waved her hand in the air to cut me off or perhaps in frustration at her daughter's involvement.

"Can we start at the beginning?" I asked.

She stubbed her cigarette out in a bronze ashtray the size of a barbeque. "Beginning? Someone better than me knows where all this began. But I'll open the door and let you have a peek." She leaned back and stared at the ceiling, gathering her thoughts.

"Cheryl babysat for the Righettis, off and on, for quite a while. After the divorce, when Ellen had to go back to work, Cheryl would watch her kids after school." Lisa shook out a new cigarette from the pack and lit it with a gold Zippo, a storyteller warming to her tale.

"One day, not long after Doc Haskins was murdered, Cheryl comes home and tells me this business about finding a gun at Ellen's house, right where the kids could get ahold of it. Now Cheryl may fib about curfew, but she's not going to make up a story like that."

"Did you call Ellen?"

"Hell no! I ain't gonna shove my nose in her business."

"Ellen denied ever seeing the gun before."

"Yeah, I read that in the paper, all right." Lisa frowned.

"The serial numbers were filed off the gun. It was impossible to trace. The cops took Ellen's photo to all the local gun shops—no one could remember her buying it or even being in the store. But the jury didn't find that very persuasive."

Lisa snorted. "You can get a gun anywhere. Gun shop's the last place you'd go if you want to keep it a secret."

"But if she wanted to keep it a secret, why did she keep the gun in the house, accessible to the kids, after she supposedly killed him? Why not wipe it clean and throw it in the river?"

Lisa's bit her bottom lip as if this was a question she hadn't yet addressed.

"Lissen, you want some coffee?"

"Sounds great," I said, wondering if my health insurance was paid up. She shuffled to the back.

"Instant okay?" she called out.

"Sure," I lied shamelessly.

She lumbered back in. "Water's on."

"If you have such a dislike of the police, how come you called them when Cheryl found the gun?"

"I didn't call 'em. Cheryl did. Then…" Her hands flew skyward. "*BOOM*. Ellen gets arrested, the kids go to the dad, wow." She shook her head as if the pace of events was too much.

"You didn't know she called the cops?"

"Not till afterwards. Then the state made Cheryl testify, and it's all over till the re-trial with your friend Sam."

"Did he call you?"

"Yep, out of the blue, and starts talkin' about this new Righetti hearing. I don't quite understand it all, but he's nice on the phone, and everything's hunky-dory, and he asks if he can come over and talk to Cheryl, and of course I say no. He says it's only fair since Cheryl's talked to the cops and she already testified and everything. I say no again and I hang up. But then I got to thinkin' about how he said it wasn't fair, her talkin' to one side and not the other. I know lotsa people doin' time cause they couldn't find no witnesses to help 'em, so I called him back and told him he could talk to Cheryl as long as I was there."

"Was that in January?" I asked, remembering the date on the phone message.

"Dunno." She shook her head.

An urgent whistling sound emanated from the kitchen and she struggled to her feet again.

"Be right back."

Lisa returned with two steaming cups on a red lacquered tray that spelled out "Las Vegas" in glitzy script.

"Cream or sugar?"

"Neither, thanks." I stirred the beverage cautiously.

Lisa remained standing, both hands wrapped around her cup, lost in thought. "I don't know that Ellen Righetti's got it in her."

I wondered if I'd heard right. Parallel universes are tricky.

"You mean to kill someone?"

"Yeah, that's what I mean." She took a gulp of coffee and gave me a sly look. "I know something that never came out at the trial."

I cocked my head. "What might that be?"

"Brenda Haskins…she was doin' some other guy when her old man was killed.

"I don't mean at the 'xact same second," she hastened, apparently taken aback at my expression.

"You mentioned that little tidbit to Sam."

"Well, we got to talking when he came over. He was nice, for a guy, like you nice for a lawyer, and yeah, I told him."

"How do you know Brenda was having an affair?" The thought of Brenda and Lisa exchanging confidences while volunteering at the hospital gift shop taxed the imagination. "Do you know who the guy was?"

She grinned at me like a cat playing with a stunned mouse. "I'm goin' to tell you just what I told Sam. I'll lay it .a…l . . .l out for you." Lisa settled herself back into the chair, wiggling with anticipation.

"First, you gotta understand that I knew Brenda before she was Brenda Haskins. We both grew up on the East side and went to Main. She graduated before I got there, but we knew each other, and we knew a lot of the same people. She went off to college somewhere, then got married and had a baby. I found out through the grapevine later that she was divorced, and then everyone in town knew when she married that doctor."

I nodded, remembering that a stepson of the Haskins' was away at school or on a camping trip when his stepdad was killed.

"So you've known Brenda for quite a while."

"Yeah, like that. I never held it against her that she married that rich dude, and she didn't care that I lived over here by the tracks." She nodded to herself. "Brenda never did me no wrong."

"So what makes you think she had an affair?"

Lisa sipped her coffee thoughtfully.

"When Cheryl was babysitting for Ellen, before Dr. Haskins was killed, I picked her up a lot. Ellen would call me when she was leaving work, and we'd both get to her house about the same time. We'd chat about this and that, you know. Turned out we both knew Brenda Haskins: Ellen showed me where she lived next door."

"A couple times I had to wait for Cheryl. I didn't want to go into Ellen's house so I waited in my car. It was late, between eleven and midnight. Both times, a man came out of Haskins' house next door and got into a big car parked about a half block down the street." She nodded at me conspiratorially.

I waited. "And?"

"And what?" Lisa was indignant.

"It was probably a friend, or maybe it was a business meeting. Docs have a finger in every pie in town and they can never meet during business hours. Maybe it was Gordon you saw, going out to the hospital for an emergency."

Lisa laughed. "Honey, you're a tough sell. Maybe I couldn't prove it in court, but this here's real life, and I don't need no avalanche fallin' down on me before I run for cover. Sam, he was kinda skeptical too. But when I told him about the car, he said it weren't none of theirs. Besides, Dr. Haskins wouldn't park his car a half block from his house."

"Do you remember what kind of car it was?"

"Sure. It was a new Lincoln, dark color, blue or black. One of the pushers in the hood drove one just like it. And I knew what Dr. Haskins looked like. He was a short man—way under six feet, I'd think. And the man that came out of the house was tall for a man, very tall."

"Did you see his face?"

"Nah, it was too dark and he was walkin' on the other side of the street. I just saw his body. He had a coat and a hat on and walked real fast."

"Same man, same car both times?"

She cracked her knuckles. "Yep."

"Did you ever tell this to the cops?"

"Cops." She spit out the word. "I don't tell cops nuttin'." She eyed me keenly. "Kessler came over here last week. You know Kessler?"

"Of course," I said wearily. When Kessler pinned on his badge, he started at aggressive and could go all the way to psycho. The guy made more busts than any other two cops combined.

"He wants to talk to Cheryl. I ask if she's under arrest. He says no, just a routine investigation. I say no, 'cause I won't let him near her if I don't have to. You know what he says then?" Lisa bounced off the chair and started pacing. I hoped she didn't have blood pressure issues.

"He says Cheryl's involved in a drug thing at school, maybe sellin' it. I seen how cops twist what you say and make it come out the way they want, especially with a kid. Then he said sometimes he does favors for the guys he busts so they owe him one when they get back on the street. And he runs his filthy hand along my doorframe, right there on the porch, and says things about my house and people being careless with matches." Her tone was belligerent but her voice caught at the end.

"Damn," I muttered. "Are you afraid?"

"Sometimes it's hard to know where mad stops and scared begins." She crossed the room in three steps and took a quick look out the peephole. "All I know is he's the biggest shit I ever seen, and I seen some big ones."

"Lisa, I'll give you my card. Next time Kessler hassles you, you tell him I'm your lawyer and I'm keeping a file on all his contacts with you. That might chill him out."

Emphasis on might.

I received a super-size grin. "That's awful good of you, Miss Marshfield."

I wrote my unlisted home number on the card and gave it to her.

"I hope they catch whoever done your friend. He seemed like a nice guy."

I nodded. "He was the best."

The Rugrats were on the TV now. Tommy was chasing some girl with blue hair down the street. Lisa's attention wandered to the screen and stayed there.

"Thanks for the coffee and the help."

"Anytime." She waved me off, grabbed the remote and powered the volume up to rock-concert level. I let myself out. Something was radically different. I stopped and sniffed: fresh air.

On the ride back downtown, I reflected for the umpteenth time on the novelty of my adopted community. Joliet's population exceeds 100,000, and every day I run into people who shouldn't know each other but do, like Brenda Haskins and Lisa Navarro. Sometimes the ties go back generations, other times only months. The burg looks like a little city, but it acts like a small town. By and large, the people here matter to each other.

Lisa's story added strength to the theory that Brenda was cheating on Gordon Haskins. If she *was* a two-timing spouse, was she also a murderer?

CHAPTER THIRTEEN

Tite's message as relayed by Yolanda seemed to signal a willingness to share information. I had misplaced his card so I called the police station but he was out. I left my name and the unpublished number that rings in my office, not at the firm.

The phone was as quiet as Wrigley Field when the Cubs are down by ten. I decided to pay a call on my neighbor.

The Blane, Kendall and Montgomery law firm encourages its associate attorneys to put in a half day on Saturday mornings. The partners didn't need encouragement: they had been coming in on Saturdays for so long they had forgotten there were other options. It was almost 1 p.m. but Griffen Bartley might still be cranking out billable hours. The oversized double doors were unlocked and the half-moon reception desk was deserted. Two hallways angled back to a Dilbert-like secretarial pen ringed by attorneys' offices. The legal talent pondered the conundrums of the day from their second floor windows where the quality of the view depended on the status of the occupant.

I chose the hallway on the right. The first two offices were vacant. In the third, two waffle-soled running shoes rested atop the desk, almost obscuring Griffen Bartley as he reclined in his chair, head resting on fist, eyes closed. I tiptoed across the room. The screensaver on his computer monitor was an image of the young associate and a very attractive blond in swimming suits. They appeared to be joined at the hip.

"Hello, Bartley," I said brightly. "Catching up or getting ahead?"

"Wha...?" His elbow slipped and his head came up with a start. "Marshfield?"

"The one and only." I circled to the front of the desk. "May I sit down?"

"Yeah, sure, yeah." He scrambled to his feet, grabbed a half dozen files from the client chair and dumped them on the floor.

"You gonna bill for the time you just spent napping?"

He rubbed his eyes, then stopped mid-stroke. "Did you come here to give me an ethics lesson?"

Bartley used a gel that made his hair do exactly what he wanted. I was willing to bet he worked the same magic on most women.

"No. I'm here to find out how you got to the hospital so quickly after Sam was attacked."

His eyes widened in understanding. "Information doesn't come cheap."

"Really. What's your price?"

He screwed up his face as if the question taxed his resources. "A glass of your favorite beverage at your favorite hang-out."

"Griffen, it's a simple question."

He leaned back, arms crossed, blue-green eyes searching my face. Being the center of his attention wasn't the worst thing that had happened today.

"Okay, simple answer." He shrugged off his bantering attitude for the moment. "I had to research some law journals so I got to the library about eight. I went to the john a little later and one of the bailiffs grabbed me and told me what happened. Most of them know Sam and I are... *were* related."

"Yeah."

"I drove right to the hospital and got there just before Aunt Betty arrived."

"Was anyone else in the law library?"

He shook his head. "It was deserted. The librarian doesn't get in till nine."

"What were you researching?"

"Constitutionality of a new provision of the Domestic Abuse Act."

"In law journals?" I asked skeptically. These scholarly publications contain articles on esoteric points of law written by ivory tower law review staffs and are capable of being understood only by other ivory tower law review staffs.

"What?" he protested. "The legislature copied the statute from other states and I was looking for a discussion of its history."

A plausible explanation, but only barely.

"Which lawyer were you researching for?"

He sipped from a designer water bottle. "I was under the impression we were having a cordial conversation, but suddenly one of us is in cross-examination mode."

"Not me. I'm still having a friendly conversation."

"I was afraid of that. Is this how you charm the rest of the world?"

"I'm not here to charm you, Griff. I'm here for a little information."

He crossed his arms across a chest that had done its share of bench presses and pouted. "Charm me first, then information."

I couldn't stop a giggle from spilling out.

"Made ja laugh." He pumped his fist in mock celebration.

"Are you ever serious?"

"Let me think. Was it nineteen ninety-seven? Once back then, maybe."

"Pardon me for asking, but how did you get into law school?"

"Ah, the lady questions my sincerity, the high purpose of my life."

"Who wrote your letters of recommendation?"

The boyish impishness faded.

"Sam."

"The name is not spoken with great affection," I observed.

The atmosphere in the office changed, like someone switched all the light bulbs from white to deep violet. Griffen stared at his computer monitor, but it was with the look of someone whose thoughts are miles away.

"My last year of law school I came here to watch Sam on trial," Griffen began. "He was defending a guy charged with armed robbery. The victim was an old man, seventy if he was a day, and the defendant had shoved a gun in his face. When Sam cross-examined him he confused the poor old guy so badly he looked like a fool."

I cleared my throat. "That's his job, Griffen. Once the witness is in the box you aim right between their eyes, if they're seven or seventy. That's what the oath you took is all about." He tapped the business end of a pen on the desktop. "I can't be a zealot like that for every client who comes along." "No problem. If you can't play to win, go plan estates. Try appliance repair school."

As a brand new lawyer some fifteen years ago, I was chagrined to learn that public defenders were somewhere south of spit in the estimation of judges and, frequently, their own clients. I decided to cut Bartley some slack.

"Law school teaches you how to think like a lawyer, but the profs don't tell you how to deal with dopers, rapists, and liars. Oh, did I mention insurance adjusters? The first year out of school is tough for everyone, Griff." I sat down in the chair he had cleared off. "I wasn't sure I'd make it to my first jury trial 'cause I was throwing up in the john. I did my entire opening statement to the jury with vomit on my black patent-leather shoes."

He looked at me with suspicion, trying to figure out how much of what I said was true. Then he smiled. "Thanks for trying to make me feel better. But honestly, if playing to win means abusing a witness like Sam did to that poor old guy, maybe I should write appellate briefs and forget trial work."

"Griff, that wasn't abuse! His client was looking at years in the joint. Sam's duty was to keep him out."

I leaned forward, careful to choose the right words. "If you ever do try a criminal case, make sure you visit the penitentiary first. Know the stakes you're playing for."

He had one of those compressed air cans for cleaning keyboards on his desk. I picked it up, pointed it at his chest and pulled the trigger.

"Ahhh!" He grabbed his chest and fell back. "Shot by the woman of my dreams!"

I leaned over the desk, can in hand. "Which lawyer did you say you're working with on the Domestic Abuse statute?"

CHAPTER FOURTEEN

"Did I wake you, dear?"

Betty's voice on the phone was like a warm, cozy comforter. I squinted at the alarm. 9:16 a.m. "No problem."

"It's Sunday, you know." Despite my status as a mid-life adult, she was reminding me to go to church.

The witty lobe of my brain was still asleep but the rest of it was awake enough to know that any response would be the wrong one.

She hummed into the phone a moment, then stopped abruptly. "I came across something in Sam's den and I'm not sure what to do with it."

"What is it?"

"It looks like that Righetti file you two worked on a while ago."

I felt a buzz like a triple espresso just kicked in. "No kidding. Can I come over?"

We arranged to meet at her house at 6:30, then go out to dinner.

I couldn't stay in bed after Betty's bombshell, so I padded out to the espresso machine, ground the beans, and a minute later was sipping the heavenly brew. I have a large deck and an enormous back yard that slopes down to a creek. It was too cold to go out, but as I watched two squirrels chase each other, a plan evolved. I showered and dressed and headed for Brenda Haskins' subdivision.

The homes were large and well-maintained, but not snooty. No in-ground pools or gated entrances. I always visit the scene of a felony trial, but the Righetti case was a post-conviction proceeding without factual disputes so I hadn't bothered to view the locale.

A Crown Victoria with four antennas was anchored in the Haskins' driveway. It had no official markings but was obviously a cop-mobile. I pulled to the curb, brimming with curiosity. Was this the site of another crime? Was Brenda all right? Minutes later the front door opened and Al Tite emerged, resplendent in a brown suit, dark blue shirt and gold tie. What was *he* doing here?

I whistled loudly as he inserted the key into the Crown Vic and his head snapped up. He looked around, puzzled, then eyed me suspiciously.

"Counselor."

He sauntered across the ten yards that separated us, leaned on my passenger side window and peered in.

"What brings you to these parts, Ms. Marshfield?"

"You know, a week ago you were a perfect stranger, and now I've seen you four times in the last five days."

"Life is strange. But I appreciate you describing me as perfect."

He tapped the roof of my car. "Why are you here?"

"Here? Where's 'here'? I'm on the way to church."

He glanced at my jeans and sweatshirt. "Try again."

"Do you get the feeling our conversations are ritualized? You ask questions, I try to answer them, then you denigrate my answers."

"No. I get the feeling you dance around whatever it is I'm trying to ask you."

"Lighten up, lieutenant. Life's too short to let me get to you."

He turned and walked deliberately around my car, dropping out of sight at the back end. Damn! He was checking to see if my vehicle registration was current. Did I put that renewal sticker on the rear license plate?

I pushed a button and the door locks popped open. After a minute he surfaced, opened the front passenger door, pushed the seat back as far as it would go and corkscrewed in.

"Third time's the charm. You're at Brenda Haskins' house because…?"

"Who came into the courthouse through the jail Wednesday morning and didn't sign in?"

His eyes shifted a fraction and I knew I had a winner.

"Ms. Marshfield, you and I are here for the same reason. We'll catch the guy who did Judge Kendall a whole lot sooner if you play straight with me and cut the games."

I tapped the steering wheel absent-mindedly. Al just admitted he's visiting Brenda because there's some connection to Sam. So far as I know, the only link between the two is Ellen Righetti's case. Had Tite found out about the post-conviction matter or was there another link? The lieutenant wouldn't give me anything out of the goodness of his heart. Time for Negotiation 101.

"Let me tell you something that could be significant. A couple weeks before he was killed, Sam had lunch at Major's with a younger, well-dressed black woman. They had a bunch of papers spread out in front of them." I hesitated. "Sam would have mentioned this to me a year ago, but as you know, we've drifted apart. It's worth checking out."

"I agree," he nodded. "We could talk to Majors, find the charge slip, and interview the waitress." He paused. "Or I could just tell you right now the woman's name is Nina Burkhart and she was pitching life insurance."

"His calendar." Tite didn't waste time.

"Verified by Burkhart and her boss. And?"

I'll never get what I don't ask for. "I want in on your investigation, lieutenant. You think it's nuts, but I can give you something in return. Sam and I handled a case together that may have some unfinished business. If we each work an angle, we might get somewhere."

Tite watched, expressionless, throughout my pitch. When I was finished, he turned to face me. "Ms. Marshfield, there's a person out there who killed your friend and did a pretty savage job of it. You see these guys in court, shackled and guarded, on their best behavior. 'Working an angle,' as you put it, is not the best idea you've had this week."

"Lieutenant, there's no law granting police the sole authority to investigate crimes. I can help you, but I need your help in return. That's my offer."

He looked out the front window pensively.

"It's the text, isn't it?" he asked softly. "You feel bad because you weren't there when Sam needed you."

I choked back the expletive that almost escaped. His words ricocheted in my head like the silver sphere in a pinball game.

A minute passed.

"It's not your fault." Tite's tone was neutral, matter-of-fact.

"It may be a while before I believe that," I said.

"Is that why you're so...relentless about wanting in on the investigation?"

"The text is part of it," I acknowledged quietly. "But there's more." I pushed the driver's seat back all the way and turned to face him. "I have to know why. When people were rotting in their cells, absolutely powerless against the state, Sam went to bat for them. He was their champion, and most of them were scum. He worked his butt off for them. He didn't deserve to die like that."

Al cast a pointed glance at my hands. They were clenched into tight fists.

"And you want to make it right?" His tone was merely curious, devoid of sarcasm.

"I'm not looking for vengeance." I shook my head. "I just need to know the reason. And the killer...when the state tries to crush him...I want him to know there's no one like Sam to fight for him anymore."

I had just committed the cardinal sin of attorneys, opening my mouth without knowing what was going to come out, but it was liberating.

"Remember the Haskins murder case, lieutenant?"

"Sure. Neighbor lady offed Dr. Haskins 'cause he messed up the anesthesia on her daughter...or son, I forget which. We don't get many murder calls from places like this." He inclined his head at the Type A neighborhood.

"Right. The neighbor was Ellen Righetti. You know what a post-conviction petition is, Al?"

"Educate me."

"P.C. for short. You have to allege and prove a substantial denial of constitutional rights: the prosecution withheld evidence of the accused's innocence; a juror was bribed; the defendant didn't have effective assistance of counsel. There are several options, but they're all tough to prove. It means something happened behind the scenes that wasn't kosher."

"So, a p.c. asks that the convicted person be released?"

"Yeah, but that almost never happens. If you're really, really lucky, you get a new trial."

"You're telling me this because…?"

"Ellen filed one on her own after she was convicted and sentenced. Sam and I were appointed to represent her. She insisted she didn't murder Gordon Haskins, and Sam believed her. I never saw him work as hard as he did on that case. He was possessed by it."

"You lost, didn't you?"

"Yeah, but not from lack of trying."

"And…?" He peered at me, totally focused.

Deep breath.

"I have a sneaking suspicion Sam never quit working on the case, even after we lost. He never let on to me; it's just a hunch. That's why I'm here today. Brenda Haskins was the main prosecution witness. Sam cross-examined her at the hearing and then, surprise, surprise, she shows up at his wake."

He unwrapped a Tootsie Pop, regarded it suspiciously, and popped it into his mouth.

"So Sam was trying to prove someone else killed Haskins?"

"It's the best I can come up with."

Al stared at the Haskins' home through the windshield. "Lawyers keep notes of everything they do, don't they?"

"We record time for billing. Some lawyers charge for every time they think about a case, even if they're in the bathroom."

"Would Sam have done that?"

I shook my head. "As a record-keeper, he was a malpractice disaster waiting to happen. What he didn't keep in his head, he wrote down on napkins, or maybe on his hand. And I doubt if he kept records at all after he got on the bench—no need to."

"Don't attorneys have to keep files for a certain time after they're closed? For appeals and what not?"

I mustered a straight face. "Right. Sam's old firm should have his file."

"And if you worked on the case, you must have a file too?"

"I do, Al. I've been through it. It's pretty straightforward, but you're welcome to take a look."

He contemplated me at some length. "Ms. Marshfield, I'm going to trust you on this one. I hope I'm not being had."

"I'm playing straight with you, lieutenant, just like you asked."

"This Righetti case may be the break we need. Maybe Sam found the murderer but then the murderer found him."

There was animation in Tite's eyes I hadn't seen before.

"Can you meet me in Sam's chambers tomorrow, and bring your Righetti file? I'll let you go through his stuff, and we'll see if we can make any progress."

"That works," I said cautiously. "I've got a trial at nine-thirty, but it might settle."

He pondered a moment. "Tell you what. Leave your file with the receptionist at Sam's firm. I'll look at yours and his together. Call me when you're finished in court, and we'll meet in his chambers."

"Okay," I nodded and continued without skipping a beat. "So what brings you from hearth and home to talk to Brenda Haskins?"

He worked the Tootsie-Pop from one side of his mouth to the other. It was like watching a tennis ball being volleyed between two solid baseline hitters.

"I'm cramped in here. Mind if we walk for a while?"

I looked at him suspiciously. "Sure."

We emptied out of the car. Neither of us spoke for the first block.

"You're not going to like what I have to tell you," he said.

I stopped mid-stride.

"Play fair," I warned. "I spilled my guts about Righetti."

A frown worked its way across Tite's face. "Right at this moment, I can't tell you why I was at the Haskins' house. It could jeopardize the investigation and maybe you too." He turned to me, a hint of something other than police arrogance on his face.

"There's one more thing. I have to ask you—in all seriousness—not to talk to Brenda Haskins."

"What?" I stared in disbelief.

"Haskins is off-limits," he said with finality.

A flood of white-hot heat ignited in my gut and rocketed to my brain. "How do *you* get off telling *me* what I can't do?" I kicked an unfortunate stone on the sidewalk and sent it into space. "Screw you, Tite! I give you the best lead in the case and then I'm supposed to let it go? You want any more 'cooperation' from Marshfield you'll have to subpoena me to a grand jury!"

I turned on my heel and spun away. He grabbed my left hand from behind. I pulled fiercely, but to no avail. I turned, bringing my right hand back to slap him. He was expecting it and caught my wrist halfway to his face.

"Marshfield, *listen.*" His eyes burned. "There's too much we don't know yet. If the wrong person finds out you're asking questions, it could be a disaster. Wait twenty-four hours. I'll make it up to you."

In spite of every instinct, in defiance of all reason, I found myself trusting him.

"How about the…the jail?" I stammered. He held both my hands. He inhaled deeply.

"Tomorrow, when we meet in Sam's chambers. Promise."

"Why should I believe anything you tell me?"

His hands released mine, gently caressing my fingers as he let go. A charge passed through me and I couldn't move, like we were a shared pair of atoms.

"Because I don't want you to get hurt."

He stepped toward me and we were inches apart. He smelled better than I did, like woods after a cleansing rain. His eyes glittered.

I drew back, feeling like a kite in a thunderstorm. A gentle smile ambled across Tite's face. We stood, not touching, then he winked and walked back to the cars. He got into the Crown Vic and pulled up to where I was standing, slightly catatonic, next to the Acura.

"See you tomorrow." He gave a casual salute and cruised away.

entirenow.

CHAPTER FIFTEEN

I don't like cops, and I don't want to. I particularly do not want to like Al Tite.

The pool is my refuge and haven. I swim when I'm feeling up, down, or maybe just dazed, like now. As I did my laps I replayed the last scene with the lieutenant a kazillion times and convinced myself that he had played me for a fool. Hadn't I learned anything from my hapless clients who had been duped by badges? It was mid- afternoon when I left the "Y," a civilized hour to call on Mrs. Haskins. Tite could go spit.

Her house hadn't changed since morning. The door chime welcomed me with a few bars of *Some Enchanted Evening*. A glance into the vestibule revealed fresh flowers in an expensive-looking vase on a chi-chi table, right out of House Beautiful.

A late model Cadillac convertible, red, top down, purred up the drive just as the song faded. Brenda Haskins' white-blond hair flashed in the sun. The bay door of the garage yawned open and the car disappeared.

I waited, then rang again. This time the lady of the house answered promptly, adorned in pale pink tights and a leotard, hair drawn back into a tight pony tail. Her tanned and deeply lined face put her between fifty and sixty, but the spandexed body belonged to an in-shape forty-something. The woman either starved herself or had cornered the market on fitness tapes.

"Hi, Mrs. Haskins. Susan Marshfield."

"I remember." She glanced over my shoulder to see if anyone more interesting accompanied me. "What in the world do you want?"

"I wonder if you could spare a few minutes?"

"No."

"I need to talk to you about Sam."

Her gaze shimmied scornfully from my blue Cubs sweatshirt down to my running shoes.

"There may be a connection between Sam's death and your husband's."

"That's impossible!" she bristled. "Look, you and Judge Kendall lost Ellen's case. Get over it and leave me the hell alone!"

"I *am* a pest," I acknowledged. "But you're the common denominator between your husband and Sam; you may know something that could help find the murderer. Humor me, Mrs. Haskins, just for a minute."

She rolled her eyes heavenward but when they returned to earth they were a shade softer. "I do feel badly about Judge Kendall. I wish it had never happened."

I bobbed my head encouragingly.

"I'll give you a minute."

I pushed across the threshold. To the immediate right, the famous staircase led upstairs to where Gordon had been shot. She led me to an expansive, sun-filled living room filled with modern, sleek furniture, better suited to a well-appointed bachelor condo than a widow's home. Everything was beige or white, including a gleaming baby grand piano. I was jolted by a sense of deja vu. The photos in Sam's file—they were pictures of this house! Had Sam taken them? I took a deep mental breath and told myself to go slow and do whatever it took to get Haskins to talk.

"Is anyone else home?" Brenda and I faced each other amidst a lustrous leather sofa and chair arrangement.

"No." She paused. "I live alone."

"Sam came here to talk to you, didn't he?"

She crossed her arms and thrust one leg out in a model's pose.

"You should know. You worked with him on the case."

"Maybe he promised to keep your conversation secret."

She looked at me through calculating eyes. "Maybe he didn't want you to know."

I nodded.

"Brenda."

I waited until she graced me with her full attention. "I think Sam was still working on Gordon's murder when he died."

She laughed derisively. "What planet have you been on? Ellen Righetti killed Gordon. She was convicted, and even you and Sam couldn't save her." She sank gracefully into the leather chair, drained by the memory of her ordeal.

"A minute ago, you said you felt badly about Sam. Tell me why," I urged in my sincerest imitation of a grief counselor.

She stroked the white arm of the chair with blood red nails.

"He was...an understanding person...quite kind," she said, clipped. A generous perspective considering his embarrassing question during cross-examination.

"How so?"

"I need a drink. Can I get you something?" She left without waiting for a response.

"Sure," I chirped to the now empty room.

A print the size of a refrigerator hung on one wall, wiggly green lines chasing after pastel-colored geometric shapes, all in a sea of iridescent pink. The opposite wall supported an oil painting with a lot of white space and sundry intersecting lines a hundred shades of gray. After each line hit another, its direction changed slightly. On a different day, in a different place, either one of these works would be intriguing.

Brenda came back with two cans of diet drinks, iced glasses and cocktail napkins on a silver tray. A slice of lime graced the rim of each glass.

"I just got back from aerobics," she announced.

"Do you work out every day?"

"I used to be an instructor. Can't break the habit." She offered me a glass.

"Thanks. I know what you mean. I'm a swimmer."

She nodded, and the atmosphere seemed a degree less chilly now that we had the common ground of physical fitness. She put the tray down on a hexagon-shaped glass coffee table.

"If you're trying to find out who murdered Sam, I can tell you from first-hand experience, the police do an excellent job."

I perched on the edge of the sofa. "They're doing their best, but they're having trouble coming up with a motive."

She cocked her head at me in response.

"How did he happen to be here?"

She bent over and lifted the cover of a small ebony box sitting on the coffee table. I watched, fascinated, as she extracted a single cigarette, then picked up a thin gold lighter, flicked it expertly and touched the flame to the paper-wrapped stick of chemicals. Amazingly her half-inch long lacquered fingernails didn't impede the production. She inhaled deeply, then sauntered to the piano and played a riff with her left hand. She held the last key down and the final note clung to the oxygen molecules in the room.

"During my testimony, Sam asked if I was having an affair when Gordon was killed." She turned back toward me. "I was totally taken aback. I didn't have to answer the question, but it was very rude, and I phoned him afterwards."

"When did you call him?"

"After the hearing." She tapped the cigarette impatiently into a crystal ashtray. "I was angry. I told him so."

"What was Sam's reaction?"

A satisfied smile crossed Brenda's face. "After Gordon died, I had an encounter with Christ. I learned forgiveness. Sam apologized for his behavior, profusely. I forgave him."

"He took pictures of your house."

"He said he kept a photo album of his cases, not pictures of people but of places."

News to me.

"What else happened between you and Sam?"

She shrugged noncommittally. "Nothing."

"You told him something that made him keep working on Ellen's case, Brenda. What was it?"

She turned away and appeared absorbed in the painting of intersecting lines. A clock ticked off the seconds. A myriad of them.

"It wasn't important," she said finally.

"Brenda, I really like that oil painting. It's like each time the lines intersect that's one person engaging another and being just a little bit changed by the encounter." Wow; where had *that* come from? I couldn't remember taking an art appreciation course in my life.

"Maybe Sam's meeting with you changed his thinking about the case. If I knew what you told him, I might be able to figure out what he did next. It'd be a huge help," I pleaded.

She took a final drag on her cigarette, stubbed it out in the ashtray and exhaled the smoke in an unbroken stream. She was quiet for a half minute, then muttered "What the hell," so quietly I could hardly hear it.

"After Gordon was killed, I was in shock. People streamed in and out of the house like it was a train station." She shivered, maybe from the scanty outfit or perhaps the memory of folks parading through her house. "After he was buried, I remembered seeing the key to Ellen's house hanging from its peg in the pantry."

I gave her statement an inordinate amount of thought. "Is that significant?"

"How do I know? The point is, I don't remember seeing the key there, in its place, for a while before that."

"The key to Ellen's house was missing after Gordon's death?"

"I didn't say that. I don't know it for a fact, and I certainly couldn't swear to it under oath. I was dazed those first days: maybe it was there but I just didn't see it. At any rate, after Ellen was arrested, the police found the key right where it was supposed to be."

"You didn't mention it to the cops but you thought it important enough to tell Sam?"

"Actually, I had forgotten about it. But when he came over and we got to talking, I remembered."

I had been fibbed to by far more accomplished liars than Brenda Haskins.

"Was the key to Ellen's labeled or identified in any way?"

"Of course. Gordon couldn't abide messiness or confusion. Everything was labeled and had a place. The key was tagged with the Righetti name."

Time for the $64,000 question.

"Brenda, who were you having an affair with when Gordon was killed?"

Brenda's face melted into something from a computer-enhanced horror movie.

"You bitch!" The contents of her glass came hurtling at me. I dodged right, but it caught my shoulder. Fortunately it contained only ice and the dregs of her drink.

"How dare you come into my home and ask me a question like that!"

I scrambled to my feet and made a show of blotting my sweatshirt.

"Brenda, I'm not saying the other person is guilty of anything," I implored. "But it looks suspicious. You had a lover and a husband. The latter is killed, the murder weapon's found in the neighbor's house, your key to that house is missing and accessible to the lover. It's a possibility, whether you want to admit it or not."

"No, it's not!" She stamped her foot. "The key was probably there all the time. You're still trying to get Ellen out of prison! You want to pin Gordon's murder on….someone else." She paused, breathing rapidly. "I guarantee you, he did not have a key to this house."

That sounded like an admission to me.

"Furthermore, that…person… was out of town the morning Gordon was killed. It's been verified." Her tone was righteously indignant.

"By whom? Sam?"

"Hell, no. I didn't tell him who it was either. Ms. Marshfield, you are seriously mistaken here, just like you were when you represented Ellen."

Time to change the subject.

"Why were the police here today?"

Her eyes opened wide. "How did you know that?"

"I saw Lieutenant Tite."

"Ask him!"

"I will. But I'm here now."

"No, you're leaving!" Brenda's cooperation was history.

"The police didn't swear you to secrecy, did they?"

She threw her hands in the air. "Get out! Now!"

"What did he want to know?"

Brenda shook her head. "You must be a helluva lawyer, Ms. Marshfield. You take the smallest opening and drive a truck through it."

"I apologize if you find my style offensive."

"You passed 'offensive' a long time ago." She grabbed my wrist and started pulling me out of the living room. I went along as far as the vestibule then I dug in my heels.

"Brenda, I promise I'll leave if you just tell me why Lieutenant Tite was here today."

She threw my arm down in disgust. "All right then. He asked about Eric...Dr. Benton, the gentleman who brought me to Sam's wake. Some kind of background check. He asked how long I've known him, what kind of person he is, things like that. He didn't mention Sam. He was decent, not rude like you," she added.

"Dr. Benton was your husband's partner. Were they close?"

She opened the front door and waited, one hand on the doorknob, the other on her hip. "I've had quite enough, Ms. Marshfield. Good-bye."

"I'm sorry if I upset you, Mrs. Haskins."

The door slammed shut behind me.

I pulled over a block away and jotted down Brenda's revelations, trying to determine where her story and the truth coincided, when it hit me like a falling tree. Brenda had been the cops' number one suspect until the gun was found in Ellen's drawer. Then she became the bereaved widow and the main witness for the prosecution. If Brenda did kill Gordon, she could have planted the gun at Ellen's to divert suspicion away from herself. Was the story about a possibly missing key an invention to send me off on a wild goose chase?

CHAPTER SIXTEEN

Betty welcomed me with open arms and a tired smile. She escorted me to the den where an inviting assortment of cheese and crackers awaited.

Books of every size and color filled shelves on three walls. The fourth was a series of sliding glass doors leading to a small patio. Paver bricks surrounded a garden that dutifully sprang to life in the summer under Betty's green thumb. The room was more than a study: it was a retreat.

"Next to practicing law, Sam loved reading best of all," she said.

"No question," I agreed. "The problem is, if you love the first as much as he did, there's not much time to indulge the second."

"Or anything else, for that matter," she added. "But after he went on the bench he'd settle in here several nights a week, happy as a clam. He never did that when he was practicing law."

"Did you see any other differences after he became a judge?"

She nibbled on a cracker. "I'll think about that while I get some wine. The usual?"

I nodded. She left and I wandered the den, running my hands over leather-bound classics, biographies of Thomas Jefferson, John Marshall and lesser-known Americans who had a hand in framing our legal system.

Betty returned with two goblets of Chardonnay and we touched glasses in a silent toast.

"To tell you the truth, Susan, since Sam went on the bench he seemed older…more mature is a better way to put it. He wasn't such a burning advocate anymore."

I couldn't reconcile the fiery trial lawyer I knew with the judge he seemed to have become.

"He actually spoke about 'balancing the scales,'" Betty added.

Hmm. The Sam I knew spent his entire life trying to tip the scales in his clients' favor. But when people are ready to move on, I guess they don't wait for the rest of us to catch up.

"Any other changes?"

She reached for a cracker, and I sensed that she was debating the wisdom of continuing. "There doesn't seem to be as much money as before."

I smiled to myself. "When good lawyers go on the bench, there's usually a drastic cut in gross income."

She nodded. "Sam and I talked about that at length before he accepted the appointment. His salary is set by the legislature, and they take out for insurance, pension contributions, taxes, everything. His gross pay is two hundred thousand dollars, but what comes home is a lot less." She cleared her throat. "It's not difficult to live on that kind of money. We don't have expensive taste, as you know. But…" Her voice trailed off.

"But what, Betty?"

She fingered a pearl earring. "I'm going through the books now. If there's a problem, I'd like to…talk to you about it."

"Of course. Just call when you're ready."

"I will." She smiled in acknowledgment.

"Susan, I've made you wait long enough to see that file." She noticed my empty glass. "Would you like another?"

"Whenever…."

Betty could make one or two glasses of wine last for an entire evening, a talent I failed to appreciate until the following morning.

She opened the door to a small closet, inside of which a two-drawer steel filing cabinet squatted. She crossed to the desk, took a key from the top left drawer, went back to the cabinet and unlocked it while I looked over her shoulder. She pulled out the bottom drawer and pointed to two large files. "Righetti" was written on both in Sam's hand.

I pulled the files out and yanked off the elastic cords. The first one held the entire transcript of *State v Righetti*, the original trial, which Sam and I had pored over in preparation for our hearing and which was conspicuously absent from Sam's file in the firm's storage. The second was stuffed with manila files similar to the ones we examined at Kevin's house, but these were in disarray. My heart skipped when I saw one marked "Brenda."

"Could I borrow this?"

"Take it. I'd be happy to be rid of it."

I riffled through the pages. "Everything's a copy, even the transcript. There's no originals."

"I thought that was curious. I assume the originals are in storage at the firm." She studied me. "Why are you so interested in this file, Susan?"

I told her about Tite's request to come up with people who may hold grudges against Sam.

"Is there something in this file, then? Should I give it to the police?"

"No!" I exclaimed. "Not until I have a chance to look at it," I added hastily.

"Susan, what's going on here?"

"Did Sam ever mention this file to you after our hearing?"

Betty pondered a moment. "I don't think so."

"He may have continued to work on it." I chose my words carefully. "I think something piqued his curiosity."

"Do the police know about this?"

"I mentioned Righetti to Tite."

"Susan, if this file has anything to do with why Sam was killed…" Her voice broke. I retrieved a box of tissues from the desk and handed it to her.

"You need to stay as far away from it as you can get," she finally managed.

"I can't."

"I know what he meant to you, Susan."

"He saved Ryan." Betty and Sam were the only ones in town who knew about my brother. I took a shaky breath and almost told her about Sam's last text but something restrained me.

Betty searched every pore of my face. "What Sam did for Ryan, he did for all his other clients, Susan. Not that Ryan wasn't special, but Sam was just doing his job the way he saw it. And he was compensated. *And* Ryan's case gave him enormous satisfaction."

She took me gently by the shoulders. "Look at me," she commanded. "You don't owe Sam a thing, not for Ryan, not for anything else." Her tone conveyed both conviction and compassion.

I blinked and turned away, meandered over to the window. "Okay," I said. "Let's say I don't owe Sam. But still…I need to know *why*."

She joined me and took my hand in both hers.

"I understand. But you need to promise me something."

"What?"

"If you get the barest hint of who did this, you tell the police right away. I don't care much for the Ross fellow that's supposed to be in charge, but the younger one, Tite, seems very capable."

I nodded ambiguously.

"Susan."

I knew what was coming.

"A policeman doesn't try a case in court. You can't investigate a murder. Leave it to the professionals."

"Hi, Mom, Susan," a bright voice said from the door.

Gina was striking in dark slacks and a cream-colored blouse, auburn hair pulled back. Did I look that good in my mid-twenties? Did I ever look that good?

"So, where are you two going for supper?" As Gina approached, she noticed Betty's moist eyes, and her exuberance changed to concern.

"Mom, have you been crying?"

"I'm fine," Betty assured her.

Gina gave her mom a bear hug.

"I remember when Agnes lost her boy, Cooper," Betty said when they separated. "She was devastated. Anytime something reminded her of him she'd burst into tears. It went on for months." Betty set her lips in a horizontal line. "I don't want to do that."

"I didn't know Agnes lost a son," I said.

"Several years ago now. Cooper had it all: looks, brains, personality. It was beyond tragedy."

"How old was he?"

"Cooper and Harry were the same age. Harry's twenty-six now, so twenty-three, twenty-four. Why?"

"I never suspected Agnes had something like that in her history."

"He died of a drug overdose. It was a huge struggle, but eventually Agnes got on with her life." Betty squared her shoulders. "I will too."

"You will, Mom. Harry and I will be around a lot more now."

Betty smiled, but the lines in her face cut deeper than I remembered.

We invited Gina to join us for dinner and she was happy to accept. In spite of the loss that brought us together, we had a good time. The world is full of topics other than death, and Gina's youthful optimism brought a refreshing perspective to the conversation.

We drove in separate cars, so I sped home directly from the restaurant, impatient to read Sam's "Brenda" folder. I got as far as my kitchen table, tore the elastic band off the file, and settled down to read, still wearing my jacket.

The police reports detailed Brenda's initial 911 call, her statements from the minute the cops arrived, and follow-up interviews. Copies of Sam's handwritten notes outlined areas to zero in on during her cross-examination: the exact amount of time she was gone from the bedroom, the healthy relationship with Ellen Righetti, and the lack of any threat or hard feelings about the death of Ellen's child. The word "affair?" was penciled in, last on the list. He had summarized his conversation with Lisa Navarro on a separate sheet. It matched what she told me and included a resumé of her various occupations: singer, cook, hostess, cabdriver, retail sales (flowers, liquor store), actress.

The last item was a copy of a letter written by Sam two months ago to the county sheriff, asking if any firearms had been registered to Eric Benton in the last five years. Our county has an ordinance requiring that gun owners register themselves and their firearms with the Sheriff. The tabulation is a public record. There was no response in the file.

I sat for an hour after finishing the file, wondering why Sam hadn't confided in me. And what had made him suspicious of Benton? Where was the original "Brenda" file?

One thing was clear: Sam had never quit the chase.

CHAPTER SEVENTEEN

I arranged for two Righetti files, mine and the one from the firm's storage, to be at the receptionist's desk for Tite on Monday morning. The third file, the one I had recovered from Sam's den, was secreted in my kitchen pantry behind the Shredded Wheat and the unpaid bills. Lawyers are information hoarders: we never give up what we don't have to.

My client for today's trial, Terrance Thomas, hadn't returned my calls about the state's offer to settle. No matter how damning the facts, clients cling to an hallucinatory hope that some natural disaster will occur and the state's case will self-destruct. Terrance needed a tempest of biblical dimensions. The hand-to-hand delivery charge was a slam-dunk for the State.

Terrance finally showed. We discussed, I cajoled, he whined. I would much rather try a case than go through this hell, but my client's best interests were paramount. If we lost at trial, a virtual certainty unless the jury was composed of his blood relatives, he'd get the full sixty months. Of course, I wasn't the one looking at state-supplied food, shelter, and clothing. Finally he agreed to the deal for four years. I hoped his resolve would last until we got in front of the judge.

It did. When Judge Wilson questioned Dave Roberts about why he was reducing the charge, Dave's explanation all but made Terrance sound like a model citizen.

After the deputies took my client away, I gathered my papers and swept through the bar separating the players from the spectators, oblivious of my surroundings. I live for the rush that jury trials bring, but the reality is that I spend much of my time negotiating deals where my clients end up with convictions. As I approached the door to the main corridor it swung open for me. Al Tite held the handle, regarding me with something vaguely resembling admiration.

"Morning, counselor."

His wardrobe today was casual: checkered shirt, khakis, and an unbuttoned blazer. Unlike many large men, he hadn't let himself get sloppy. Not a bit.

"I heard your plea in there. Sounds like your client got a gift"

"The state was very reasonable."

"My sources in the state's attorney office tell me you're one of the best in the county."

"You get an affidavit?"

"Can you take a compliment?"

I expelled a gust of pent-up emotion. "Sorry. I always feel inadequate when they take my client away in cuffs, even if it's a good deal."

The door closed behind us.

"But you're bound and determined to put Sam's killer away."

I stopped. "No, that's not true. This…" I gestured back to the courtroom. "This is business. The person who killed Sam…that's personal. I need to know why, pure and simple."

"No burning desire to punish them?"

"I don't know the why or the who. How could I want to punish what I don't know?"

"Most people wouldn't be so open-minded," he observed.

I gave him a sidelong glance, but his expression was unfathomable. We headed toward Sam's chambers.

"Judge Kendall's Righetti file was a little thin."

"Thin?" I echoed.

"I didn't see anything about Brenda Haskins. You said she was the main prosecution witness."

"Hmm. That *is* strange."

Al fit the key into the lock and opened the door to the anteroom, then repeated the procedure at the door to Sam's office. I took one step inside and surveyed the room.

Chairs were overturned on their sides, cushions ripped apart. The sofa and the desks had been pushed aside and were scattered about the room. The bookshelves were a mess: papers and legal volumes were scattered on every surface.

"The evidence people came back for a second try," Al explained as he closed the door behind us. He removed a manila envelope from his briefcase and handed it to me. Inside was a thick spiral-bound calendar filled with Sam's writing. I righted one of the chairs and sat at the working desk to read it. On Tuesday three weeks before the murder, the entry for the noon hour was "Majors—Burkhart—insurance." Other routine items were noted: associate judges' meetings, committee for courthouse renovation, an afternoon seminar on new developments in search and seizure law. On the Monday before he died, Agnes was in his book for 10 a.m.

I examined the plaques and awards that decorated Sam's walls: the Italian-American Society lauded him for dedicated service, ditto Easter Seals. The local bar association recognized his fairness and integrity, the governor acknowledged his commitment to equal justice, etc.

His framed photos were lying around like leaves scattered by November winds. Several caught Sam shaking hands and showing teeth with various political personages. Most were informal pictures of Sam and Betty accompanied by the kids in various stages of growth. A recent formal family portrait showed Gina and Harry standing, resting their hands on the shoulders of Sam and Betty, who were seated.

"Have you spoken to Betty yet?" I asked.

"Should I?" Al's eyebrows rose and fell. "She's not a suspect, if that's your concern."

"Betty would never hurt Sam!"

"Good thing you're impartial about this."

Something he said made me pause. "Why isn't she a suspect?"

He pulled out his notebook and flipped through the pages. "Moore did the initial interview. Mrs. Kendall says the judge left at seven-thirty that morning. She cleaned up breakfast and started laundry. She showered and was going to do some computer work when she got the call on her land line at eight forty-seven. She remembered because of the digital clock on the microwave in the kitchen. Judge Knapp verified the time of the call, and he knows her voice. There's no way she could have gone to the courthouse in her own car, gotten in before it opened without anyone seeing her, killed him, and gotten home soon enough to receive the call. She'd be an Olympian."

"And a murderer, neither of which she is."

Al regarded me through half-closed eyes.

"Weren't you going to give me the jail list? And tell me why you were at Haskins'?"

"They're related. You saw the ledger, and you know how someone could get in through the jail without signing the book."

"You talked to Yolanda?" I asked flatly.

"Of course I talked to Yolanda. My job is to talk to people."

"And…?"

"Judge Frederick came in at seven forty. He had a friend with him, an Eric Benton. Benton was bending his ear about a case on the judge's docket where Benton's medical group is involved. In the course of our investigation, we discovered Benton is a good friend of Brenda Haskins. I had just interviewed her about him when you appeared on the scene yesterday."

"What else did Frederick say?"

"The judge was very forthcoming."

"I would think so. He doesn't want anything to do with a murder investigation."

"Nor did he want anything to do with Benton that day. They've known each other for years, and Benton had set up an early coffee with the judge on the west side. They chatted about this and that, then the judge left for work and Benton tagged along in his own car, which Frederick thought was strange. They came in through the jail together. Since Benton was with a senior judge, the deputy in the jail waved him on through. Didn't even ask for I.D." Al shook his head in amazement.

"When they were in the elevator, Benton broached the subject of the pending lawsuit. The judge tells us it's highly unethical for him to discuss a pending matter with anyone who's involved, so he told Benton to button it. Benton kept talking, so the judge says he pressed the button for three, took Benton to the coffee shop, which had just opened for early employees, sat him down and left him there."

"What time was it?"

"Early. The judge said it didn't take more than five minutes for him to sign in and deposit Benton in the coffee shop."

I was quiet.

"What do you know about Benton?" Al finally asked.

"I met him at Sam's wake. He was with Brenda."

"Is there a Benton/Sam connection?" Al took a step toward the window and looked out. "You said Brenda Haskins was a witness at the P.C. hearing you and Sam did, the one you told me about yesterday, right?"

"Uh-huh."

He turned back toward me. "How come when I looked at Sam's file this morning I didn't see anything on her?"

It was my turn to shrug. "Sam cross-examined her, so he should have a sub-file with police reports, areas he wanted to cover on cross, maybe specific questions…case law to meet objections."

"So where would that file be? And what else might be missing?"

He didn't seem to be asking me, so I didn't respond.

"Is the fact that Brenda's name keeps popping up just a coincidence, or is she at the center of it all?" I mused.

Al's expression changed from thoughtful to perplexed. "Was Benton a witness at your hearing?" he asked.

"No. I never heard of him till Brenda introduced us at the wake. Have you spoken to him?"

"Anything else you want to know?"

"I'm just a cog in the wheel of justice, trying to help the proper authorities cover all the bases."

He crossed to the chessboard and studied the pieces, profile of a man in deep concentration.

"Okay," he said with resolve, and turned to me. "Benton admitted he was trying to explain his side of the case to Frederick. Says he didn't know it was against the rules until the judge told him. Felt put out when the judge left him in the coffee shop. Says he sat for a minute, the coffee was terrible, then he left and went straight to his office."

Benton was one floor below Sam's chambers at 7:45. Sam had signed in at 7:55.

"Anyone verify Benton's story?" I asked.

"All United Anesthesiologists employees have to punch in and out for security reasons. They keep drugs on-site. Benton punched in at eight thirty, according to the computer records." Al grimaced. "By car, if you get the lights, his office is eight minutes from here. Add a couple minutes on both ends for getting to and from the car. Time of death was between eight and eight thirty. The text to you went out at seven fifty-eight, so Sam was alive then. Even if the timing worked, what's Benton's motive?"

"Let's take it a step at a time. Could he have doctored the computer record at his office, no pun intended?"

"I had our geek take a look at his system. It's tamper-proof, at least on the sign-in program."

"Hmmm. What's your take on Benton?"

Al gazed into the distance. "He's a character…stuffy, formal. Misses his old partner, but enjoys running the show. He's pretty wrapped up in his business and his patients. Admitted to a friendship with Brenda Haskins. They go out now and then."

"Was he telling the truth?"

He gave me a quarter-smile. "Does anyone?"

I decided against bringing up Sam's question to Brenda during our hearing. Even if she was cheating on her husband at the time he was killed, I had no credible proof that her paramour was Benton. She could have been carrying on with half the males of Joliet back then.

We lapsed into silence, two pairs of eyes searching the shambles of Sam's chambers for a hint of what happened here a mere five days ago.

"Can I go through the drawers?"

"Help yourself," Al waved.

I settled in at Sam's working desk. The top drawer held the usual assortment of paper clips, ink refills, business cards, rubber bands, picture hangers, and other debris. Outdated fliers for legal seminars, months-old news clippings, and a broken shoelace resided in the middle drawer of the working desk. The bottom drawer seemed devoted to computer stuff: manuals, CDs, pamphlets, cables, a couple of discarded mice. I removed the contents of each drawer and sifted through it in painstaking detail, then dumped it back and repeated the process with the next drawer. When I was finished with the bottom drawer, I stared into the empty cavity. The lining appeared a trifle askew. I felt idly along the surface where the bottom and the side came together, watching Al's profile across the room as he sat reviewing reports. The interior facing of the drawer felt flimsy and loose. I played around with it until I could pry it up with my fingernails, careful not to interrupt Tite. He was turned three-quarters away from me, deep into his work. Finally I lifted the lining far enough to stick one hand underneath. My fingers wrapped around a rectangular object that felt like a notebook. I palmed it and tucked it into my briefcase without examining it, then I slid my hand back into the concealed space and felt all around. Nothing else was hidden there. I pressed the lining securely back in place and returned all the sundry computer equipment to the drawer. I stood and stretched. We had been in Sam's chambers for more than an hour. I walked to the couch and collapsed on it.

Al looked up from his papers.

"Who's the perp?"

I made a face. "Beats me."

"Ready to go?"

I had studiously ignored the bloodstained carpet behind the desk, but I was drawn to it like some are attracted to the twisted pile of metal after a fatal car wreck. My eyes crawled inch by inch across the rug until they found the henna-colored blotch. An apparition of Sam being savagely beaten by a faceless attacker appeared in the window. I shook my head to make the ghastly image dissolve.

Tite stood in front of me. I looked up curiously. He reached down, grasped me by the shoulders and gently lifted me till we were standing toe to toe. He released me, then, starting at the top of my blouse, his fingers softly traversed my throat and up my neck. When he got to my chin he lifted it slowly till our eyes met. He bent his head and brushed my lips with his. My whole body went tingly, like when you whack your funny bone. He wrapped his arms around me and we kissed warily. His tongue found mine and I suddenly felt like a washer on the "agitate" cycle.

He pulled back and his eyes searched my face. I stepped into him, put both arms around his neck and pulled his face down to mine. I met his lips with a passion or maybe a need that was shocking when I thought about it later. He came alive against me and in a moment was kissing my neck, my ears, my eyes. My legs wanted to crumble underneath me. As if he read my mind he lowered me onto the couch.

"Not here!" A voice in my head screamed. Tite's hands were suddenly everywhere, squeezing, caressing, making me crazy. If I let him go another ten seconds I'd be at the point of no return.

"I want you!" I panted and entwined my fingers through his. "But this place, Sam's chambers…I can't."

He pulled back, breathing like he had run up three flights of stairs. For a fraction of a second, I thought he'd run through the stop sign.

"Right." He swallowed hard.

I struggled to a sitting position and ran my hand through his short bristly hair. He looked at me with a bashful smile and all my good intentions vanished quicker than a witness trying to avoid a subpoena.

My arms encircled his neck and our lips came together like the opposite poles of a magnet. He pushed between my knees and pressed me backward into the couch. His tongue explored my lips, my mouth, while his hands undid the buttons on my blouse and cast aside the bra. I felt his shoulder holster under his blazer; seconds later, he had stripped. His upper body was thick and heavily muscled, more like a fighter than a runner or swimmer. He found the zipper on my skirt and slid it and everything else down my hips. When he reached my ankles he discarded the clothes and started working his way back up. Somewhere an animal moaned.

"You're beautiful," he murmured in my ear. The couch became our playground, used in ways the designers never intended. He brought me to the edge of frenzy and I never wanted it to stop.

"Are you ready?" he panted, eyes glittering.

"You mean there's more?"

He grinned and found his pants, pulled out a wallet and fumbled with a wrapper. Finally he shook out a condom.

As he took care of that, I caressed the contours and crevices of his body. He filled me and I savored every inch of him as we rocked toward delirium, then whooped simultaneously. When we were spent he rolled over on his back, taking me with so I was on top. We lay like that, waiting for the adrenaline to subside and the heart rate to return to normal. I combed his light brown chest hair with my fingers.

He opened one eye. "I think we found an area where we're compatible."

I smiled dreamily. "You found places I never knew I had."

"Oh, there's more. I'll get to them."

I smiled to myself at his confidence that there'd be another time, then my smile widened when I realized he was right.

We gathered our clothes. I felt like I was on the moon, free of gravity's anchor. We dressed and regrouped in silence. What do you say after an encounter like that with someone you've known less than a week?

Tite took care to lock the doors behind us when we left chambers. I made it to the elevators, well aware that I was not striding with my usual assurance. Once we started to descend I had to fight a temptation to nuzzle up into him. We exited the courthouse and crossed the large plaza in front, keeping a business-like distance between us till we got to the corner. The police department was two blocks away.

"See ya." He gave me a lopsided smile, touched my hand, and sauntered across the street. He stopped in front of the bank and stood motionless for a minute. Then he crossed back to me, deep in thought.

"Maybe Brenda told Sam something that incriminated Benton. Or maybe it's the other way around: he found something incriminating about Brenda from Benton." He looked at me quizzically.

My ears heard the words but the rest of me was still in Sam's chambers. Al nodded and crossed the street again, continuing toward the station. He turned and waved before he disappeared into headquarters.

CHAPTER EIGHTEEN

How could a guy who was such a klutz of a cop be such a wizard in the sack? I basked in the memory of our encounter, then with Herculean effort put it out of my mind and focused on the task at hand.

I locked the door to the office and fished around my briefcase for the object I had retrieved from Sam's desk drawer. A checkbook, standard issue, blue plastic wallet. I turned it over gently and opened it like a treasure. The checks were drawn on an outfit called Great Midwest Securities. The face of the checks bore only Sam's name and a statement that they were valid only for an amount greater than $500.00. I thumbed through the check register, scrawled in Sam's chicken scratch. According to the ledger, he wrote one check on the last day of each month, starting in May almost three years ago. All the checks were written to cash. The first one was for $2,500. The checks remained at that amount until the following October when they increased to $5,000. Deposits were recorded every three months: they averaged twenty grand a pop. Sam didn't keep a running balance but every couple of pages or so he totaled things up. The last line reflected a balance of $75,000. I ran a total on all the deposits and came up with $240,000 in round numbers.

I tugged the printed checks and the register out of the plastic wallet and felt inside their little compartments. Empty. I put it back together again, closed it up and willed it to talk to me. It remained mute. The account was innocent, I told myself: investments Sam and Betty made, monthly withdrawals to pay bills. But why did Sam keep it at the office, and why wasn't Betty's name on the checks?

The Internet revealed that Great Midwest was a regional brokerage firm that catered to the small investor. I called them, pretending to be a potential client and the phone rep gave me the rush about all their products and services. I asked about a checking account and was told that it came with a stock trading account, but checks could only be written for $500 or more.

I needed answers. I dialed Betty at home.

"You were concerned about finances yesterday. What's going on with that?"

"I hate it when you beat around the bush, Susan."

"Sorry. I'm wired like that."

A hefty silence ensued.

"The numbers aren't adding up the way they should," she finally said. "Have you found out anything?"

"Does Great Midwest Securities ring a bell?"

A pause.

"Could you say that again?"

"Right. Sorry, Betty, I wasn't making myself clear. Great Midwest Securities is a brokerage house, stocks, bonds, investments. One of the things they offer is a cash fund that's like a checking account. Did Sam have an account like that?"

"What are you talking about? I never heard of them."

I groaned mentally.

"Tell me what's going on," she commanded.

I have no problem telling clients the hard truths. But once in a while, with friends, the waffle urge kicks in and I try to protect them from pain.

"Well, after we talked yesterday, I remembered Sam had mentioned something about an investment account. I...I thought that was the name but I was probably mistaken..."

"No, dear. Your mistake is that you are trying to cover something up and failing miserably."

Heat flashed through my face.

"Do you have a lie-detector in your phone?"

"Tell me what you know. Now."

I told her about the checkbook and what I had learned from my phone call with Great Midwest.

"So if there's seventy-five thousand in it now and he wrote checks for five thousand each…how much money are we talking about?"

I did the arithmetic in my head, couldn't believe the number I came up with, and re-did the math on paper.

"I think the checks total a hundred sixty-seven thousand, five hundred dollars."

"Where did all that money come from?" Betty gasped.

"And where did it all go?" I countered.

"Sam's paychecks are automatically deposited in our joint checking account. We have investments, but we live on his salary."

"Who spends the money?"

"I've been paying bills for the last several years. Sam used to, then I felt the need to get a handle on our finances. If Sam needed clothes or a new suit, we'd go together. If we took a vacation, we generally could afford to do it out of our checking account or otherwise we'd borrow a little from savings."

"Betty, after a lawyer leaves a firm, there's usually residual payments as cases cash in and outstanding bills get paid. The lawyer gets compensated for work he did on the files when he was with the firm. Do you know if Sam received payments like that from the firm?"

"Not that I know of," Betty said slowly.

As a name partner, Sam would have had a financial interest in every case in the office. Kevin would know the details.

"He didn't gamble, did he?"

Her laughter boomed back at me.

"Susan, come on. He was too busy working to even think about that kind of thing. Besides, five thousand a month is a lot of poker money."

"Good point."

"Wherever it came from, it was legal," Betty said confidently. "We certainly didn't want for anything, so I can't begrudge him his own account. But I don't understand how he could have spent that kind of money. I mean, if he needed cash, he'd just go to the ATM."

Except you can't just get 165,000 smacks from an ATM.

"And besides," she added, "he'd start off the week with enough cash in his pocket for lunch, gas and things like that. So, I…I just don't know."

"Me, neither." But I was starting to suspect that wherever this led it wouldn't be pretty.

"I need to find out more about Great Midwest," Betty declared. "Do you have a number for them?"

I gave it to her and we promised to talk again soon.

Griffen Bartley had told he was working for Nancy Hunsacker, one of the senior lawyers in Sam's old law firm, when he was researching in the law library the morning Sam was killed. I called Nancy and she confirmed his assignment, but when I asked specifically if she had requested that he search in law journals, she told me that he turned in such exemplary work that he had free rein to perform the assignment however he pleased. Why did I ask? I made some noise about law journals being more complicated than rocket science. Thankfully someone rushed into her office just then with a more pressing issue and she had to terminate the conversation. Griffen's explanation for his whereabouts at the time of Sam's murder could be the truth or a clever fabrication, coin flip. I didn't see him as a killer but his early entrance into the courthouse on the day of the murder was a red flag. On the other hand, if he was going to kill his uncle, why would he leave such an obvious trail by signing in at the jail just after Sam?

Kelly was my last call.

"Where have you been?" she chided. "I've been leaving messages since Friday."

"I know. I'm sorry. Way too much to talk about on the phone. My trial settled, wanna run?"

"I did that this morning. My back's killing me."

"How about this? I'll go home and change and run in the forest preserve. Then I'll meet you at the Y for a whirlpool at…" I consulted my watch. "How about two?"

"That's great." Kelly said with enthusiasm. "It'll work out perfect for picking up the kids."

"See you then."

***

Fur raced into the kitchen as I opened the door from the garage into the house. I kneaded her till she moaned like an out-of-control timber saw, then I kissed my index finger, touched it to her pink nose and told her I loved her. I had never done anything so ridiculous in the entirety of our lives together. What was going on?

I changed into my running tights and tee shirt and drove to the forest preserve. It was three miles from the house but well worth the short drive. Years ago, in a rare display of farsightedness, the county had carved out this slice of thick undergrowth and tall oak trees from the middle of hundreds of acres of similar landscape. With all Joliet's growth and expansion, the site was now an island of nature surrounded by housing developments. I turned off the main highway and rolled down a quarter-mile blacktop road to the empty parking lot. The main trail is about two miles long and loops around the perimeter of the forest. It's mostly flat but there are tree roots and brush so you have to pay attention. Lesser-used paths crisscross in the forest but they are narrow and can be impassable. At this time of day, someone might be taking their dog for a romp, but it's often deserted. I parked, locked the car, and stretched for a few minutes. The late winter sun made the barren forest seem more inviting. The air held an irresistible crispness. As I tightened the laces of my running shoes, I heard the first birdcall of spring, but there was no answering warble. I tucked my car key in the pocket of my tights and headed into the woods.

CHAPTER NINETEEN

After a third of a mile, I started to air it out, gradually shedding the concerns of the day. Eighteen minutes later, according to my stopwatch, I finished my first loop and arrived back at the parking lot, not having seen another soul. The Acura had been joined by an orange Plymouth of uncertain vintage. It looked as if it had been totaled at least twice and miraculously escaped the junkyard. Probably some high school kids playing hooky, I thought, and dismissed it. On the second time around the loop, I began with some wind sprints, then settled into a pace which pushed me beyond comfort, but you don't get better by being complacent. The usual aches and pains that accompany a run were plaguing someone else today, probably because of the spongy dirt cushion, softened by winter's deposit of dead and decaying leaves. Most of the trees were still winter skeletons, but a few were starting to bud. My constant motion seemed effortless. I was breathing deep and even, my legs were tireless pistons, and my world, at the moment, was in harmonious balance.

The trail gradually ascends, then drops quickly to a flat quarter mile, ending at the parking lot. As I cruised up the rise for the third time, a wild thrashing in the bushes startled me. I glanced quickly to the right, thinking it might be a deer or a coyote. A human figure shrouded in black from head to foot rose up out of the woods about twenty feet off the trail. His face was concealed by a ski mask, but his eyes were small and mean. He brought his right hand up high over his head. Sunlight glinted off the long, slightly curved blade of a hunting knife. For a moment I was frozen jelly, then the fight-or-flight reaction kicked in and I chose flight. I scorched the path to the parking lot, hurtling rather than running, thinking only of escape.

Thirty yards ahead, another human form, this one twice as large, sprang directly into the center of the path, brandishing a short, thick tree limb. He readied it over his right shoulder like a batter and eyed me like I was a hanging curve ball. The growth on either side of the trail was impenetrable: roots and brambles would trip me instantly if I tried to evade him by cutting across the forest. I glanced desperately over my shoulder: the other thug loomed in the middle of the trail, blocking my retreat. He was crouched low like a defensive tackle, knife upraised, advancing on the balls of his feet. His quickness was obvious even at this distance. I chose the tree limb rather than the blade. I barreled directly at the giant, then when I was almost on top of him, darted to his left then shifted my weight and cut quickly the other way. My peripheral vision caught a blur of motion. I dove for the ground, hoping to roll past him and avoid the blow, then spring up and run like hell. I heard a shriek, then darkness crushed me.

CHAPTER TWENTY

I floated through a forgotten galaxy, novas exploding in my head like erratic fireworks.

"Susan."

Something warm wrapped around my hand. I willed my fingers to squeeze back but they weren't working.

"This is Kelly. I'm going for help."

I struggled to understand but the effort was too great and I fell back into blackness.

Later—an hour—a day—other voices buzzed indecipherably. I gathered everything I had and forced out a cry for help that even to me sounded like a screech from a back-alley catfight. The chattering came to an abrupt halt, then a cacophony broke out.

Blurred shapes of gray collided with each other, then glided into place like pieces of a jigsaw puzzle, finally resolving into a familiar face.

"Ryan?" I called weakly.

"This is Dr. Lopez. You're in the hospital. You're going to be all right."

I let go and slipped back again into a coma-like slumber. I was swimming through clouds, drifting past childhood playgrounds. When I awoke again, I felt more like myself. Well, myself with the world's worst hangover. I was in a hospital room. Some yellow pudding-like stuff was on the tray table. It looked as beat-up as I felt. A newspaper appeared. I tried to open it and discovered my left arm was useless and in a sling. The story at the bottom of page three was headlined "Local Attorney Victim of Mugging." According to the article, I had suffered a concussion and severe bruises and contusions. The police had no leads but were encouraging anyone with information to come forward.

Dr. Lopez came in and told me if I had been smacked eight inches higher I'd either be dead or a quadriplegic. I told him that was more information than I needed.

Late in the afternoon a colorful bouquet of blossoms marched into my room, a familiar face peeking out from behind.

"It's good to know where I can find you." Al put the vase on the bed table.

"Not for long. The doc says I can leave tomorrow if there's no infection."

"Are you serious? Have you looked at yourself lately?"

I grabbed the remote control and killed the ghastly overhead glow from the fluorescent tube.

He tried unsuccessfully to hide a grin. "A good night's sleep will do wonders."

"Do you want to sit down?"

He bypassed the hospital chair and hitched himself up onto the bed. "What day is it?"

I gave the question a lot of thought. "Monday?"

"Oh-oh. Try Wednesday."

"Know-it-all."

A searing shock of fire chose that moment to shoot through my shoulder. I shuddered and involuntarily grabbed the sling that kept my left arm affixed to my rib cage.

"Are you all right?" He leaned forward anxiously.

The pain faded. "Yeah." I took a deep breath. "As long as they keep the pain pills coming. Are you here officially?"

"The flowers are unofficial." He grinned. "Officially, I need to know what you remember of the attack."

I told him everything.

He nodded. "Any idea on height, weight, nationality?"

"They wore knit ski masks, the kind that fit over your head and cover everything but your eyes. One was David, the other guy was Goliath. It happened so fast…I can't tell you much else."

"They followed you from home, maybe from the office." He drummed his fingers restlessly on the bed. "The smartest thing you did was to tell your friend Kelly exactly where you'd be. When you didn't show up at the Y she got concerned and went looking for you. After she found your car she didn't quit till she found you."

His expression changed. "If I could, I'd put a guard on you twenty-four/seven. Someone sees you as a threat."

"No way! It was just a couple of freaks who got their jollies beating up on a stranger," I protested.

"An ambush in the forest when the victim obviously has no money, there's no evidence of a sexual assault, and they leave your car keys in your pocket? After they flattened you, it would have been the easiest thing in the world for them to bash your brains in. But they didn't. This was a warning, Marshfield. They followed you till you were alone and far from help."

"That's crazy. I haven't found out squat about who killed Sam."

"You're getting close to something even if you don't realize it." His mouth was set in a grim line. "What haven't you told me?"

I leaned back into the pillows and closed my eyes. A minute passed. I felt my cheek being stroked, then his finger traced my lips. When I opened my eyes his face was inches away. The shadow of a beard hadn't been there this morning. No, that was several mornings ago. I brushed my hand gently over the bristles.

"Susan, listen. This isn't about you and me. It's about stopping a killer and making sure you're not the next victim."

"Oh." An intriguing idea jumped into my head. "Are you *sure* it isn't about you and me?"

He leaned back uncertainly.

"Let's disconnect this." I grabbed the IV eagerly.

"*Listen!*" He vaulted off the bed and glared down at me. "Next time it won't be a sling and some pain pills. Next time, we'll find you in a Dumpster. Tell me what you've been doing!"

"I know there's something between us," I said in a measured tone. "Something very nice. But if you think you can intimidate me like some third-rate car thief, you better go back to the frickin' police academy."

If I was my normal, healthy self I'd be doing a hair-standing-on-end rant but today a heavy fog slowed me down. Tite started to retort, then caught himself. We remained motionless for several seconds.

"Okay. I'm sorry I came on so strong." He looked right at me with gray eyes that were now soft. "I need to tell you something."

"I bet you don't bully other witnesses like this!"

"No," he said evenly, "I don't. But other witnesses don't go off on their own, dig under rocks, and generally make themselves targets."

"The only rocks are the ones in your head!" I retorted.

His mouth tightened and his eyes lost their softness. "You're way too stubborn to stop chasing whoever you're chasing. And to be honest, you bring a…unique insight to the process. So here's my offer. You promise to tell me ahead of time what you plan to do and let me clear it. In return, I'll keep you in the loop."

I stared at him. "I have to clear stuff with you?"

"Play it this way and the investigation moves forward. You stay out of trouble, and even though I'm breaking all the rules, I get to keep my badge as long as our little deal stays between us."

His proposal filtered through my cerebral cortex. "It's all about you, isn't it, Tite? Keep the show rolling, hang on to your badge, throw me a bone so I don't gum up the works. That's what's going on here, isn't it?"

His eyes squeezed shut. When he finally opened them, I saw only pain.

"Offer's open. You decide." He wheeled and was gone. Too bad I didn't have anything to throw at him.

CHAPTER TWENTY-ONE

Kelly brought me home from the hospital, fluffed up my pillow, and turned off the ringer on the phone. I wondered what mayhem my clients had committed during my three-day absence and whether any of them had been caught. Then the feel-good pills kicked in, and I didn't worry about anything anymore.

Monica, who handles my work at the firm, stopped by in the afternoon. I devoured the chocolate Bismarcks she brought, but the briefcase full of mail made me gag. We patched up my wrecked schedule, put out the worst fires and battled through the mail and phone messages. An old client and friend, Jimmy Ray Peterson, had called the office several times but wouldn't say why. We penciled him in for eleven the next day, Friday.

George Vollrath, the first assistant state's attorney, called late in the afternoon. George possessed a keen legal mind and, unlike most prosecutors, could work with and had a sincere respect for the defense bar. He had survived several regime changes in the office of his boss, the elected state's attorney, and was the main reason that office enjoyed a reputation for integrity.

"How's the loyal opposition?"

"I have a grave head injury which causes an inability to negotiate anything. I demand a speedy trial on all my files."

"Susan, you sound like your ornery old self."

"Come witness the carnage."

"I'll drop by about five."

I chanced a look in the mirror. Jagged scratches littered the face that stared back at me. A nasty yellow-green bruise decorated one cheekbone. No make-up, arm in a sling. I looked like a victim of serious domestic abuse.

A few minutes after five, the bell rang and I opened the door to a sight out of a French cartoon: George, whose girth matched his height, clutched a bouquet of balloons in one hand while he examined me over the top of his half-glasses.

"What's the other guy look like?"

"Not as pretty as me. Want a drink?"

"Scotch, thanks."

I escorted him into the great room. A crescent-shaped, plum-colored leather sofa sat in the middle of the large space. In front of it, a sheet of oval glass was balanced on top of a large, egg-shaped black marble rock. A large Persian rug lent some color to the stark setting. I don't have a lot of material possessions, but I enjoy the ones I have.

I poured him a stiff one, no rocks. His imbibing habits were familiar to me from hours spent waiting for jury verdicts together in bars where a glass of Two-Buck Chuck was the most expensive wine in the house.

"Where's yours?"

"Pain pills." I looked longingly at his glass.

"Well, here's to ya." He saluted and sipped appreciatively. The balloon bouquet he brought was weighted with a heavy mouse. We amused ourselves by watching Fur bat it around and chase madly after it.

"Word is you're nosing around about Sam."

"Whatever happened to the right to privacy?" I groaned.

George shrugged noncommittally. "Did you know he worked in the state's attorney's office when he first started out?"

I shrugged. "Everybody's a little misguided at the beginning of their careers."

"Did he ever tell you how he came to leave the office?"

"Can't say we ever talked about it."

"Well, I'll make it brief. There were so few of us back then that you could be trying a murder case a year after you hired on. Not like today where you spend two years in misdemeanor and DUI court before you can touch a felony file. Well, Sam got a homicide over in Flagger's Park—a ball game that got out of hand, lopsided score, too much beer.

The cops turned up a couple of eyeballs who swore the guy we had in custody didn't do it. Remember, this was the dark ages, before we had to give exculpatory material to the defense. Matter of fact, in those days we didn't give 'em anything. We tried cases by the seat of our pants."

The exchange of witness lists and statements between prosecution and defense in criminal cases was a fact of my legal life, mandated on the theory that if each side knew the other side's case, more trials would settle and judges wouldn't have to work so hard. But these rules of engagement were of relatively recent vintage in the history of the law.

"In any event, Sam thought it only fair that the defense attorney know about the witnesses. He told the boss, guy named Bassini, that he wanted to give the attorney the statements, and the boss put his foot down: absolutely not; we had no legal obligation; our job was to convict the bad guy; there was lots of evidence, etcetera."

"So what happened?"

"Sam argued with Bassini, gave him all the reasons cited later by courts in support of open discovery: due process, fair trial, fifth amendment, the defendant's limited funds for investigation versus trained police professionals…" George shook his head sadly. "Bassini tore up the witness statements in front of Sam and told him the next thing he wanted to hear about the case was a conviction."

I looked at George expectantly.

"Sam gave copies of the reports to the defense attorney, the witnesses testified, and the case ended in a hung jury. Sam was fired when the boss found out about it, but his letter of resignation was already on Bassini's desk."

"You're telling me this because…?"

He swirled the contents of his glass, frowning deeply.

"I had the highest respect for Sam after that incident, and in the thirty years since, he did nothing to diminish that respect. Ditto for you, Susan, although we don't have that kind of history. But here's the rub: you're a *lawyer*, not a homicide investigator. What you do, you do very well. But you're dealing with a killer here. He'll get desperate if he thinks you're close, and you won't know what hit you."

Fur grew bored with the mouse and wrapped herself around George's ankles. He scratched her ears absent-mindedly.

"Who've you been talking to?" I asked, although I knew the answer.

"*Susan.*" His glass crashed to the table. Startled, Fur darted away. "Are you listening, or am I wasting my time here?"

I stared out the window till George's voice ceased reverberating through the room.

"I'm listening. George, what happened to me was random. It has nothing to do with Sam. I know you've been talking to Tite. He's just all huffy because…whatever."

George eyed me over the top of his glasses. "Tite whispered in my ear, yes. I don't know what's going on with the two of you, and it's none of my business." George belched quietly. "Al's just trying to keep the homicide statistics down."

I rolled my eyes.

"Susan, you're in way over your head on this."

"Don't look at me in that tone of voice."

"We lost one great lawyer this week. Don't make it two."

CHAPTER TWENTY-TWO

Jimmy Ray Peterson strolled in at 1:30, wearing a straw Fedora and painted-on blue jeans.

"Hey, Ms. Marshfield." He inspected my face. "Either everything I hear is true or you got one mean kitty cat."

"She's a nice kitty," I said. "What do you hear?"

Jimmy Ray was a former drug client for whom a court-ordered rehab program actually worked. Now instead of dealing dope, he deals information, mostly to the cops. I don't know what he gets in return, and I don't want to.

He gave me a sideways glance. "This place ain't bugged, is it, Ms. Marshfield?"

"What do I look like, the President of the United States? I'm an attorney, Jimmy. There's a law in this state that says I can't tape you without your permission."

"Right." He slid into a client chair, lanky legs outstretched. "Ms. Marshfield, you must be feeling better if you're back at work."

"Yeah." Jimmy's attempt at small talk was as transparent as Cling Wrap.

I waited while his eyes searched every corner of the room. Apparently satisfied, he leaned over the desk, motioning me to lean toward him. "Someone put a hit on you," he whispered.

My pen halted above my legal pad. "Tell me more."

"Word is some Mexes got paid to take you out."

A strange tingly feeling swept over me. Fear? Vulnerability? Bad eggs for breakfast?

"You okay, Ms. Marshfield?" He looked as concerned as I felt.

"Been better. What else have you heard, Jimmy?"

"Weather's gettin' nicer, you know, and folks is startin' to hang out again. I ran into three Mexes I know and we started talkin' about you."

"Me?"

"Not that you're my lawyer or nuttin', just about what was in the paper. Kinda unusual, y'know, lady lawyer getting' um…" He looked sheepish.

"Uh-huh."

"They rappin' and tellin' me a coupla their buddies took off outta state that day 'cause they was paid to mess you over."

"Who paid them?"

"Dunno, Ms. Marshfield," he shook his head. "I truly don't."

"Who were the guys in the woods?"

"I tried to find out without looking too…" He searched for the word.

"Nosey," I supplied.

"Yeah. I can't let them think I's a snitch, ya know."

"Of course not, Jimmy. What did they say?"

"They didn't. They mighta knew but they weren't gonna tell me."

"How about the guys you were talking to? Who are they?"

"I only know their street names. The one with lots of muscles, his name Moby 'cause he's so strong. The other two are normal size. Younger one is Teach; the other they call Nasty."

"You know where they live?"

"I guess with all the rest, over by Du Champs on the east side."

The Hispanic enclave, probably more than ten thousand people.

He leaned forward. "Whacha goin' to do, Ms. Marshfield?"

I expelled a lung full of air. "For starters, I'm not going to jog alone in the forest preserve anymore. You think you can dig a little deeper?"

"I'll keep listening, Miss Marshfield, and I'll let you know." Jimmy unfolded himself from the chair.

"You can leave a message anytime, day or night. I want to know who paid those guys." I found a fifty in my purse and handed it to him. "For your trouble."

"I didn't do this fo' the money, Ms. Marshfield," he protested. "You been there when I needed you: I just thought you should know what's goin' on."

"You're right about that. But it'd make me feel better. You've spent time here you could've been out…working."

"Since you put it that way..." He grinned and stuffed the bill in his pocket. "You think there's a chance of finding those guys between here and the border?"

A straight line between Joliet and the border would cover about twelve hundred miles, but there was no straight road. There were hundreds of ways to get there and thousands of places to hide on the way. I trusted Jimmy to tell me exactly what he heard, but it could be Moby, Teach, and Nasty were just running off at the mouth.

"Zip," I replied sadly. "It's too big a country."

Jimmy touched his fingers to his hat in a mock salute. "Be in touch."

I did a mental checklist of the people I had sought information from since Sam's murder. The list didn't make me quiver with fright. But Al was right when he said I was getting close to something. What?

I fought to keep the image of a garbage-filled Dumpster out of my head.

CHAPTER TWENTY-THREE

The good news was I caused someone to be concerned. The bad news was I had no idea who or how I had done so. I left the office, walked north up Chicago Street past the mix of last-century office buildings and brand new commercial pavilions and sat on a wood bench a few blocks from the office. I reviewed everything I'd done, every conversation I'd had, since Sam's death. Who was trying to scare me off? How was I a threat?

The bright sunshine allayed the vague sense of dread that bubbled up in my gut like bicarbonate of soda. On the way back, I saw Moses on the other side of the street. There was no reason for me to cross, but I did. He was sitting on his canvas camp chair, staring straight ahead with a hint of a scowl on his face. An open cardboard box lay at his feet, a few lonely quarters in the bottom. I saw no evidence of his radio.

"I miss your music."

He lifted his head up at me and shrugged. I pulled out a twenty and dropped it in the box. His eyes grew large, and he quickly snatched up the bill.

"Did you run out of batteries?"

He shrugged again but a smile spilt his face revealing teeth the color of butternut squash.

"You get something good to eat. Okay?"

When I got back to the office, I e-mailed Monica and asked her to make a list of the local gun shops and their hours. Then I caught up on paperwork before a doctor's appointment at five. He told me no swimming for a few weeks, but easy biking and walking were fine. No weights with the upper body and physical therapy was a good idea.

I picked up the paper on the way home and read it with dinner. A story about a local cop being on the take caught my attention. The article said Larry Malone allegedly took bribes to "divert" investigations. He was suspended pending review. I knew him: a big, beefy sergeant who looked like he passed his last physical a decade ago.

I put on some Eagles but couldn't get into the music. Jimmy's news and Malone's suspension gnawed at me like carpenter ants feasting on new construction. I called Al but he wasn't in, so I left a voice mail. I fed the cat and was getting comfy with a book when the phone rang. It was Tite.

"Hello."

"What's going on?"

"When will you be off?"

"Say what?"

"I…I need to talk."

The phone was quiet.

"What about?"

"I was a little…snippy the last time I saw you."

"Snippy." He tested the word.

Bedlam erupted in the background.

"Gotta go."

Click.

I had little to lose by pushing the good lieutenant for information: the worst he could do was to tell me to get lost, and he'd probably do that anyway.

***

Saturday morning was sunny, no wind, temperature in the fifties. I dutifully checked in with Kelly and told her I was going for a walk. I warmed up slowly, and was soon churning along at a twelve-minute-mile clip. But when I tried to jog, the forest preserve incident was brought back with sudden, painful clarity.

Back at home, I let Kelly know I was safe and sound. Then Al called.

"What happened yesterday?" I asked.

"Patrolman was shot from an alley in the south end. He's in the hospital; could have been a lot worse."

"Did you find the shooter?"

"We think so, but he's clammed up so far."

"You okay?"

"There's a lot going on right now," he said in a subdued voice.

The evil of people who do bad things and the desperation of those who have bad things done to them are the front lines of a cop's life. We lawyers have the luxury of sorting it out later. Sympathy for Al fluttered up and tried to fly.

"I know what you mean. Why don't you come over for dinner tonight?" The words were out of my mouth before my brain realized it.

Al paused. "That's a nice invitation. I'm working tonight, but I'm off now. What were you saying about being 'snippy' the other day?"

Big breath. "I acted like a moron, Al. I'd like to apologize, maybe get together."

The second hand crept slowly around the face of my dress watch.

"You *are* full of surprises. Somehow I got the feeling the words 'Marshfield' and 'apologize' never appear in the same sentence."

"It could be a first," I admitted.

"I'll be at the Loading Dock at one o'clock if you want to chat."

"That works. See you there."

CHAPTER TWENTY-FOUR

The entrance to the Loading Dock is halfway down a nondescript alley no one would venture into unless they knew about the restaurant or were searching for a good place to hide. A small hand-painted sign identifies the establishment and points to concrete steps leading below street level, where a weathered door opens into a sixties netherworld of Formica tables, red plastic booths, and dusty artificial plants. An old geezer with a patch over one eye runs a small corner bar where he's been pouring drinks since Reagan was president. Sliced pickles accompany every order.

I debated the selections on the antique jukebox where a buck still buys five songs. Elvis' *Jailhouse Rock* seemed like a good start.

I was moving to the beat, drumming on the tabletop when suddenly Al was on the other side of the booth. He wore a White Sox baseball cap with the sides of the visor curled in so you couldn't see his face unless you were looking straight at him. Which I was. His face was drawn and noncommittal. A faded red tee shirt peeked out from under a leather jacket.

"I have an idea," I said. "I'll say hello, you say hello, and maybe we'll have a conversation."

His eyebrows arched heavenward.

"No, huh? New game. I'll say a crime that begins with 'A,' you say a crime that begins with 'B' and so on. The crime can be modern day or biblical. What d'ya say?"

The waitress left menus. Al requested a club soda, coffee for me.

"Adultery."

"Blackmail."

"Conspiracy."

"Debauchery."

"I don't think that's a crime in Illinois."

"Wow, that's a relief."

I mustered a tentative smile. "Thanks for meeting me."

"The offer of an apology was more than I could resist."

"I was hoping you'd forget about that."

Chin on fist, elbow on the table, he waited.

"I don't respond well to statements like 'Tell me what you've been doing!' But I realize where it came from—and I overreacted. I'm sorry."

His expression went from barely engaged to mildly attentive.

"That's it?"

"My best effort."

He leaned back and scratched the stubble on his cheek.

"Your *best* effort?"

The waitress returned with the drinks and took our orders.

"I'm not gonna grovel, Al. Take it or leave it."

He peeled the paper wrapper from the straw and very deliberately rolled it between the palms of his hands for a minute. Two minutes. He shrugged.

"Okay. It is what it is. We'll go from here."

I reached over and found his hand. "Thanks."

The stone visage relaxed and the corners of his mouth stretched a centimeter.

"What about my offer?" he asked.

"What you said in the hospital? I have to clear any plan with you and in return you'll keep me in the loop?"

"That's the one."

"You know I can't quit on Sam, but you want me on the sidelines."

"I want you *safe*."

"You want *control*."

He leaned back and crossed his arms across his chest. "This is going nowhere."

"I agree." I ran my finger around the rim of my coffee cup, eyes downcast. "Can we start over?"

He rubbed his forehead. "Why not? They haven't even brought lunch yet."

I put a mental padlock on my mouth to avoid escalation. Within a minute, our plates arrived. BLT for him, huge salad for me. We ate non-stop. Halfway through, it seemed like the food had worked a bit of a healing: I felt the combativeness dissipate.

"I read the article about Larry Malone in the paper."

He looked at me blankly.

"I have a gut feeling there's a link between Malone and Sam."

His glass stopped halfway to his mouth. "What?"

"If Malone was taking bribes to back off certain investigations, maybe Sam got wind of it and confronted Malone, or confronted whoever gave him the bribe. Sam was a bit of a crusader, and he wasn't above taking matters into his own hands if he thought he could get the right result." I warmed to my subject. "He took on the city once when they tried to push a group of homeless people around. He did it for free, wrote letters to the editor, even filed a lawsuit. He'd do anything to fight an injustice."

"Your theory is…imaginative. But how would Sam have crossed paths with Malone?"

I cleared my throat. "To answer that, I'd have to know what cases Malone sabotaged."

Al locked his fingers together in a wing pattern, eyes searching everywhere but in my direction. He leaned back and gave me a wry smile. "I get it."

"Get what?"

"The reason you called, the reason you wanted to meet me. It wasn't to apologize: it was to pump me on Malone."

"No. Well, sort of. But I meant it when I said I was sorry. Cross my heart."

As if on cue, the morose strains of Brenda Lee's *I'm Sorry* came over the sound system. 1960. I leaned back, arms outspread and gazed upward. "Fate." I picked up my fork and held it poised above my food. Al hadn't moved. I put my fork down.

"Al, it's the truth. I needed to say I'm sorry because I didn't want that scene in the hospital to be the end of us. And when I read about Malone, it hit me like a bolt of lightning that there could be a connection."

"Lightning flashes randomly and disappears quickly — have I got that right? We cops tend to connect the dots: I'm sure you're familiar with the concept. Gather evidence, interview the players, analyze, figure out what makes sense."

"At least tell me how he got away with it."

"That's the easy part. Bad chain of command, no accountability." Al shook his head in disgust. "Malone started doing investigations about three years ago. They weren't part of his regular duties—he wasn't trained. As a matter of fact, he was only called on when supervisory manpower was stretched to the breaking point. If he caught a case he was supposed to run the show in-house, assigning patrolmen, pursuing leads as he chose. Theoretically a superior officer oversaw him but…" Al shrugged.

"How many cases was he assigned?"

"Fifteen, maybe twenty. No master record was kept of what was assigned to him."

"What kind of cases?"

He regarded me through half-closed eyes. "Here's where I'm keeping my part of the bargain. Malone got the usual assortment: run-of-the-mill burglaries, robberies, hit-and-run vehicular with injuries. Your grandmother could have solved most of them. Malone did the easy ones by the book—he couldn't afford to arouse suspicion—they were closed with arrests and convictions."

"And the tough ones?"

"Couple, three homicides, an arson and a home invasion." Al scowled. "He chose carefully. These were the kind of cases that, as the newspapers say 'baffled the local police.' They all needed solid investigation and some luck to crack. If they didn't get solved, victims, witnesses, families might not complain too loud, you know?"

"How did the supervisors on these cases let him get away with it?" I was incredulous.

"Don't forget, everyone was swamped at the time—that's how he got the assignments. He'd bullshit his way past 'em, told them things were going to break any day, or that he was on the verge of arresting the perp." Al grimaced. "Dumb luck."

"What finally tipped you off?"

"Some guys were concerned because he's been drinking a lot lately, and he's going through a divorce." He shrugged. "Happens to most cops one time or another. Then, on the home invasion, the vic's father is an alderman. He called Malone's supervisor and things unraveled fast after that."

"So now what?"

"They'll try to burn Malone: lock him up, throw away the key. Cops don't do well on the inside."

"What about the cases?"

"That's the rest of the bad news. The reports have disappeared. They think Malone sensed Internal Affairs closing in and destroyed them."

I slathered a pad of butter onto a hard roll that was probably baked a week ago. "And without the reports you can't trace who bribed him, or maybe I should say who he was shaking down."

"Plus it puts us in a huge hole. Damn difficult to solve the case without even a starting point."

"The currency of the realm is information," I pointed out. "Malone has it, and you guys need it to get your investigations up and running again. Time to play 'Let's Make a Deal.'"

Al was uncharacteristically quiet. Was he pissed off that a dirty cop could cut a deal or was he worried about the fallout from the scandal?

"You think there's a chance Malone stashed the reports somewhere as a sort of insurance policy?"

Al stopped chewing. "That's a thought. If we get the reports back, it'd sure make the next couple weeks a lot easier. I'll whisper into some ears."

We lapsed into a hunger-satisfied silence.

"Donna Gillespie called in sick the day Sam was killed."

Salad dressing dribbled down my chin.

"What?"

"Her parole officer's been very helpful."

"Was she really sick?"

"Gillespie is off limits." Tite's eyes were ice. "After what I've told you about Malone, I could end up in the same bleep he's in. "

"Off limits. Cool."

The waitress cleared our plates.

"You've been stirring your coffee for five minutes."

"You said most cops get divorced or have a drinking problem." I stopped stirring. "I was wondering if that included you."

He searched my face for an unreasonable length of time. "Yes to both." He shifted his attention to the salt and pepper shakers and regarded them like they held the key to existence. "It's not something I'm ready to talk about yet."

"I understand. You don't strike me as a guy who loses the tough battles."

A world-weary smile materialized. "It's a day-to-day life."

Silence floated between us like a balloon neither wanted to puncture.

I smoothed out my napkin on the table in front of me. "Can you give me the names and dates on those five cases?"

"When do you want them?"

I looked at him, wide-eyed.

"Just kidding. Imagine my head on Ross's plate. *Not* a pretty picture." The tone was non-negotiable.

"I had to ask."

The bill appeared on a plastic tray with two cellophane-wrapped peppermints. We each paid for our own lunch.

The walk back down the alley felt so different from the walk—was it just last Monday?—from Sam's chambers across the courthouse plaza. We paused at the entrance to the alley. He looked down at me, all stern and serious, then flashed that great all-boy grin. Even when he was being a cop, like now, I felt right in his presence, like a loose photograph finally fitted into the perfect frame.

"Make sure to let me know when they throw you in the river," he said. "I'll try to come fish you out."

I watched him slide into the undercover car. He pulled away without a backward glance.

CHAPTER TWENTY-FIVE

I drove to the medical building where United Anesthesiologists had their offices, and pulled into a parking spot with a clear view of the entrance. I called and asked for Dr. Benton. When the receptionist wanted to know who was calling, I responded "Dr. Watson" and was put through immediately. When Benton came on the line, I hung up. That seemed the most efficient way to find out if he was still at work. I waited, eyes glued to the entrance. It was almost five o'clock. An hour later the object of my curiosity emerged wearing a three-piece suit that was fresh off the cover of a men's fashion magazine. The red carnation in his lapel was striking, even from this distance. He folded his tall frame into a low-slung yellow sports car that sprang to life and growled out of the lot before I could get the Acura in gear. I caught him at the first light and stayed four or five cars behind him as he drove across town. The yellow car wove in and out of traffic like a soccer player dribbling the ball through a field of defenders, making moves I couldn't match and increasing the distance between us like he was an eagle and I was a pigeon. Fortunately he drew the line at running red lights, so I was able to keep him in sight. We left the city limits, and after a mile or so, he turned into the road that goes to the Joliet Country Club. I accelerated to the threshold of stupidity, but the sports car pulled steadily away.

From a quarter mile back, I saw him turn into the long country club driveway. I knew from attending a few parties here that the parking lot was open to the public, but for a low-life like me getting into the club was going to be a problem since I was neither a member nor a legitimate guest. I'd have to catch Benton before he went in.

The parking lot was huge as befits a golf/workout/spa/restaurant retreat. Benton was approaching the entrance on foot when I swerved into the handicapped space closest to the front door.

"Hi, doc." I waved as I jumped out of the car.

"Ms. Marshfield, what an unexpected pleasure." His expression changed to concern. "What happened to you?" He indicated my arm, still in a sling.

"Turns out there's still a few wild animals left in the forest preserve," I said, unsmiling.

"You were attacked by an animal?" He seemed startled.

"Yeah, the kind with hunting knives and ski masks and clubs who take off for Mexico after their dirty work's done."

He appeared puzzled, then his face cleared. "You were being humorous," he said, bemused. "You were really attacked by people. How terrible. Have they been arrested?"

"Not yet. Do you know any Mexicans, doc?"

He looked at me, seemed to consider a response. "I don't think so," he said uncertainly.

"Do you own a gun, doc? A twenty-two?"

His goatee seemed to bristle. "Ms. Marshfield, whether I do or not, I fail to see what business it is of yours." He was wary now, but still polite, as if I might be clueless as to how out of bounds my questions were.

"You know judges can't talk to parties about pending litigation. How come you waylaid Judge Frederick at the courthouse the morning Judge Kendall was killed?"

"What kind of game are you playing? Why are you trying to antagonize me?"

"Brenda Haskins was having an affair with you at the time of her husband's murder, wasn't she?"

He drew a deep breath and seemed to expand in all directions. "Mrs. Haskins' personal life is none of my business. If I see her in passing I'll be sure to pass on your slanderous allegations. Now, if you'll excuse me…" He turned to enter the club. As he did so a foursome exited.

"When did you last talk to Judge Kendall?" I asked, loud enough for the newcomers to hear. They stared at us, wide-eyed.

Benton inspected me calmly. "Your questions give you away, Ms.

Marshfield. You are desperately seeking a scapegoat for your friend's murder and for some unfathomable reason you've settled on me." He came to within a foot of my personal space. "If you do not cease harassing me with these unfounded allegations, I will take legal action."

He turned and walked away. I waited till his hand was on the entry door handle.

"Where were you the morning Dr. Haskins was murdered?"

He hesitated mid-stride, half-turned, then disappeared inside the club. The foursome was motionless as if caught in some giant neutralizing beam from outer space. I manufactured a smile for them, sauntered to the car and drove off.

Benton won that round. His placid demeanor in response to my attempt to press his buttons was weird. The doctor was either totally innocent or guilty and supremely unflappable. If the latter, I would have to be very, very careful.

CHAPTER TWENTY-SIX

An unfamiliar Buick sat in my driveway. As I pulled up, the front doors of the other vehicle flew open, and Betty emerged from the passenger side, Agnes Hart from the driver's. My welcoming grin faded when I saw the consternation on Betty's face.

"Susan! What happened?"

I had become so accustomed to my sling and a face that caused mothers to clutch their infants and run that I forgot how shocking my new appearance could be.

"Little accident. Nothing serious."

Betty came to a standstill. "What kind of 'little accident?'"

"I was running in the forest preserve and a couple guys didn't want me around."

"Omigosh! I saw the headline in the paper. I didn't realize it was you!" Betty squeezed my good side. "No permanent damage?"

"No, it's okay. I've got to take it easy for a while."

"Susan, does this have anything to do with the things we've been talking about?"

"I don't have a clue, but I'm open to the possibility."

"This is too much," she said, clasping her hands in distress. "Can we go inside and talk?"

I unlocked the front door and led them through the foyer into the twenty by thirty-foot great room. Agnes looked suspiciously at the plum-colored sofa and the modern coffee table. "Would you like some tea?" I asked.

"Water's fine," Agnes said. Betty nodded.

"Wine?"

Betty nodded again. Agnes put her arm around her friend's shoulder and gave her a hug.

I fetched the beverages. The two of them settled on the couch, I sat cross-legged on the rug. "What's going on?" I asked.

"Susan, I'm sorry for dropping by with no warning. But I spoke to Great Midwest and then I started thinking about this account and how much money is involved." She took a deep breath, steadied herself. "I'm worried. It's not like Sam to do this and not mention a word to me. It's not how we treated each other." She looked beseechingly at Agnes, then me.

"Betty, I can see how this could be devastating. I think to make sense of it, we need more information. The first place to look is the firm—I'm positive most of the money came from there."

"It's not about the money—can't you see that? It's about him doing all this in secret, concealing it from me!" Betty was almost hysterical. Agnes and I exchanged a quick glance.

"I trusted him," Betty whispered. "*That* was a mistake."

"You don't mean that." I took her hand. "I know Sam, and I know you. He would never betray your trust. There's things we don't know. We need to get to the bottom of this."

"I couldn't agree more," Agnes chimed in. "I remember how upset I was when Cooper…died." She studied the contents of her water glass. "There were moments, I'm ashamed to admit, when I doubted him, blamed him somehow for what happened. I never got the answers I needed. That's been difficult, and it still is. So find out everything you can, then at least you'll know what you have to deal with."

Agnes's words grabbed me and wouldn't let go. According to Betty, Cooper died of a drug overdose. This was not the time to explore that incident, but I needed to know the details.

We sat in a long but not uncomfortable silence.

"You're right. Susan," Betty said. "Have the police looked into this account?"

"Uh, would you like some more water, Agnes?" I busied myself gathering up glasses for a refill.

"Susan?"

"I don't think they're aware of it."

"You *cannot* withhold information from the police. If you don't tell them about Great Midwest, I will!"

I knew when I was defeated. "Uh, Betty, if you tell them, it might be better if you don't mention my name."

"How did you find out about it?"

I told them about fishing through the drawer and discovering it under a false bottom. No need to share how I surreptitiously slipped it into my briefcase.

"The police could learn a thing or two from you," Agnes said.

"I'm just glad we found it before they did."

Agnes sat up straight. "I wish you had been around when Cooper was killed. I don't think the police were as thorough as they could have been in his case."

"His *case?* The police were involved?" I echoed.

"My son died of what they call a 'drug-induced homicide.' It was never solved."

Neurons sizzled in my brain pod. "Agnes, I don't suppose there was a Sergeant Malone involved in the investigation?"

"Yes, he was the one I dealt with. I believe he was in charge."

Tite had said Malone's dossier included two or three homicides. Cooper Hart might be one of them. I segued back to the original topic. "I think we need to find out if the firm paid Sam after he went on the bench. Betty, you're the executrix of Sam's estate: they should give you the records with no problem."

Agnes agreed to help Betty obtain the financial data. I made a mental note to talk to Kevin about how the current and former partners split the revenue pie.

When Betty excused herself, I asked Agnes if I might visit her tomorrow to discuss Cooper's case. She seemed a bit taken aback but agreed to meet at eleven o'clock and gave me her address.

Having a plan of action had a calming effect on Betty. I escorted them to the Buick, but as I opened the passenger door, Betty planted both feet firmly on the pavement and placed a hand on my good shoulder. "Susan, I think it's hands down that what happened to you in the forest preserve is related to Sam. I want you to tell Tite *everything*. Will you do that, for me?"

I cleared my throat. "I'll do my best, Betty."

CHAPTER TWENTY-SEVEN

Drug-induced homicide is an offense created by the legislature in its never-ending campaign to give prosecutors more tools they can use to bludgeon defendants. The law is a double-whammy for pushers: they're prosecuted once for the traditional offense of manufacture, sale, or delivery (six years minimum), then whacked again for an additional fifteen to thirty if anyone dies as a result of taking, ingesting, snorting, shooting, or inhaling the controlled substance, even if the delivery is a gratuitous, no-money-exchanged deal.

Agnes Hart lived in an established, genteel neighborhood with large oak trees that provided shade in the summer and wore out rakes in the fall. She answered the bell attired in a yellow nylon workout suit with brilliant swaths of turquoise and purple. Her resemblance to a butterfly was unsettling.

She welcomed me into a foyer done in textured silver wallpaper and ushered me through a sunken living room into a solarium where plants too numerous to count exuded the bracing scent of newly turned earth.

"Will this be all right?" She indicated a small glass-topped wicker table and two chairs.

"That's fine, Agnes. You have a wonderful home."

She smiled wistfully. "My husband Ed built the house. This was his favorite room."

Quiet strains of classical music flowed around us. We sat opposite each other at the table.

"If I was a plant, I'd want to live here," I sighed.

"They're all my friends," she said indulgently. "But you didn't come to hear me go on about horticulture. How can I help?"

"Well, let's ease into this. What did you think of Malone?"

She cast a lingering glance over the rows of flora. "I must confess, looking back on it, I didn't treat Mr. Malone very well at first. It was upsetting that the police were involved. Cooper was gone, so what was the point? I wanted him to rest in peace."

She closed her eyes and swayed gently with the rhythm of the music. The violin section was playing a particularly soothing segment. I was learning that some folks are more forthcoming when they felt comfortable and unthreatened. If I wanted to gain their confidence, I'd be wise to adapt to their concept of time and not force them into mine.

"He wasn't as gruff as he looks," she continued. "He said that whoever *gave* Cooper the drugs was the evil one, and ought to be punished. He never said anything bad about Cooper. I spent quite a bit of time with him. He needed to know all about Cooper's school and friends and work."

She interlocked her fingers together on the table and took a deep breath.

"To answer your question, I came to like Malone. I thought he did a good job."

"But there were no arrests made?"

"He didn't have to tell me it was a hard case. It happened just when the weather started to get nice, May, a grand reunion out at Badger Lake. The kids who went away to school and the kids who stayed here in town all got together. There were over two hundred people. They had a live band, everybody brought friends—that type of thing. Young people are so casual."

Badger Lake was about forty minutes from town. Many Joliet families had vacation homes there, and a few commuted back and forth to work.

"Malone said there was a lot of drinking and some kids were smoking marijuana. Apparently no one saw Cooper take anything. He just…convulsed on the dance floor." Agnes spoke in an absolutely monotone, as if reading a train schedule.

"I'm so sorry, Agnes."

"Ed was busy with his business when Cooper was growing up, so I was the one who went to all his games, helped him with homework, talked his problems through." Tears filled her eyes. She got up and adjusted a potted plant.

"Do you know what kind of drugs he took that night?"

She stood with her back to me. When she finally turned around, her face was colorless, like a sidewalk that had been trod upon far too much. "They said it was heroin laced with hashish. I know he never used drugs until that night."

"Were there any suspects?"

"Malone talked about some Gangster Disciples who showed up at the party. No one knew them. But he couldn't find anyone who said they had drugs."

The Gangster Disciples are a black street gang that originated on the South Side of Chicago. They are known for drug dealing and related crimes. Joliet has several state prisons, and a lot of gang members stay in town after their release. I like to give them the benefit of the doubt, but quite often they are not model citizens.

"Did the sergeant keep you informed of his progress?"

She lowered herself heavily into the chair. "He called regularly at first, telling me who he'd interviewed and what he'd found out. After a while, the leads just seemed to peter out. I'd call and he'd say he was working on it. He always had time to talk." She smiled at a memory. "Usually he'd mention something nice about Cooper that someone had told him."

She looked at me with a fox's eyes. "Susan, why all the interest in Mr. Malone?"

I wasn't seeing any connection between Sam and Malone, and I didn't want Agnes to worry about the possibility or repeat it to Betty.

"Well, Cooper's case was unsolved, the reports are missing…"

Her head jerked up. "What?"

I repeated my last sentence.

"Cooper's reports are missing?" Her eyes swiveled in disbelief

"No, no, I misspoke." I raised my hands in denial. "*Some* reports from Malone's cases are missing; I don't know if Cooper's is one of them."

"Maybe they're just lost, or misplaced."

"Could be. Did Malone ever dodge you, not return your calls?"

She shook her head. "Not that I remember. He seemed very diligent." Apparently she hadn't read the article in the paper about the possibility that Malone took bribes in exchange for allowing the guilty to evade the consequences of their crimes. I decided not to enlighten her.

"If Cooper's reports are missing, what does that mean? Will they have to start the investigation all over again?" Dread, horror, fear—all were etched on her face.

"I don't know. Agnes, I'm sorry. I didn't realize this would upset you so. And remember, Cooper's reports may not be missing. His case may just be unsolved."

She looked right through me, her eyes overflowing.

"I…I can't believe this. I need to be alone now. I'm sorry. Can you show yourself out?"

She buried her face in her hands. I reached out to reassure her but my outstretched hand hung in the air between us as a small groan momentarily drowned out the classical music. I pulled my hand back and looked to the plants for guidance but they were mute. I tugged my jacket tighter around me and felt helpless. As I exited the solarium, I stole a quick glance back at Agnes. She was slumped over the wicker table, head cradled in her arms, her body racked with sobs.

CHAPTER TWENTY-EIGHT

"I faxed a copy of Sam's autopsy report to your office." Al's voice on my home answering machine was matter-of-fact. No preamble, no farewell, no "can't wait to see you again."

I chopped up a few veggies that were still the right color and threw them into some couscous. I ate, then called Al at the station.

"How ya' doin'?" he drawled.

"No complaints. You sound good."

"Took the day off, got away for a while."

"Where did you go?"

"Up to Chicago, saw some buddies, chilled."

Nice of you to invite me.

"Thanks for the autopsy."

"Yeah. No surprises. What's up with you?"

"Is the Cooper Hart case one of the homicides Malone messed with?"

Long pause. "Mm...m...ay...be," he drawled. "You missed your calling. Think you could pass the police academy exam?"

"Depends on the search and seizure questions."

"The answer is search everywhere, seize everything and worry about the law later."

"I was afraid you'd say that. Hart's mother is Sam's wife's best friend."

"No kidding," he said. "So Sam probably knew the deceased."

"Yeah, probably," I said, less confident now.

"Sounds like one of those 'six degrees of separation' things. Maybe four degrees. Stories like that happen all the time in this town. You might find connections in some of the other cases too, considering the business Sam was in and how many people he knew."

"You think it's too tenuous."

In my mind's eye, his face turned thoughtful. "If that's all there is, affirmative. What's your plan?"

"Well," I said hesitantly, "I was wondering what you're doing right now."

Silence. Then a chuckle tickled my left ear. "I live in the world's last great bachelor pad," he said. "It's not the place I want to entertain the opposite sex."

I swallowed something large. "Would you like to come over?"

"Where's 'over'?"

I gave him my address. He told me he was at the station to pick up some paperwork and could be at my place in twenty minutes. I hurriedly cleared away the dinner debris. When the bell rang, I belatedly checked the mirror. I had discarded the sling, and the bruise on my face had faded to a green/orange medley. My eyes were strangely luminous. I tugged the door open with an unbridled eagerness.

His tee shirt was purple today under the brown leather jacket. The White Sox baseball cap was stuck to his head. A grin split his face.

"You don't look like a cop. You don't even look like you."

"You gotta get past this cop thing. I don't get all hung up because you're a defense attorney."

Whoa. It was like someone splashed cold water on me, without the wetness. I stood, one hand on the doorknob, lost in the thought his words provoked. I had indeed been looking at him through a prism of my own making, rife with distortions and biases. Just what I tell a jury not to do when judging the facts of a case.

"Ahem."

I invited him in, still ruminating.

He strolled into my house like he'd been there a hundred times before, stopped in the middle of the great room and looked around.

"I think your office has more...personality. This house...you don't spend much time here. It's not very lived in."

"You must be a detective."

We gauged each other from opposite ends of the sofa.

"Want some coffee?"

"Do you have any tea?"

"I'll look."

When I returned, he was sprawled out on the rug next to the glass table, eyes closed, hands folded across his stomach. I set the steaming cups on the table. As I straightened up, a hand encircled my ankle, squeezed, and slowly massaged its way up my calf.

I turned and straddled him from above. He massaged both legs with slow, strong fingers, all the way up my thighs, then he raised to a sitting position and unbuttoned my jeans. He unzipped them slowly and drew them down, inch by inch, to my ankles. I stepped out of them and lowered myself so a knee was on either side of him. I tugged his tee shirt out and pulled it off over his head. His hands crept from my thighs to the leg band of my panties, slipped underneath and went exploring. I put my arms around his neck and pulled him up so we were chest to chest. The first kiss was cautious, but seconds later every scrap of clothing was tossed and we were writhing against each other. We plunged into the same wonderland as before; a wild place where the usual constraints are forgotten and life is reduced to white-hot urges and moaning "yeses."

***

The tea was cold, but we drank it anyway. He told me about being a football star in high school, a starter all through college, but failing to make a career in the pros. He tried business school but couldn't stay awake in any of his classes. He became a cop when a friend asked him to take the police entrance exam with him as a favor. The friend failed, but Al got the highest grade in the group and found his calling.

"What was your nickname?"

"My nickname?"

"Every football player has a nickname: Gonzo, Shredder, you know. What was yours?"

He reddened. "Jackal."

"Isn't that a wolf?"

"Wolf, wild dog," he shrugged. "I played middle linebacker where you have to be able to read what play is coming. I did it by instinct and I was almost always right, but it looked like I was taking chances, not exactly doing what we were told. I think coach wanted to call me a jackass but he wimped out. The name stuck."

We sipped in companionable, naked silence.

"Why did you go to law school?"

Sam and Betty were the only two people in town who knew about my brother Ryan. The topic was like a favorite pair of jeans that had grown too small and were now buried in the back of the closet. You hope things change and you can wear them again in the future. Something urged me to share Ryan's story with Al, and I did.

"That's a shame." He sighed. "So law school and your practice are your way of making sure no more Ryans happen on your shift?"

I considered my response. "I suppose, but don't confuse me with Donna Quixote. There will always be more Ryans because there will always be people who have too much power and get too greedy for wins."

"Everybody's greedy for something."

I looked a question at him.

"Money, happiness. . . " He lowered his voice conspiratorially. "Sex."

"Which one are you greedy for?"

"Every single one of them." He hurled himself at me and pretended to gnaw my neck.

"Enough!" I cried and shoved him away. We wrestled each other all over the floor till I gave up. We separated and lay on our backs, hands interlocked, gasping for air.

"This is the best evening I've had in six months," he said as his breathing returned to normal.

Hmm. I probably shouldn't tell him it's been the best evening of my last decade. Sex had been an occasional by-product of several relationships in the past, but those experiences were like a quiet night at home watching TV compared to the rock concert experience with Al.

"It's been fun," I concurred. "Guess what? I just remembered I need your help with something."

"The sun, the moon, the stars," he said grandly.

"There was an old man at Sam's graveside service." I rolled over and planted my chin on his chest. "Shabbily dressed black fellow. I got his license plate number and I was wondering if you could run his registration."

He contemplated me with one eye closed, like he was sighting down the barrel of a gun.

"Your enthusiasm is overwhelming."

"I thought maybe you needed help with putting in a screen or fixing a computer. Silly me," he said, reaching for his jeans.

I got up and padded to the kitchen, found a piece of paper and wrote down the Nova's number. When I came back into the great room, Al was pulling on his tee shirt.

"Guess I ruined that mood."

"It's okay. I gotta get going," he said shortly.

I gave him the paper. He glanced at it and stuck it in his pocket.

"One last thing. Do you have access to gun registration records?"

"That depends. What do you want to know?"

"I want to know if Eric Benton ever registered a handgun, specifically a twenty-two."

"Still shaking his tree, huh?" A moment's silence. "There was no gun involved in Sam's death. We had the doc specifically check, because when the head gets as…bad as that, it can be a cover-up for another cause of death. The autopsy is definitive: blunt trauma to the head, no evidence of gunshot." He combed his fingers through the bristle on his scalp. "What are you driving at?"

"Well, Benton and I had a chat. He wasn't very enamored of me. I hope he won't try anything, but I wonder if he has the means."

"Benton? What kind of a chat?" he demanded.

I told him in non-specific terms how the doctor had resisted my efforts to rattle him.

"What if I check and he's registered a three-fifty-seven? Will that put your mind at ease?"

"I'll have to get a bigger one."

"And learn how to use it."

"I played laser tag once," I said brightly.

Al's face turned hard and his lips formed a narrow line. "When you were in the hospital, I made you an offer. You don't seem at all interested, so I have no obligation here. You're good at finding things out—you did a great job on the Hart kid. You can figure out the rest of this stuff." He pulled on his socks and shoes.

"Al, I'm sorry. Sometimes I just get carried away." I picked up his belt and held it out to him. "I'm not used to asking permission."

When he looked up, his eyes were flat. "What now?"

I wrapped myself in a throw blanket. "I sit tight and wait for you to get back to me on the license plate and Benton."

His gaze danced slowly from where the blanket started across my chest and stopped at my knees. For a moment I thought he'd grab it and pull it off. Instead he very deliberately threaded the belt through the loops of his jeans and buckled it. Keeping his eyes above my neck, he gave me a slow-motion, one-handed wave and let himself out.

In my dream that night, I was skiing down a steep slope toward Al who was yelling and waving his arms frantically. I skied past him, way too fast, to the bottom of what turned out to be a blind drop and I was falling, falling through the air.

CHAPTER TWENTY-NINE

There were fifteen Malones in the phone book, none with the first name Larry or initial L. Directory assistance was no help, ditto the Internet. The sergeant knew how to stay off the radar. Al could get his number, but I knew better than to ask.

Tom Oberg was the Joliet city attorney and a friend from law school. He had clawed his way up the legal department ladder and was wired to everything of consequence in the city. We had become reacquainted when I arrived in town years ago. I called and congratulated him on a recent victory in federal court, and then we talked Tom's lifeblood, politics, for an interminable length of time before I could get to the point.

"Tom, I hear Larry Malone's in trouble and I thought I'd give him a call, just to let him know the whole world's not beating up on him. He was on a couple of my cases, and he's always been decent. Do you have his number?"

"Out of character for you to cheer up a cop, isn't it?"

I laughed. "Most of the time, yes. But Malone treated me real well."

"I'm not supposed to give that information out. Besides, he's not your type."

First rule of negotiation: understand the way the other side thinks. "True, but I heard this disciplinary thing is goin' nowhere, and I may need another favor in the future, you know?"

Tom hesitated. "I hear ya, lovely. Give me a minute to access that data base." I heard keystrokes in the background. "Ready?"

"Shoot."

"Phone is 731-1465. Says he lives at 2975 Beacon if you want to send a card."

"Thanks, Tom."

"No problem, just don't let on how you found him."

"We never had this conversation."

Tom warned me not to go jogging in unincorporated areas. After we hung up, I made a mental note to email my city council member about what a great job the legal department was doing under Tom's leadership.

The autopsy report Al had faxed was long and filled with medical jargon. The cause of death was blunt force trauma to the cranium, instrumentality unknown. If the killer went to trial, DNA on the golf club would presumably be matched to Sam and it would be identified as the murder weapon. I waded through the morning's appointments and checked voice mail before lunch. Al had left a message that the Nova from the funeral was registered to a Digger Cullerton in South Lombard, a rural community about thirty miles south of Joliet. Since we had parted on ambiguous terms, his message was a surprise, albeit a pleasant one. He also left his personal cell phone number.

My calendar was clear for the afternoon. I locked the office and grabbed a sandwich to go.

As I headed down the interstate it occurred to me that maybe I should call Al and thank him. He answered on the fourth ring.

"It's Susan."

"Yeah."

"I just wanted to say thanks for getting Cullerton's address. I…I didn't know if we were still friends."

The pause was so lengthy I thought the call was dropped. "I don't know if we're still friends, either. It seems to be a one-way street. I'm giving information; you're holding back and going your merry way."

A gust of wind hijacked the car and tried to blow it into the other lane. I gripped the wheel tightly and fought for control. The blast moved on.

"I thought there was something more between us than information-swapping."

"Swapping is back and forth, give and take. You do not swap. You take and then you want more."

"My, we *are* being blunt today, aren't we?"

"Blunt and truth are usually the same."

"Okay." I sounded way too loud, even to my own ears. "I did give you Righetti. There's something there."

"Point for Susan," he said in a somewhat softer tone.

"Al, I'm on my way to Cullerton's now. Why don't I call you afterwards?"

A gap of silence.

"Do that."

CHAPTER THIRTY

If a real estate agent described 925 West Poplar as "modest," he'd be flirting with fraud. The clapboard house, which was more like a shack, slouched on a narrow, overgrown lot. A concrete stoop led to a fatigued wooden porch. I rapped twice on the weathered door. The paint that still clung to it was green; the rest had peeled off a long time ago. I waited, then banged with the side of my fist.

"Hold on!" A hoarse voice cried out. The door opened by inches and the whites of the occupant's eyes materialized from the dim interior like two puddles of cream in a dark chocolate pudding.

"Mr. Cullerton? Digger Cullerton?" I asked.

"Says so on the mailbox." His voice rumbled from a place deep within and was not unfriendly.

"I'm Susan Marshfield, from Joliet. I'd like to talk to you for a few minutes, if you don't mind."

Misshapen flaps protruded from the side of his head. Pouches under his eyes hung halfway down his cheekbones.

"What do you wanna talk about?"

"You attended Sam Kendall's funeral. I was wondering how you knew him."

Cullerton shaded his eyes with a slightly trembling hand and surveyed the area in front of his house. Apparently satisfied, he teetered out, leaning heavily on a cane, and lowered himself to a sitting position on the edge of the porch. He motioned me to sit beside him. I did so, hoping my trench coat was thick enough to absorb splinters and rusty nails. Even though it was only early spring, the porch was a little harbor of warm sun.

"Good to get out of that house once in a while," he said.

"Yeah. Gets a little close." Crevices in his face intersected and forked off each other like lines on a county road map.

"Could be I just like going to funerals of rich, important people."

"Yeah, it's probably a hobby," I replied. "But it was a cold day to come all that way on a lark. And you looked like you were having some pretty serious thoughts."

A sudden whirring noise grabbed our attention and an object struck Cullerton's house with a sharp crack. I turned just in time to see a stone bounce off his front window. I shot down the stoop to the sidewalk. To the left, hidden from the porch by a hedge, two boys who couldn't have been more than nine or ten snickered and slapped each other on the back. When they spotted me they almost choked on their laughter. One took off on foot, abandoning his bicycle. The other tried to pedal away, but his coordination deserted him. I grabbed his jacket firmly at the collar.

"What's your name?"

"Lemme go." He squirmed mightily.

"I asked you a question."

He started to cry. "Joshua."

"Do you know you just committed a crime, Joshua?" I asked pleasantly.

"No, Robert did it. He threw the stone," the boy wailed.

"Settle down, Joshua. You were with Robert and you knew what he was doing. That makes you just as guilty as him. In fact, it's two crimes. Assault and property damage."

I pursed my lips. "Let's see. The chief of police here is Pershall, right?"

I knew him, a benefit of having represented several DWI clients from this town.

"Uh…I guess so."

"I think we're going to go see him," I said and started to guide the boy to my car.

"No!" he yelped and pulled away. I tightened my grip.

"Hmm…let me think. What's your last name, Joshua?"

"Gardner." He stopped struggling.

"Okay, Joshua Gardner. I have a proposition for you. You know Mr. Cullerton, the man who lives in the house you and Robert just threw the stone at?"

The kid nodded miserably.

"Well, Mr. Cullerton's a special friend of mine. If he has any more problems, I'm going to find you and Robert and we're going to the police station, understand?"

The boy's eyes grew very large. He nodded. "We won't give Mr. Cullerton any more trouble."

"Okay, Joshua." I relinquished my grip. "You make sure Robert gets my message, and you give him his bike back, okay?"

"Yes, ma'am." He agreed eagerly.

Mr. Cullerton had hobbled out to the sidewalk to observe the proceedings. After the boy rode away, I examined the window.

"No damage."

"Kids've been doing that for a long time. Broke the window last month. Had to get me a new one."

"Well, I don't think it'll happen again, at least from those two. If it does, you call the police and ask for Chief Pershall. I'll let him know what happened today and he'll take care of it." In South Lombard, the cops might actually pay attention to this kind of nuisance.

"I'll do that, missy." He looked at me thoughtfully. "Thank you."

"You're welcome." Our eyes met. He was little more than an apparition, but something about him was so authentic that I felt drawn to him in a way that was almost spiritual.

"Kin you help me sit down again?" he asked after a quiet moment.

I took his elbow and guided him gently back to the steps. Once again, he settled down awkwardly and I balanced across from him.

"Why do you want to know 'bout me and Judge Kendall?"

"He was a good friend of mine. I'm…I really need to know why he was killed."

"But you're not the police."

"No."

"If you went to all the trouble to find me and then drove down here to talk to me, this must be pretty important."

I shrugged. "It is to me."

His gaze swept to the distant horizon and back again. "If you're his friend you might not like what I have to say."

I sat up straight. "It doesn't matter if I like it or not."

He laid his cane across his lap and studied me unabashedly. "I see."

I basked in the sun's warmth. My usual impatience to get down to business was in recession: Mr. Cullerton had time like Bill Gates has money. I took my watch off and stuffed it in my pocket.

"I had a grandson once," he began, kneading his thigh. "My son was home here on leave from the Army. He met the momma and they spent his whole leave together. Nine months later when she had the baby, he was overseas. The momma and the baby lived here with me till she went off with someone else and left the little guy." He nodded at the recollection. "So I raised him up. Took care of him every day, fed him, got him into school." He looked at me for understanding.

"What was his name?"

"Anthony."

I had to strain to hear.

"What happened to Anthony?" I asked after a lengthy silence.

His upper body swayed from side to side like a metronome set at super slow speed. "September two and a half years ago he was a senior here at South Lombard High. He was a real good basketball player, and three colleges were talking to him, offering scholarships.

"After he got his driver's license, I'd let him borrow the Nova. One night the damn fool car quit on him and he had to walk home. They say he was probably walkin' right where he should be on the side of the road. But there was no sidewalk and no lights over on Stanley Street." He gestured to the north. "They fixed it now."

"Uh-huh," I said uneasily.

"Anthony didn't make it home that night."

"What happened?"

"They found him the next morning. He was thrown 'bout fifty feet, broke his neck, inside injuries."

He reached into a pocket of his overalls and pulled out a dingy handkerchief. He twisted it until it disappeared in his bony hand. "They told me he died right away."

I had heard too many hard luck stories from too many hard up clients. But Cullerton's narrative was different, raw and palpably genuine.

"The police called it a hit and run and tried to find out who done it, but after a while they had to close the books." He rubbed a thumb across the worn handle of his cane. "That's the part of the story everyone knows," he sighed.

Minutes passed. I thought Cullerton forgot I was there. Then he lifted his chin. "This here's the part you might be interested in. After Anthony died, I started getting money orders every month, like clockwork. They were from the post office, always dated the first of the month.

"Nothin' like that's ever happened to me. I put two and two together and figured the money had to be coming from whoever hit Anthony. But the 'from' part on the money order was always blank, and my name was printed. The envelope it came in was typed with no return address, ever."

What did you do?"

"I got it in me that I just had to know who did this." A slow, sad smile crossed his face. "Maybe kinda like you need to know why your judge was killed. So I took one of the money orders to my post office here in town and they told me which post office sold it. They can tell by the numbers. Every one of 'em came from the main post office in downtown Joliet."

He had my total attention.

"Finally, 'bout six or eight months after I started gettin' them, I went up to that post office. I was the first one in the door on the first of the month. I got me a chair and I waited, all day. I told the post office people why I was there, so they wouldn't throw me out. I did that, on the first of the month, for three months in a row."

The handkerchief hung, limp and forgotten, from his hand.

"And for three months in a row, Sam Kendall came in and bought a money order, early, before nine."

Some geese honked as they flew north overhead. I watched until they disappeared.

"What then?"

"The post office people were nice, but they wouldn't tell me anything about the money order he bought. And they don't ask for I.D. when someone buys a money order with cash."

"Circumstantial," I commented flatly.

"Yep," he agreed. "So I got smart. The next month, I got in line right after Mr. Kendall and I bought the next money order. And when the check came in the mail the next day, I compared 'em."

"And?" I asked softly, knowing the answer.

"Same everything, 'cept my serial number was one more than his." Cullerton's tone was apologetic.

The post office was only a couple blocks from the courthouse, right on Sam's way to work. I knew what to think; I just didn't want to think it.

"I wonder if he knew who you were, waiting there."

The old man let out a low, mirthless chuckle. "I weren't wearing no sign. I knew who he was, cause I got cable TV here, living alone, and he was on the local station, and I seen him in the paper once in a while. After this happened, I seen where he made judge."

If Sam was the old man's gravy train, Cullerton had every reason to want him to live long and prosper. Except that Sam might have killed his grandson. And if he was smart enough to track Sam as the source of the money orders, was he smart enough to get into the courthouse and ambush him?

"When did the payments start?"

"Anthony was killed September fourteen. The first one came in October."

"Did you ever confront Sam about any of this?"

Mr. Cullerton traced invisible designs on the ground with the business end of his cane. "I've thought long and hard 'bout what I'd say if we ever met," he mused. "But he got his sack to carry and I got mine. I loved that boy more'n anything I've loved in all my life…"

He couldn't hold the tears back any longer. They trickled down the lines of his face, silent as deer slipping through the forest.

"No," he answered brokenly. "I let him go his way. Good Lord's got a way of takin' care of things, better'n mine." He wiped his face with his sleeve.

I wanted to disbelieve Cullerton, to find a flaw in his story.

"What did you do with the money?" Maybe he spent it all on liquor and the lottery.

"It's all in a savings account. I haven't spent a dime. My will says that when I die, half of it goes to Anthony's father. He's settled down now, over in Ohio. The other half will be in a college scholarship fund at Anthony's high school. Lawyer set it up for me, Miller here in town."

"That's very wise, Mr. Cullerton."

He nodded. "I think it's best."

"Why don't you use some of it for a vacation, or to fix up your place here?"

His grin was like a jack-o'-lantern, more empty spaces than teeth. "Ain't no place I want to go that bad, and it's just me livin' here. I like the house the way it is."

We lapsed into silence again.

"It must be pretty tough to hear this, Judge Kendall being your friend and all," Cullerton ventured, turning to face me.

"How much did Sam send you?"

He shook his head disapprovingly. "Is money all you lawyers ever think about?"

I hoped he was being funny. "Mr. Cullerton, I have no desire to pry into your personal finances. Sam left a money trail. I'm trying to follow it, match up numbers, make sense out of things. If I know how much he sent you, I'll know how much I still have to find. Maybe he sent you all of it."

Cullerton shook his head. "I don't know 'bout no money trail, but I do know money's not worth killin' for. Anger...fear...jealousy..." He raised his eyebrows. "I'd be thinkin' along those lines if I was you."

"I agree, but if I can figure out the money trail, I might find one of those motives."

"We all done things we ain't proud of," he rumbled on as if he hadn't heard me. "I suspect your judge was tryin' to buy his way out from feelin' bad about Anthony. Most of the time, dealin' with what you done ain't as easy as writin' a check." He gave me a baleful look.

"Have you told anyone else about the money orders?"

"Haven't told nobody. You the only one."

"Can we keep it just between us?"

The throaty rumble escaped again. "Missy, I done kept it secret going on three years now. I kin keep it another thirty."

"Thanks, Mr. Cullerton."

The old man's eyes drifted closed and he appeared to doze off. A sudden chilly breeze sent a shiver through me.

"Are you okay, Mr. Cullerton?" I whispered.

His eyes opened quickly, like the shutter of a camera. "Yeah, I'm okay." A smile tried to raise the corners of his mouth. "I feel better now someone else knows."

I swallowed, wordless. The old man's cane slipped to the ground. I handed it to him.

"May I help you back into the house?"

He looked up at the blue sky. "It's nice out here. I think I'll just set a few more minutes."

I dug out a card and handed it to him. "If the kids give you a hard time, call me."

He rubbed his thumb across the raised lettering.

"Sure thing, Ms. Marshfield."

"I know this wasn't easy, Mr. Cullerton. Thank you for telling me about Anthony."

His eyebrows raised slowly like a curtain over a stage. "Maybe I should be the one thankin' you."

We sat on the porch as the shadows lengthened and the warmth ebbed. I didn't want to say goodbye so I touched his hand in farewell and walked to the car. As I rolled past the house I glanced back at Cullerton. He was staring at the clouds, looking for someone he alone could see.

CHAPTER THIRTY-ONE

"I will not allow you to interrogate my friends. You are *out of control.*"

"Betty, hang on a second. I didn't 'interrogate' Agnes. I never intended to upset her, and I apologized. I had no idea she was still so torn up about Cooper's death."

She spun her Starbucks cup around the table. "You wouldn't intentionally hurt Agnes," she admitted. "The problem is, you're like a horse with the bit in its mouth. You run right over people, and they get hurt. Negligently, as you lawyers say, but hurt nonetheless. You need to remember people have feelings!"

Somewhere deep inside a lid flew off. "I have feelings too!" I protested. "What do you think I am, some heartless monster?"

She regarded me over the top of the cup. "No, of course not. But there's a difference between a healthy emotional life and a temper."

On the drive back to Joliet from Cullerton's, I had tried to reconcile the Sam I knew, brave and honest, with the one who was apparently guilty of vehicular homicide resulting in the death of Cullerton's grandson Anthony. I went to a little place I knew of on the river and just sat and listened to the water. It was an intellectual exercise, not an emotional one, and I left with nothing resolved.

"I'm a much better thinker than I am feeler," I said after a minute. "In court, a big part of my job is swaying jurors' emotions. Judges' too. So I have to stay above it all. If I let my feelings show, it has to be for the right reason and with the right effect, you know?" I sought her eyes. "And it's carried over into real life."

Betty squinted into my face like a botanist examining a unique plant life. "You have emotions—you've just pummeled them into submission.

Let them rampage a bit…well, at least admit their existence and let them out of their box. That's not too difficult."

I clutched my head. "First Kelly, now you. I'm surrounded by pop psychotherapists. Help!"

"You're surrounded by people who love you," she retorted.

I flung my arms outward. "I *feel* the love."

She looked at me like I was a car that inexplicably stopped running and she was considering kicking the tires. "Well, we don't love you *that* much."

We lapsed into agreeable silence. I was perfectly happy in my own emotionally-challenged existence. Why would I change?

"Susan, I'm fine with this topic, but I *am* curious. What does Cooper's case have to do with anything?"

I debated how to answer. Betty deserved honesty, to a point. I told her about the accusation against Malone. She had read the article in the paper.

"Something about the proximity of Sam's death and Malone's suspension is…unsettling. Throw in that one of his cases was Cooper Hart's DIH and it's pretty intriguing."

"What possible connection could there be between Sam and Malone?"

"I think Sam kept his own counsel on some things. As an attorney and then a judge, he was privy to information the rest of us have no clue about. If he somehow found out what Malone was doing, I wouldn't put it past Sam to try to fix it."

We looked at each other, thinking the same question: had Sam been killed because he tried to remedy Malone's injustices?

"Susan, do you have proof of any of this?"

"Nada," I shook my head dejectedly. "The truth is, it's all speculation and guesswork on my part. I didn't really want to tell you. I hope I did the right thing."

"You did," she said reassuringly. "But this is definitely something Tite should know about."

"He knows," I said. "He thinks I have an over-active imagination."

She stirred her coffee. "I've been gathering the records. Apparently there's a lot of money I never knew about."

"From the firm?"

"Yes. Theodore was very cooperative about giving me the documentation. I don't think he suspects that I never knew." She bit her lower lip. "Since Sam went on the bench, the firm's paid him over eighty thousand dollars."

I whistled. Sam had been a founding partner of the firm, and the partnership agreement undoubtedly provided that a departing partner, depending on the reasons for the departure, got a piece of every fee generated for a specified period of time.

"How about before he went on the bench?"

"He got a regular salary, which matched the deposits into our checking account. Then every quarter the firm would pay a bonus, depending on revenues."

There wasn't a delicate way to ask this question. "How much of all this did you know about?"

Betty sighed. "I never had a clue about the eighty thousand since he went on the bench or the bonuses before that. I don't think they made it into the checking account."

We cogitated, separate and somber.

"He opened the Great Midwest account three years ago and he's deposited roughly two hundred forty thousand dollars."

Hmm. When I had added up the deposits into Sam's checkbook I got the same number. "Do you have copies of the checks?"

"Yes. He wrote them all to himself."

I rotated my neck. The tendons popped like corn in hot oil.

"What does all this mean?"

It meant Sam had laundered money through the Great Midwest account and some, if not all of it, was in Digger Cullerton's savings account.

"Sam was hiding income so he could use it without your knowledge."

Betty drew back as if an habitually docile dog just tried to bite her hand. "Subtlety isn't your strong suit, Susan." She crushed her paper coffee cup in both hands. "But you're right. I guess I had to hear it to make myself believe it."

"Betty, you knew him better than anyone. You must have some

thoughts on all this."

"Thoughts." Her eyes clouded. "I've thought about it till I'm blue in the face. I believe Sam used this money to somehow protect me from something...shield me." She shook her head. "That's the saddest part. If he didn't know after all these years that I'm strong enough to handle whatever it is, I guess maybe he really didn't know me."

I couldn't tell where the pain in her voice ended and the bitterness began.

"It's time to tell the police about this."

"No!" I yelped.

"What?"

I leaned forward anxiously. "What I mean is, there's nothing to connect this money with Sam's death."

If this story leaked, the press would have a field day speculating about what Sam did with two hundred and forty thousand dollars. "It might get ugly."

She sighed heavily. "That's what I'm trying to say. I guess you don't understand either," she said. "Susan, you've known us for what, three, four years?"

I nodded. "Five, I think."

"The law was Sam's tool for leaving this world a better place than he found it. Fortunately, he made a very good living at the same time, but that was never a priority. Whatever he did with all this money..." She covered the lower half of her face as if protecting herself from the stench of a dead and rotting animal. "He did it for a good reason."

I nodded mutely, the image of Anthony Cullerton lying dead on Stanley Street plastered in my head. "Betty, we need to keep this between us for a few more days."

"Is that what you're advising me to do? Keep it quiet?"

Time for a cell phone to ring, or maybe there'd be an earthquake.

"Give me a couple days to go through the records from the firm," I asked.

She stared at me, or maybe through me.

"All right. Two days. But you have to let me know what you find."

"Of course."

"*When* you find it."

Al, now Betty, were singing the same song to me. What had I done to deserve this treatment?

"Right."

If Al found out about the Great Midwest account, he'd think he'd found the motherlode and would use his resources to track every dime. And if Digger and his payments came to light, I could see Ross try to pin the murder on the old man. I trusted Al's instincts and integrity, but the powers that be might need a scapegoat.

Betty and I separated, her to run errands, me to return to the office. I needed to find out exactly how much money Sam had sent Digger Cullerton in the anonymous money orders.

CHAPTER THIRTY-TWO

Malone's small bungalow sat in a grid of cookie-cutter homes, remnants of the middle of the last century when men went to work and women found fulfillment ironing shirts and changing diapers. A decades-old Chevy Silverado with a smashed-in rear quarter panel called the driveway home. The lawn was mostly crabgrass, the landscaping was non-existent, no toys littered the front yard.

I took up a vigil about four doors south of the sergeant's house on the opposite side of the street. The next hour was a bevy of activity: a white-haired woman walked north, accompanied by two Chihuahuas, and a thermal-clad jogger labored by in the opposite direction.

By six my bladder was groaning. No Porta-Potti in sight. What do real surveillance people do? I recalled a gas station on the main street a mile back and made a quick trip there. As I hustled back, Malone's front door blew open and a burly form lurched out of the house and down the sidewalk. I drove past him, then swerved to the curb and peered into the rearview mirror. The fellow was a poster child for an aging cop: surly, grizzled, and rotund. It was either Malone or a former KGB agent in the Witness Protection Program.

I abandoned the car and followed discreetly on foot. Three blocks later the shapeless hulk turned into a corner tavern. These blue-collar saloons dot the eastside like baseballs in the outfield after batting practice. I've found myself in one or another of these establishments on occasion and always left with the feeling that they'd be happy to scrimp by without my business.

I waited to make sure Malone was settled in, then raced back to the car. I gunned it past his house, swerved around the corner and found the alley. I counted the dark garages till I got to the sixth one and squeezed the Acura in close to his bay door, leaving enough space for another car to pass.

The sun was long gone. The city had erected vapor lights that cast a surreal yellow glow throughout the alley. A few homeowners had mounted outdoor lights on the top of their garages, but not Malone. He probably had a gun.

Flashlight in hand, I exited the car. Malone's house squatted in the late winter gloom. Pretending like I belonged there, I walked to his back gate and reached over to raise the latch. At that moment a white light blinked on at the rear of the house. I turned to cement for an instant, then shrank back into the alley. Perhaps a child was home or maybe the estranged wife was collecting her belongings. Didn't matter. What was I doing here anyway? If this guy had any smarts, he wouldn't keep stolen police reports or records of payoffs buried in his backyard.

Certain now that the house was occupied, I was cured of any thought of unauthorized entry. My law license was safe for another day. But Malone's garbage receptacle was outside the gate, in the public alley. It was thick, heavy plastic with a hinged lid, and far too tempting. I watched the house for signs of people leaving or glancing out the window, but all was quiet. I flipped the lid of the garbage receptacle open and aimed my light at the interior. Two black plastic trash bags were crammed tightly inside. I tugged the top one loose, carried it awkwardly to my car and heaved it into the trunk. It was full but not terribly heavy.

As I scurried back for the second bag, a merry little jangling sound cut through the silence. I peered into the darkness and was appalled to discover a giant canine prancing eagerly in my direction. Hopefully he was attached to a human being. I slid into the narrow space between the car and Malone's garage and crouched down low, hoping the dog would find scents far more interesting than mine to pursue. The clinking noise abated. I got down on my knees and peered underneath the car. Six feet were visible: four furry ones and two shod in hiking boots. The dog was nosing around the opposite rear tire of my car. I remained as still as a stone in the desert, breathing in just enough oxygen to maintain life. Suddenly, without even glancing my way, the dog lurched across the alley on another search, the hiking boots stumbling to catch up. I waited until the jingle bells were too faint to be heard, then got up cautiously. The alley was deserted. I hoisted the second bag out of the garbage bin, flung it next to the first and slammed the trunk lid. I fumbled with my key ring, unable to find the ignition key. Finally I shook it free, but it wouldn't fit into the slot. I jammed it, wiggled it, cursed at it, then coaxed it gently and finally it slid in. The car started immediately. It took every ounce of self-control I possessed to refrain from heavy-footing down the alley. Once I was safely on the street I covered the three blocks to the tavern in less than a minute.

If the number of cars surrounding the tavern was any indication, business was gangbusters. I parked a half block away and brushed myself off, hoping I looked more like a lawyer than a garbage thief.

A swinging sign proclaimed that I was about to enter The Hospitality Suite. Tiny red and green Christmas lights blinked cheery greetings despite the early spring weather. I pushed through the door and was greeted by low-pitched male rumbling and alcohol-driven guffaws. A loud and enthusiastic darts game occupied one corner. Both pool tables were busy. The remaining customers nestled at the bar. As the patrons became aware of my presence they stared unabashedly. The bartender gave me a cursory glance, decided I wasn't an immediate threat, and continued pouring drinks. The noise level surged back to a congenial roar.

Malone wasn't hard to find: his derriere was propped up on a barstool like a mushroom cap on a narrow stem. His black and white plaid shirt, frayed at the edges, hung out over stained khaki pants. He was deep in conversation with the man on his left. The two stools on his immediate right were unoccupied.

I shook out of my coat, hung it on a peg, and sauntered to the empty seat farthest from Malone. I hesitated as if debating what to do. The customer at the end of the bar looked as if he had been rooted there for a week. He was fixated on the glass in front of him, which looked to be a straight-up Manhattan. The giant TV screen was tuned to a pre-season Cub game. No one was paying much attention. It was that kind of year already.

The bartender approached, towel slung across his shoulder. He was in his twenties, stocky with a dark complexion, likely related to the owner. "What can I getcha?"

"Two things, actually. You want the easy one first?"

"Whatever," he shrugged with a genial smile.

If I said "Chardonnay," they'd all look at me like I was Rush Limbaugh and had just wandered into the Democratic national convention. I glanced at the handles of his draught beers. "Old Style."

"You're right, that's easy." He drew down a glass and placed it on a coaster that proclaimed the goodness of some unknown lager.

"Now," he leaned toward me, elbows on the bar. "I love a challenge."

"I'm a lawyer. I've got a big trial coming up, and I need to find a witness. I heard he comes in this place a lot."

The bartender tugged at his ear. "I'm subbing for my dad tonight. I don't know many of the regulars."

"This guy, his name is William Glidden, was a passenger in a car that was in an accident. If Glidden testifies and I get a good verdict against the driver, chances are Glidden can settle his case for decent money too."

"I see." He seemed to follow what I was saying. "Only problem is, I don't know anyone named Glidden. What does he look like?"

"I don't have a picture, but he's in his late forties, thin sandy hair, medium build, about five foot ten. At his deposition he said he was a truck driver. Any help you can give me would be great."

"Lotsa guys like that come in here." He started to speak to the Manhattan customer, then shook his head. He spotted Malone who was still oblivious to my presence. "Let me ask this gentleman. If anyone would know, he would." He waited politely for a break in Malone's conversation with his buddy, then leaned over the bar and spoke to my quarry. I couldn't distinguish their words but the bartender gestured in my direction and Malone nodded a few times. I sipped my beer, ecstatic. This was working out better than I could have scripted.

Malone finally turned towards me. "Nick here says you're lookin' for someone named Glavin?"

I turned my 100-watt smile on him. "Glidden. William Glidden." I repeated the description.

"There's a foo…few truckers who come in here, but none of 'em look like that." He squinted. "Who'd you say you were?"

I dug my cardholder out and handed him a card. "Susan Marshfield. He's an important witness."

"Yeah, yeah, Nick told me." He brought the card close to his face, then extended it as far as his arms could reach, then put it on the bar in front of him.

"You know Kyle Galvin?" he asked.

Kyle was a divorce lawyer in town. "Sure, I've known him for years. Guy knows his way around the courthouse."

"Yeah. Well, good."

"This guy Glidden…he may not be a trucker anymore. Do you know anyone around here who even looks like that?"

"Like what?"

I again described the non-existent witness. Malone scanned the faces of the patrons. "How old's this clown supposed to be?"

"Late forties, give or take."

"Well, you can give 'em to me. I need all the extra years I can get." He winked and elbowed the guy next to him. "Really, honey, I know some guys who look like that, but their names aren't Glidden."

"That's okay. Thanks for trying." I smiled remorsefully.

My glass only had an inch or so left. "You ready for another brewski, honey?" He motioned to the bartender.

"No, thanks. I should ask around."

"You can ask whoever you want, but if I don't know him, chances are none of these other rummies does either." He threw his head back and guffawed loudly.

I studied his face long enough to be impolite.

"Whacha starin' at honey? Haven't you seen a handsome man before?" He patted his medium-sized belly which rested happily atop a far larger one.

"None as handsome as you."

I was kidding. I hoped he was too. "Actually, I was thinking that I know you from somewhere. Are you a police officer?"

He took a long toke on his beer, then carefully replaced his glass on the bar. "None of your business," he mumbled.

"Oh…okay."

His buddy on the left resumed their conversation, and Malone became animated again. I slid off the barstool and approached the pool-playing crowd, watching the sergeant out of the corner of my eye.

Faking a witness search was easy, having done it countless times for real. My empty glass finally gave me an excuse to return to the bar. Malone glanced at me. I shrugged.

"No luck."

"Maybe you should try the sexy state."

I frowned, then realized he meant the Secretary of State.

"Yeah, trace the address on his license. Or run a skip trace." I looked at him in the mirror. "Do you do that kind of stuff in your off hours?"

He frowned. "Uh-huh."

I took a calculated risk that he'd forget our entire conversation by morning. "Did you know Sam Kendall, the lawyer who was killed? He knew a lot of cops."

"Not personal…not personally," he shook his head. "Everybody knew him by reputation. He tried to fry some of the guys in court."

"He ever fry you?"

"Naw, not me." He focused his attention on a stuffed parrot perched on a swing in the corner of the bar. "I don't do many street investigations."

"You ever see him outside court?" I persisted.

He shook his massive shoulders. "Fuckin' a, lady. You understand English?" He spun on the barstool so quickly his knees crashed into my legs and I had to grab the bar to keep my balance. Malone clutched my good arm above the elbow and yanked me close. His breath was sour and made me feel sick to my stomach.

"What are you, some kind of plant? Did Internal Affairs send you?"

I grasped his thumb where it wrapped around my arm and bent it back the wrong way. He yelped in pain and released me. We now had the undivided attention of every half-sober patron in the establishment. The bartender came from nowhere and slid between us.

"You're outta line here. Chill, botha ya," he commanded.

"Goddamn bitch. Tell her to leave me the fuck alone."

I drew back. "Sorry. I was just trying to start a conversation. I guess I asked one question too many."

Neither the bartender nor my apology mollified Malone. He swayed on the barstool, then steadied himself.

"Lar, it's okay. She's gone." Nick was making the rules now.

"Miss, I have to ask you to leave." He inclined his head in the direction of the door.

"What do I owe you?" I reached for my purse.

"On the house." The barkeep faced me with his back to Larry. Brave fella.

"Thanks, Nick. Sorry about the ruckus."

I had a clear view of Larry's face over the peacemaker's curly mop. Desperate for any indication of his possible involvement with Sam, I asked loudly "What about Cooper Hart, Malone? Who killed him?"

It took a couple seconds for my question to penetrate his alcohol-soaked brain. Then, eyes bulging, he lunged at me, knocking Nick aside like an insect. Three of his cohorts jumped up and, with great effort, wrestled him back to the bar. Nick collected himself, grabbed me firmly by the shoulders and pushed me unceremoniously to the door.

"Out."

"My coat."

He loosened his grip, allowing me to retrieve it, but stood with his arms crossed, blocking any idea of reentry.

"We don't like people bothering our customers. Don't come back."

I swung past Malone's house on the way home. The driveway was deserted, and the house was dark. I thought about taking a quick peek in the windows, but I'd had enough of Larry Malone for one night.

***

The answering machine winked in the dark kitchen.

"Got a positive on your gun registration inquiry. Subject owns a three fifty-seven Magnum, purchase date 2/21/08. Also a twenty-two, same date." A long silence.

"You sure know how to pick your friends."

I turned my back to the machine. In the darkness I brushed against something on the counter. It crashed to the parquet floor, and I let out a shriek. I reached wildly for the light switch, flipped it on and stared at the broken and slivered glass that was scattered across the kitchen floor.

CHAPTER THIRTY-THREE

The next morning before work, I found a pair of Latex gloves, spread a large tarp on the garage floor, and gently shook out the first of Malone's garbage bags, hoping the contents weren't lethal or toxic. Papers, Styrofoam food containers, and beer bottles rolled out. He didn't believe in recycling, but he did believe in potato chips, apparently any brand on sale. Battle-scarred stuffed animals were liberated next, most with serious parts of their anatomy missing: eyes, ears, appendages. Broken costume jewelry, clipped newspaper articles once believed important, outdated women's magazines, school announcements, homework, and lots of junk mail followed. I scanned everything carefully, then broomed it all back into the first bag. I upended the second sack. Discarded pizza crusts and dozens of empty junk food bags tumbled out. Malone needed a dog to take care of this stuff for him. My friend Kyle Galvin's business card was partially obliterated by tomato sauce. Torn halves of a photograph fit perfectly together: Malone posing with a woman who looked like a doll next to his hugeness and two towheaded boys wearing awkward smiles and ill-fitting suits. If I hadn't known there was a divorce pending, I would've guessed it after reviewing this debris. The bottom of the second bag was filled with ashes. I located a magnifying glass, sat cross-legged on the floor and strained to find anything legible that had escaped the flame, but the arsonist had done a thorough job.

An hour later I surrendered, having scored nothing remotely connected to Sam, finding not a shred of a police report. I showered, did what was necessary to present myself to the legal world, and drove downtown.

The prosecutors were particularly disdainful at morning pre-trials. Monica called during lunch, frantic. The firm was short-handed due to a flu bug. Could I cover a deposition? These question-and-answer sessions with a witness under oath are intended to allow each side in a civil case to discover the strengths and weaknesses of the other side's case but often devolve into posturing skirmishes and pointless stonewalling. Thankfully my opponent was not the sort who objected to the form of every question and it went smoothly. It was also a welcome break from the Malone conundrum.

It was after five when I returned to my office, and the building was dark. The firm's staff leaves messages and phone calls on my e-mail during the day, but after hours my answering machine picks up the calls. I punched the play button. A raspy voice that identified itself as "Digger" had called at 5:15 and would try again at 6:00. I started typing a summary of the deposition while I waited for him to call back.

I picked up the phone before the first ring faded. "Marshfield Law Offices."

There was a clanging sound like someone dropped the receiver, then static. "Miss Marshfield?"

"Mr. Cullerton. How are you? Are those kids bothering you again?"

"No, no. Haven't had any more problems with them. Hope it stays that way."

"Me too."

"I'm callin' from the pay phone down at the grocery store."

He paused.

"Somethin' happened today, I thought maybe you oughta know."

"What is it, Mr. Cullerton?"

"A policeman came by and wanted to know why you were here the other day."

Cold clamps tightened in my gut.

"Did you get his badge number?"

"He weren't wearing no badge. He was in a suit."

"Did he give you a name?"

"Yeah, and a card too. I got it right here."

"What's the name?"

"Wait, I gotta get it in the light."

"Says 'Lieutenant Al Tite, Joliet Police Department.'"

Surprise and puzzlement chased each other like squirrels around my innards.

"You there, Miss Marshfield?"

"What did you tell him, Mr. Cullerton?"

"Well, I felt a little funny, him being a police officer and all. But what we talked about was private, just between you and me. I thought it should stay that way."

My grip on the phone loosened to a mere chokehold.

"So what did you say?"

"Well, I hemmed and hawed for a while 'cause I couldn't think real fast. Finally I told him that one of your clients died, and I was listed in the will so you had to come see me about what I get."

I laughed out loud. "Mr. Cullerton, that's inspired. You're a genius."

He chuckled delightedly. "I thought it was pretty good too." Then his voice became somber. "No reason to put down the dead. Can't do nothin' for Anthony anyway. But I hope you know what you're doing here."

I hoped so too.

"What you did was very special. I owe you."

"You don't owe me nothin. You scared those kids off. I can sleep good now."

"That's worth something."

"You bet it is."

"When I get some time I'll be down to visit you again, okay?"

I squeezed the "never quit" stone while I awaited his response.

"That'd be real nice."

"I'll see you soon, then."

"Okay, Miss Marshfield.

***

Al would know Digger lied to him: after all, Al had located Cullerton for me and he knew why I went to see him. Why hadn't Tite reamed Cullerton out or cited him? What kind of cat and mouse game was he playing? I had a glass of water halfway to my mouth when another thought paralyzed my arm. Was Al having me followed?

I closed up the office, made sure the building was locked behind me and strode to the parking lot with all my antennae out. I recognized the few remaining cars left in the parking deck. They all belonged to the usual group of conscientious late workers. No shadow stirred, no garbage cans were out of place.

By this time of day, the downtown swimmers have finished their laps, and the pool is usually deserted. I had been faithful to Dr. Lopez, but I was desperate for a chlorine fix. Casey Aubury, who works the front desk and lifeguards for the family swims, greeted me warmly and buzzed the electronic gate open. Halfway to the women's locker room, I stopped and retraced my steps.

"Casey, if anyone asks for me can you tell 'em you haven't seen me?"

"You in trouble? You're a lawyer. You're too smart to get in trouble."

"Sometimes being smart gets me in trouble," I groused. "I'm just being careful. Some bad stuff's been going on lately."

He grinned. "Haven't seen ya in a week."

"Thanks."

I changed, showered and made my way to the pool area. The sole occupant floated on his back, occasionally kicking up small ripples.

"Frankie! I'd recognize that flaccid body anywhere."

"Flaccid. That means trim and muscular, right?"

Frankie was between seventy and a hundred pounds overweight. He claims to love swimming because it's the only sport he can participate in horizontally.

"Muscular?" I retorted. "How can you be muscular when the only exercise you get is dealing pinochle?"

"Oh, I get plenty," he winked. "I just don't do it in front of people."

"Where are all those juvenile delinquents you hang around with?" Frankie was the clown of the senior citizen group at the Y.

"I wore 'em all out."

"Frankie, tell me the truth. How many laps did you do in the two hours you were here?"

"Laps? You think I want to hurt myself? I played beach ball. That's enough."

The Social Security set amuses themselves by batting a beach ball around and trying to keep it airborne.

"Can you spare a lane?" I adjusted my goggles to a tight fit.

He gave me an impish grin. "Sure. I'm almost out of here. The old lady says I reek of chlorine when I stay in too long."

"Drives 'em wild, doesn't it?" I pushed off.

"Have a good one," Frankie yelled and waved.

My overhead stroke on the left side was painful and stiff, but with some adjustments I could swim in a straight line. The sheer joy of being back in the water again carried me through half my workout though I wouldn't set any speed records today. How could I get Malone to lead me to the missing reports? Al's face kept popping up. I tried to stuff it back wherever it came from, but he was insistent. Finally the rhythmic breathing and repetitive motion made all my concerns melt away and I ascended into endorphin heaven.

I stopped for a breather at the edge of the pool. Frankie had disappeared, and a lifeguard isn't required for adult swim hours, so I was the only person in the entire pool area. As I reached for my water bottle, a grip like a vise clamped onto my skull and an equally crushing one dug into my bad shoulder. An instant later, another body plunged on top of me, forcing me underwater. Panic and pain flooded through me and I flailed wildly. Steel arms pinned mine from behind and rock-hard legs encircled me. Within seconds I was captured and helpless.

My attacker propelled us deeper. I'd drown if I didn't do something. I willed my body to go limp and crossed my arms in front of my chest as if I had lost consciousness. The tentacles that encircled my upper body loosened, and my arms had a window of movement. I drove both elbows backward with what I hoped was the force of an erupting volcano. I struck flesh and bone with a satisfying *whack,* and the restraints on my limbs dissolved. I leapt off the bottom of the pool, angling away from the human octopus, and kicked for the surface in an adrenaline-fueled frenzy. I broke through like a torpedo and gulped in oxygen through every pore. It hadn't yet reached my brain when a forearm locked around my throat and I was whiplashed back underwater. He swam with one arm and towed me with the other so my face was bobbing in and out of the water. I tried to inhale but took in mostly water. Dozens of wet hands slapped my face. He was headed for the side where he could get enough purchase to keep me under. If I could dig all ten nails into the arm choking my neck deep enough to draw blood, I might jerk free, but it would be temporary: he was much stronger than I and extremely determined. I angled my head to keep as much water as possible out of my mouth, filled my lungs with air and forced myself underneath him. I brought my knees up close to my chest and drove my feet into his groin with all the strength I had left. Immediately the arm around my neck vanished and I was unleashed. I broke the surface and stroked helter-skelter for the side of the pool like a crazed sailfish. I grabbed the edge and hoisted myself up, but my legs dangled for an instant. An iron cable wrapped around my waist and I was flung backward like a rag doll. When I struck the water it was like hitting concrete: pain detonated in every part of my brain. Fingers like talons closed around my throat and I was helpless against them. Semiconscious, I stared into my attacker's eyes and saw my own terror-stricken face in his reflective goggles. Then everything disappeared.

CHAPTER THIRTY-FOUR

I was buried in a thick glacier, encased in a tomb of black ice.

Something pulverized my chest. Bile gushed from my mouth. I tried to breathe but my lungs wouldn't expand. Again, a huge weight crushed me.

"Stop!" I shouted, but only a hoarse whimper emerged. Something terrifying had occurred. I reached for the memory but couldn't grab it. The pressure eased.

"Susan, say something."

I struggled to a sitting position. Kind hands cradled me, other hands whacked me between the shoulder blades. Liquid spilled down my chin.

Two shapeless blobs evolved into gray spheres. Long spiral curls were attached to one of them. The hair, I knew that hair.

"Casey?" I croaked weakly.

"Yup, me and Frankie." His worried face broke into a smile. The other sphere morphed into the aforementioned, wearing an anxious grin.

I struggled to form words. "What happened?"

"You are the latest recipient of the Casey Aubury mouth-to-mouth resuscitation…uh…effort," he responded.

"What d'ya think about brain damage?" Frankie asked.

"No more than she started with," Casey answered confidently.

Without warning, short bits of a terrifying event leaped into my consciousness. Hands around my throat, legs around my middle, my brain siphoned down a black hole. A wave of nausea started in my stomach and rose up in my throat. I started to retch and they held me vertical while my insides erupted.

"Think we should get a doc to check her out?" Frankie asked.

"Shower," I chattered. "Hot shower. Be fine"

They exchanged glances.

"I'll get towels and clean up," Casey said. "You okay here, Frankie?"

"Ten-four." He wrapped his big arms around me and, like a grandfather with a baby, held me close and rocked gently back and forth. When Casey returned, they draped me in layers of warm towels and I rose shakily to my feet, leaning on them for support. An unpleasant thought struck.

"He's gone, isn't he?"

Frankie's jovial expression turned grim.

"Yeah, he's gone. Ran out that door." He pointed to the emergency exit that led directly into the alley behind the Y.

I didn't realize I was holding my breath until I expelled it. "Good."

We staggered in the direction of the women's locker room like three drunken sailors, their arms around my shoulders.

"Which one of your two hunks saved my life?"

"He did," they answered in unison.

Casey blushed, while Frankie looked pleased.

"There's only so many decent lawyers," the senior citizen shrugged. "We gotta keep the good ones."

When my core temperature approached that of a cooked turkey, I wobbled out of the shower. I had to focus on what this attack meant, but the part of me that needed to think was still waterlogged.

The welts around my neck stuck out like tree roots. Good thing I had a turtleneck.

A two-man reception committee waited as I walked with studied coordination to the front desk.

"I don't recognize you with your clothes on."

Frankie was dazzling in a red and white vertical striped shirt with blue stars on his left shoulder, an American flag on steroids.

"Do I hug you or salute you?"

Casey's replacement had arrived, so the three of us climbed into Frankie's antique red Cadillac and drove to Zina's, a Greek restaurant that offers breakfast 24/7, plus lunch and dinner at the appropriate times. After some discussion, Frankie and Casey requested a large clam, shrimp, and Canadian bacon pizza. The waitress never blinked.

"So tell me how you saved my life."

They exchanged embarrassed glances.

"I forgot my beach ball," Frankie began. "I figured it'd only be you in the pool, so I grabbed a towel and came out. You were jumping out of the water like you'd just seen a ghost. Then this guy swoops up behind you, grabs you and slams you back into the pool. I thought it was a friend of yours and you were just playing around, but then he pounced on you—I mean he was puttin' on the big hurt. That's when I knew something was wrong. I yelled as loud as I could and ran like hell for the pool."

Elbows on the table, Frankie peered at me over pudgy hands. "My towel came off."

I burst out laughing at the idea of Frankie charging my assailant in the altogether.

"He rolled off you and swam like hell for the other side, then he ran out the emergency exit. I made like a lifeguard and fetched ya. I got you up on the deck and yelled as loud as I could for Casey. I don't know how to give mouth-to-mouth resuscitation," he concluded sheepishly.

Casey took up the story.

"I heard Frankie scream and beat it for the pool. You were lookin' a little blue, so I got busy." He nodded approvingly. "You came around pretty quick."

My scotch was delivered. Bliss.

"I can't for the life of me figure how the hell the guy got in. And I have no idea why he attacked you, but I think there's a lot you haven't told us. Yet."

The last word was spiked with expectation.

"Frankie, could you recognize the guy again? What did he look like?" I slurred my words like I had had three drinks instead of one small sip.

Frankie thought a moment. "Silver cap and fancy goggles — the kind that reflect back and you can't see in. As soon as I figured out what was going on, I was more worried about you than him."

"So this guy magically appears in the pool with a swim suit and goggles, then takes off in 50 degree weather, soaking wet, down an alley?"

We gazed at each other, hoping someone could explain such bizarre behavior.

Our plates clattered to the table.

"Maybe the guy left his street clothes." I said brightly.

"There's so many nooks and crannies in that old building: if he knew where to hide 'em we'd never find them." Frankie shook his head.

The building was a certified antique. There had been so many make-overs and rehabs in its long history that I doubted anyone knew all the secrets of the three story labyrinth.

"Susan, who was it? I think you got a real good idea. This doesn't just happen out of the blue."

"Anyone in the rest of the club?"

"There was a bunch of guys in the weight room. Couple people might have been shooting baskets." Casey rubbed his chin. "They were all regulars."

The pancakes and bacon renewed my spirits. Their pizza disappeared so fast I wondered if they threw it on the floor.

"Susan, I gotta report this. It's the rule. And my boss Terry will have to turn it over to the cops. I should actually call him at home now." He shook his head.

"Can we skip the report this once?" I asked.

Casey shook his head sadly. "It's my job if Terry finds out."

I couldn't be the cause of Casey's unemployment after his heroics on my behalf.

"Right, okay." I massaged my eyes. "But it's late. Can we let it go till tomorrow? I can't deal with cops tonight."

Frankie crossed his arms across his massive chest. "Only if you get a friend to stay with you," he said firmly.

"Good idea." I was cooperative. "I'll make a phone call."

My cell phone was in my car, but there was a pay phone near the restrooms. I went through the motions of depositing coins, dialing and talking to someone in case my friends were peeking, but I never put money in.

"Kelly'll be over as soon as the kids are asleep," I nodded reassuringly when I returned to the table. "Makes me feel better."

"Me too," Frankie said, in a relieved voice. "Now that we got you squared away, I gotta scram. The old lady's gonna have a fit."

I paid the tab, and we dropped Casey back at the Y. I got in my own car. Frankie insisted on following me home. I pulled into the garage, then came out to tell him I was dog tired and really wanted to go to bed after the evening's ordeal. He wanted to wait till Kelly came, but I offered to call his wife to tell her he'd be quite late. Apparently the idea of his spouse hearing that from a woman a few decades younger changed his mind and he decided to go home.

It was ten o'clock, and most of the houses on the street were dark. No cars had followed us. I walked into the house, thinking I should be ashamed of myself about the deceptions I had worked on my two friends.

Fur wove her way between my ankles and caressed my legs with her tail. I washed her bowl, humming "Stayin' Alive" from *Saturday Night Fever*. She meowed hungrily, and I gave her the full meal deal. What would have become of her if Frankie hadn't forgotten his beach ball?

I retrieved Sam's Righetti file, the one from his locked cabinet at home, and pored over it once again. I thought about Ellen's wasted years in the pen and wondered about her children's lives. I ran my fingers gingerly over the welts on my throat. Time to fight back.

I pulled on black running tights and a matching turtleneck, shoved matches, a small but powerful Maglight, gloves, my phone and a pocketknife into an old fanny pack. I called the office and left a detailed message on my own answering machine regarding the attempted drowning, and my plan for the rest of the night. Then I left a note on Monica's voice mail telling her that if I didn't show up in the morning she should play back the message I had left on my own answering machine. Fur was busy cleaning herself after her repast, but I took a few minutes to scratch her ears. It was 11:30. Perfect.

I went in the garage and sat in the Acura's driver's seat. My whole body was tingling. For a moment I thought it might be a delayed reaction from the events in the pool, but then I figured it out. It was the thrill of anticipated revenge.

CHAPTER THIRTY-FIVE

Eric Benton lived in an exclusive subdivision in a recently annexed part of town. The phone book divulged his home address, but his phone number was not listed. That was okay: I wasn't going to call first. I Googled the address and printed the directions. His street, Sunset, branched off the main road of the development and appeared to dead-end after a few blocks.

If I had to admit to a secret desire at this moment it was that Al or his minions were indeed shadowing me. But no pinpoints of light followed at a discreet distance, no black-and- whites cruised vigilantly. I was flying solo.

The sky was thickly overcast, stars and moon nowhere to be seen. I parked on the subdivision's main thoroughfare a hundred yards from Sunset. The streets in this upscale neighborhood were bare because the vehicles that lived here were comfortably tucked into three-and four-car garages.

Eleven-fifty. Too late even for walking a dog. I hunkered down in the driver's seat, eyes seeking the slightest movement, ears attuned to the tiniest rustle. After ten minutes of empty streets and gusting winds, the time was right.

On the theory that boldness would draw less suspicion than slinking from bush to bush, I strode brazenly up the sidewalk and turned onto Sunset. Dazzlingly bright streetlights theoretically kept the neighborhood safe from people like me. Numbered mailboxes at curbside made the postman's job, and mine, easy. The twenty or thirty residences on this street were set on such huge lots and so far apart from each other, you'd have to drive to chat with your neighbor.

Benton's place was two stories high and about as wide as a football field. It loomed beyond a long, half-oval-shaped driveway that divided a lawn you could practice tee shots on. I skirted across the property to avoid the illumination of the obnoxious streetlights and arrived at the opposite end of the structure, which had to be the attached garage because three separate bay doors faced the street. 12:05 a.m.

This side was pitch black. I took out my flashlight and played it on the wall, hoping for some kind of entry. Sure enough, there was an extra-wide service door, probably made for lawn-tending equipment. I opened my fanny pack and pulled on knit gloves. My right hand reached out and gently grasped the doorknob, while my heart wildly attempted to break out of my rib cage. A gentle nudge to the knob, to no avail. A harder twist, but the knob refused to move. I wasn't felled by electric current; no siren whooped. I forced myself to breathe in, hold, and exhale.

I sidled over to a small window, raised my head, and peered into inky blackness. I aimed the flashlight inside, cupping my hands around it so the reflection couldn't be spotted by a roving insomniac.

The yellow sports car was in the near bay. Next to it, in the middle section, my light picked up the distinctive hood ornament of a Lincoln. I couldn't make out the contents of the third slot.

I wasn't in the mood to admire his car collection. I snapped the flash off and crept to the front corner of the building, scanned the street carefully, and scooted past the three bay doors, hugging the dark bulk of the garage. A second service door appeared near the junction of the garage and the house. I huddled into its frame. It occurred to me, belatedly, that my plan was illegal, immoral, and somewhat inconsistent with my ethics. Dangerous too. But the rules change when someone tries to subtract forty years from your life expectancy.

I encored my actions from the first door with a heart that was still thudding like a boom box. This time the knob turned easily, and the door swung open. A tiny voice whispered that this was too easy, but the welts on my throat still stung and the memory of what he did in the pool made turning back impossible. I ducked inside, pulled the door closed and willed myself to absolute stillness. Welcome to the world of felons.

I played the beam around the interior to get my bearings. Some people live in houses smaller than this garage. I picked my way to an aisle that ran the entire width of the structure behind the vehicles. At the far end three bicycles hung upside down from hooks on the ceiling: a Raleigh road machine, a Fisher mountain bike with about 25 gears, and an antique Schwinn. A top-of-the-line Trek leaned against the wall, probably four grand new and built for pure speed. I test rode one once, my shoes securely fastened to the pedals like a professional racer's. It was like being on the starship Enterprise when it hit warp speed and disappeared into a tiny dot on the screen. Two shelves jutted out from the rear wall. The top one at eye height held bike paraphernalia: tools, oil cans, inner tubes, see-through plastic boxes containing nuts and bolts. The lower shelf was knee-high, more like a workbench. He could run a repair shop out of this place.

I bent down for a closer examination of the Lincoln. A "click" severed the silence and the garage was lit up like a stage. My bowels froze.

"Officer, my silent burglar alarm alerted me. When I turned on the lights, someone came at me. I shot instinctively. I had no idea it was a woman. Imagine my surprise when I saw it was Ms. Marshfield, the lawyer. What could she possibly be doing in my garage?"

I turned back toward the door. Benton's neatly-creased trousers and crisp white shirt belied the .357 which was aimed squarely between my shoulders and knees. Anywhere he hit me, the rest of my short life would be quite miserable.

"Come here, my dear."

The blue eyes that were bemused and polite at the funeral parlor were flat and hard.

I shuffled ruefully in his direction. "You unlocked the door."

He regarded me like I had just requested anesthesia for a paper cut.

"STOP, right there," he commanded as I got within five feet of him.

I took one more step. His left hand, the one that wasn't holding the gun, shot out like a striking python and grabbed my right wrist. Using that arm as a fulcrum, he spun me quickly so my back was flush against him.

"You won't talk yourself out of this one, Miss Nosy Lawyer," he growled into my ear. A flood of sweat blossomed on my forehead. He jerked my arm a notch higher and my shoulder caught fire. I fought to hold on to consciousness.

"You're going to tell me what you know and who else knows it. *If you cooperate, your death will be quick—in the blink of an eye. If you don't, you will experience pain beyond anything you thought possible.*" He shoved me roughly onto the bench. "*Then,*" he bent toward me and licked his lips, "you'll die."

Why hadn't I told Al everything? Why hadn't I bought a gun?

"Take off your left shoe and sock. I'll inject you between your toes so they won't find a puncture mark in the autopsy."

I envisioned myself writhing on the ground in unspeakable torment, a victim of some exotic drug.

"Why in the world do you want to kill me?"

His eyebrows rose in the unspoken comment that I was a complete moron.

"You're convinced that I killed your loathsome Judge Kendall, in spite of no proof. You blab to Brenda, you plant ideas with the police. You are indestructible, or perhaps just lucky, and you won't quit. So, Ms. Marshfield, you have to be excised."

His indifference was paralyzing.

"Like you 'excised' Gordon Haskins?"

In the silence that followed I pulled myself up into a sitting position on the bench. In that moment, he reached over to the light switch and plunged the room into darkness.

I felt for my fanny pack. What the hell had I put in there? The puny flashlight had long since disappeared, dropped somewhere in the garage.

A blade of light stabbed through the darkness. His torch was one of those high-tech instruments that singed my eyeballs.

"Why would I kill Gordon Haskins?" Benton snickered.

Somewhere there was a creak. He probably bumped against a car.

"You and Brenda were having an affair," I prompted. "My guess is she wouldn't leave Gordon, and that made you crazy. Maybe Brenda was in on it with you; I don't know. She's a hell of an actress." I struggled to keep my thoughts straight and the words coming.

"Killing doesn't bother you. You see it as ridding yourself of a problem. Gordon stood in the way of what you wanted: Brenda. So you offed him."

"Very good. Exactly what I expected from you. Have you told the authorities your suspicions?"

"No! I don't have proof. And they're hot to trot on Sam's case, not a years-old murder where someone's doing time."

He laughed. "Liar's poker doesn't become you, Ms. Marshfield. Did I mention that I made out a police report about the incident when you followed me and harassed me at the country club? I told them I wanted a stalking order against you," he added pleasantly.

"So you see, your showing up here in the dead of night solves my problem. It confirms your obsession about Judge Kendall, tragically misdirected at yours truly. It gives me a…what do they call it—justifiable homicide?—when you shoot a burglar in your home. And if the police do get nasty, I'm ready. When Sam Kendall started focusing on me after he represented the Righetti woman, I began liquidating my assets. I now have an extremely large and very untraceable account. If the police don't buy my story about what happens here tonight, I'm on a plane for parts unknown. I'd lose this house, but it's mortgaged to the hilt. No equity, big loan. I have your good friend the judge to thank for that bit of foresight."

"Can you please turn that damn thing off?"

The room went black, and I let out a sigh of relief.

A car door opened, the interior light flashed on, and for a moment Benton wasn't focused on me. I fumbled in my fanny pack, located the puny pocketknife and silently opened it, then slipped it behind my back.

"How did you kill Gordon?"

His light came on again, knife-bright and directed right into my eyes. I shut them tightly.

"All right, Ms. Marshfield, here's how we're going to play this. Open your eyes and I'll keep the light below your neck."

I followed his direction and the beam settled on my midsection.

"You want to hear about Gordon, and I find myself quite willing to tell you. However," he added, "there's a quid pro quo here. *You* are going to tell me everything you know and who else knows it. If you choose not to do that, or to lie, well, I've got a little cocktail here." He aimed the flashlight at the syringe in his left hand and pushed the plunger so a sprinkle shot straight up. "When I inject it you'll be able to speak and have normal brain function but you'll be completely paralyzed, unable to wiggle even your little finger. If you persist in failing to cooperate I'll prepare a main course that will cause every joint in your body to feel like it's on fire. The pain can only be endured for a very short time. The long term effects are horrendous, but you won't have to worry about those."

His words terrified me but I couldn't let him see that. I had to keep him talking, buy time, figure something out.

"I'm dying to know about Gordon, no pun intended."

He cleared his throat professorially and swung the light back at me. I felt like an escapee from some prison, skewered by a brilliant searchlight emanating from the guard tower.

"My plan started to jell when the Righetti child died on the operating table. Gordon and I played golf at the country club every Thursday. We talked business, sorted things out. The next time we golfed I took a wax impression of Gordon's house key when he was in the shower. A locksmith friend duplicated it for me—I told him I was planning a practical joke. Brenda wouldn't give me a key to their home," he added wistfully.

"I knew from visiting the Haskins that they had keys to several of their neighbors' homes, all neatly tagged on a board in the pantry. Of course, I was well aware of the Righetti family because of the son's death, and I knew they were neighbors. The next time I was at Gordon and Brenda's, I simply took the Righetti key from its hook and replaced it with another harmless key so no one would notice an empty hook. I duplicated the Righetti key and replaced the original at the Haskins' the day of Gordon's funeral. I was there often, comforting Brenda."

"So far you're pretty lucky."

"Luck is for ball games," he said scornfully. "Every detail was meticulously planned."

The atmosphere in the room suddenly became unsettled, charged with emotion. Was my psyche playing tricks on me?

"I'm fascinated. Go on."

"I had to have an alibi. I knew Gordon slept late on Saturdays. I arranged for a friend to call me long distance at the office on a Friday, and I told everyone the call was a family emergency, and I had to go to Wisconsin for the weekend."

I shifted my weight. The light stung my eyes like a hundred needles.

"Stay still," he commanded. I complied meekly and the beam dipped again.

"As you see, I'm a bit of a bicycle nut," he resumed, weirdly pleasant again. "That Saturday, before dawn, I biked to the Haskins' house. No one recognizes a bicyclist: helmet, spandex, wrap-around sunglasses. It's a great disguise.

"I locked the bike to a tree a block away and waited. Their paper was delivered, and Brenda got it. It was still too early for most people to be out, so I circled to the back of their house. Brenda was reading the paper in the kitchen. I opened the front door with the key I had copied and crept upstairs to the bedroom. That was the chancy part. Gordon never woke up. One shot with the twenty-two, silencer of course, checked his pulse, and left. I wasn't in the house more than two minutes. I rode home and immediately took off for Wisconsin and let myself be seen up there, just in case. Of course, I was shocked to hear the news."

"Brenda wasn't in on it?"

"Absolutely not," he declared. "She couldn't be tainted with anything like that. It was up to me to make our destiny."

I thanked my fairy godmother that I never had a maniac like Benton hit on me. Then I remembered my current predicament.

"What about a mother who's wasting away in the pen? What about her kids? How many lives do you have to ruin before you see what you're doing?"

"My dear Ms. Marshfield," he chuckled. "You don't get it. You play by the rules. You even help enforce the rules, after a fashion, because as a defense attorney, you encourage the belief that everybody gets a fair shake."

There was a rasping sound, and the light source moved again but the beam remained trained on me like a spotlight. "Rules are made for people who can't think for themselves."

"After you offed Brenda's husband, you used the Righetti key you copied to plant the murder weapon in Ellen's drawer."

"Yes. I knew she worked, and the kids wouldn't be home alone in the middle of the day. It was easy. In and out."

"Dr. Haskins was killed years ago. You're in the clear. Why do you and Brenda keep your relationship so low key?"

"Brenda." He echoed the name with an ethereal reverence. "Gordon introduced us shortly after I came to town. She was a sculpture, delicate, and polished to perfection. I had never known real love." Benton sighed and the beam wandered slightly. "Merely being in the same room with her was exhilarating. I coveted her, secretly of course. I couldn't throw myself at her; she'd only be contemptuous. I knew enough about women to know that."

"Gordon didn't suspect?"

"Gordon asked me to be his business partner: that's how much he knew," Benton's tone was sneering.

"And Brenda, did she know?"

"I fooled her too, for a long time. But one night I made a mistake. We were at a medical association party and, quite by accident, I found myself alone with her on a balcony at the country club. It was a warm summer night...I lost control and told her how beautiful she was..." His voice trailed off.

"Did she respond?"

"Somewhat," he said crisply. "We developed a...relationship. But she wouldn't leave Gordon. Whenever I brought up the subject of our future, she'd change the topic. I could see she was afraid to leave him."

"I get the picture."

"She never understood it was our destiny to be together, that it was bigger than both of us."

This guy watched too many soap operas.

"So Gordon became 'excisable'?"

"Without him Brenda would be free to give me all her affection," he explained simply.

"She still doesn't know what you did?"

"Of course not. I had planned to make an anonymous phone call to the police about the gun after I planted it in Righetti's house. But when the babysitter found it, Brenda and the police were convinced your client did it. I never had to make the phone call." He coughed depreciatingly.

I wanted answers, and I needed to keep him confessing.

"You paid those guys to tag me in the forest preserve," I said.

"I was sending you a message, dear. Not my fault you ignored it."

"How did you get into the Y tonight? And how did you know I'd be there?"

"You told Brenda you're a swimmer, so I've been keeping a swim bag in the car. Once in a while I follow you. Tonight that buffoon desk clerk went to the bathroom after you arrived. I reached inside his little glass box and buzzed myself in, changed and hid my clothes. If it wasn't for that fat old man in the pool, we wouldn't be having this conversation."

I shivered involuntarily.

"The police will figure it out. The Y reported the attack."

"That's enough," he said curtly. "I hope you finally understand that I've committed the perfect crime. And to give you something to ponder as you lose the ability to control your muscles, I'll tell you one last time: *I did not kill Sam Kendall.*"

His light loomed ever closer and more intense. I clutched the pocketknife, hoping I could do some damage before he emptied the syringe into me.

"Don't do this," I begged. Without warning, he extinguished the torch. A cold band closed around my ankle and I was jerked off the workbench so quickly my head bounced off the concrete floor and the knife spun out of reach. In a flash, Benton wrestled me into a helpless, face down position and tore off my shoe and sock.

"It's been fun, Ms. Marshfield."

BOOM! The sound sucked the air out of the garage and I was suddenly deaf. An awkward weight collapsed on top of me; I was stunned. What just happened? Was some crazy drug coursing through my body? I lay paralyzed, wondering if I should be alarmed or thankful. The reverberations faded and oxygen rushed back in.

"Son of a bitch."

A woman's voice, dripping with venom.

I tried to swallow. It felt like Benton's .357 was stuck in my throat.

"I won't hurt you, Miss Marshfield." The same voice, without the hate.

I scrambled out from under the suffocating weight and grabbed the workbench like it was a lifeboat. Brenda Haskins stood at the door, a gleaming gun in her right hand. An invisible rod connected it to an object on the floor.

I didn't want to look.

I had to see.

Eric Benton lay awkwardly on his left side, facing away from me. Red liquid drained like sap from his head into a puddle on the concrete floor.

"Is he dead?" she whispered.

My eyes swung from Benton to Brenda and back again, all in slow motion. Sometimes what the brain knows to be true the conscious can't fully absorb.

"Is he?" Her voice was an octave higher. She was losing control, and I didn't have any extra to loan her. I willed myself to reach out and touch Benton's neck where the carotid artery should be pumping life.

"Yes."

"Bastard. Fucking bastard."

"I won't argue the point."

This was not the glamorous woman who had attended Sam's wake. Flesh sagged from her cheekbones. Lines previously concealed with makeup ran deep patterns around her eyes and mouth.

"Give me the gun, Brenda."

She looked at me like I had asked her to leave me everything in her will. I nodded with feigned confidence and held out my hand.

"How long have you been here?"

"From when you said that he and I had an affair."

She closed her eyes and sagged against the Lincoln, her hands falling to her sides. "I think I'm going to be sick."

"Let's get you outside." I staggered over to her, pried the gun from her hand and placed it on a shelf just inside the door.

"Sit," she breathed, and sank to the garage floor, bracing against the Lincoln. I slumped next to her, so close our knees touched. My brain sloshed like pancake batter, unable to collect itself.

"What an ass I've been."

"Everybody's Somebody's Fool." Connie Francis, 1960.

"You were manipulated by a highly intelligent, extremely psychotic individual," I said thickly.

"I should have suspected," she groaned. "No other woman in his life; we were a constant threesome."

I bit my lip till it hurt. "When did the affair end?"

"It wasn't an affair," she shook her head vehemently. "It was barely a flirtation. He misread all the signals. I was flabbergasted when he asked me to leave Gordon."

Oh, brother.

"What did you do?"

"I told him I couldn't lose Gordon."

"Why didn't you tell him to take a hike?"

"I…I was afraid he'd walk away from the business, and Gordon would blame it all on me."

"Brenda!"

Her eyes sought sympathy, or maybe understanding. I wasn't coming up with either. That was a shame, considering she had just saved my life.

"What happened after that?"

"Nothing, really. Things went back to normal. Eric lost interest, or seemed to, and I thought we had put it behind us."

I had enough proof now to help Ellen Righetti, possibly get her a new trial, maybe an outright release on the grounds of newly discovered evidence, especially since Brenda heard Benton admit he killed Gordon Haskins. I doubted the police would even charge Brenda for Benton's death, given that she'd shot him just as he was about to inflict great bodily harm upon yours truly. It was a perfect "justifiable homicide." She'd walk with any jury.

Was Benton's final cruel joke to leave me wondering who killed Sam?

"I just can't believe he did that to Gordon and he was still…after me." Brenda's body started shaking uncontrollably.

"Brenda, how did you happen to be here tonight?"

"Mmmm…" She rubbed her temples like she was trying to bring events into focus. "Yeah, I remember. Eric and I had planned to go to Chicago for dinner. He called this afternoon and said he had a terrible flu and couldn't make it. That was odd: he had never broken a date, so I was concerned. I called and came over earlier, but the house was empty. I looked in the garage window and one of the cars was gone." She frowned. "I figured he was lying to me. I came back just now and saw light in here. That was strange, so I came closer and heard voices. The door wasn't locked, so I came in and listened."

"Why the gun?"

She looked surprised, as if she had already forgotten it. "Eric talked me into it. After Gordon died, he said I needed protection. We picked it out together, and I took some shooting lessons. It's been in the car and I just brought it in." She stiffened. "I wasn't going to kill him, if that's what you're thinking. It was the first time he lied to me and…I thought he might be in some trouble."

The first time he'd lied to her? Was this woman delusional?

"You cared about him."

She stared at Benton's corpse for an uncomfortably long time, oblivious to her surroundings. "I suppose I did," she sighed. "After Gordon died, Eric was solicitous, concerned. A gentleman. He never pushed himself on me, we never talked about the earlier thing. He was always there if I needed advice or help. At first, I was afraid he'd go back to…"

"Adoring you," I supplied.

Her eyes found mine but they were empty.

"He never did. He was quite distant, emotionally. After a while,

I started to feel real affection for him. He'd respond to my affection, but he'd never initiate it." Her chin sagged to her collarbone. "It was comfortable, so I kept the relationship going."

I watched Brenda Haskins contemplate her husband's killer. When I grew tired of playing voyeur, I gave the crime scene a once-over, careful not to touch anything.

Benton's gun rested on the front seat of the Lincoln where he must have left it when he retrieved the syringe. I found that little item under the workbench where it probably dropped after he collapsed. I pulled out my cell phone, dialed 911, and reported a homicide on Sunset Lane.

CHAPTER THIRTY-SIX

Sirens screeched like caged banshees. Uniformed cops scurried from one garage door to the other like paparazzi jockeying for the best camera angle. Their plainclothes counterparts stood in small groups talking and gesturing. Oscillating red, white, and blue lights created a crazy carnival-like atmosphere that stretched from the perimeter of the homicide scene down Sunset as far as the eye could see. Two detectives hustled Brenda out of my sight. I was escorted into Benton's house and invited to sit at the kitchen table. I couldn't leave: a uniformed guard was positioned at the door. The kitchen reminded me of an art gallery: the lighting was a combination of indirect and track; gleaming copper pots and pans dangled from ceiling hooks. Sensuous works of pottery rested on a glass shelf that encircled the room.

Al arrived, shot me an indecipherable look, and didn't say a word. Ross said quite a few, at excruciating length. At his request, I told the story once from beginning to end, starting with the pool attack which seemed like days ago. His eyebrows reached new heights when I related my method of entry into Benton's house. To explain the doctor's hostility, I had to lay out almost everything I'd found out about the Haskins/Righetti case since Sam's death. Ross questioned it all, skipping around like a good cross-examiner. I told him the absolute truth, as much as he asked. Al lounged against the kitchen counter, his eyes darting between me and Ross like he was watching a tennis match. Finally both cops left me alone, and I dozed off in the chair. It was not a restful interlude: rapid-fire discussions and the occasional glare of light jolted me awake. Finally Ross told me I could leave. His final words were right out of the old TV shows: "If you have to leave town, call us. Don't go out of state."

I was numb with exhaustion. Al put his hand under my elbow, lifted me to my feet, and propelled me out the door. In the east, the night reluctantly surrendered to a pink lemonade dawn.

"Do you have your keys?" he asked as if we were returning from a movie. I dug into my jacket pocket and gave them to him. Next thing I knew we were in my driveway, and Al was wrestling me out of the car. Putting one foot in front of the other was a challenge, but somehow we got into the house. Blankets were pulled over me and Fur cuddled up by my feet. It was good to be in bed. It was better to be alive.

***

I came to wakefulness slowly, like morning frost evaporating from a blade of grass. The clock read 12:30. P.M.? I reached frantically for the phone, certain I had missed court. No dial tone. I followed the cord to the wall where the plug lay on the floor. Pushing my electronics skills to the max, I jammed the plastic thingie back in the wall and reconnected to the world.

The doorbell chimed. On the other side of the peephole, Kelly shifted a small grocery bag from one arm to another. I opened the door and made a mental note to tell her how funny she looked when her mouth dropped wide open.

"You're here!"

"I live here."

"Are you okay?" Emphasis on the last two syllables.

"I think I missed a court appearance."

"I take it you…you don't know what's happening today."

I shook my head. "Just got up."

She brushed past me on her way to the kitchen. I followed meekly.

"Your name's on every news program between here and Chicago. You've been up to no good." She inspected me head to foot, wrinkling her nose. I followed her glance, amazed to discover the same stunning outfit I wore last night.

"How 'bout some coffee?"

I made espresso while Kelly unpacked the bag. Ten minutes later we sat down to bacon, poached eggs, and buttered English muffins. Between mouthfuls, I related the events of the previous evening. The phone rang three times during the telling. She told each caller I was unavailable. The fourth time she disconnected it.

Kelly was a good listener. I finished up by telling her I was convinced Benton did not kill Sam.

"Susie, in the last two weeks you've been mugged, almost drowned, and an inch away from being shot up with some lethal drug. You have a repressed masochistic streak?"

"I *am* a defense attorney." I nibbled on crispy bacon. "Seriously, trying an aggravated murder case used to be the biggest rush in the world, but this last week…it's been like jumping out of a plane. Life is so…*vivid* now."

"Susan, being an eyelash away from dead is not most folks' idea of 'vivid.' First, I track you down in the woods. Then your friend Frankie saves you, now Brenda. Has it occurred to you that you may not have enough friends for the next time? You think Sam's killer is still out there. What happens when you find him and ain't nobody around to save your sorry butt? What then?"

"C'mon, Kelly. I always thought you were a glass-half-full kind of person."

"I am, but I also touch base with reality on a regular basis, a little stratagem that seems to be eluding you. You're not trained for what you're doing. You don't even *know* what you're doing. Let the pros take it from here." Her imperious tone booked no argument. "Did you tell the police everything?"

"Pretty much."

Ross hadn't brought up Cullerton, Malone, or Sam's finances, and I had seen no need to enlighten him. Apparently, Tite hadn't either. That was interesting.

"You tell the cops the whole story," she ordered. "With Benton out of the picture, they'll find the killer right away." She leaned forward as she sensed a point of persuasion. "Sam tried to prove Ellen Righetti's innocence. He failed."

I winced, not enough for her to notice.

"You just succeeded. You've accomplished what Sam couldn't. Let that be your tribute, your payback to him. Go back to your law practice. Your clients need you."

I studied the dregs of my espresso. "I can't. It's not just about Sam anymore. It's kind of about me too." I searched her face, seeking empathy.

She got up and soaked some pans in the sink, then turned and faced me, arms crossed. "Okay, you've taken up a mission here. I get that. You're passionate about it. But passion is not crazy. Crazy is what you did last night. If you keep tempting fate by chasing Sam's killer, I can write your eulogy this very moment."

Fur jumped up on the counter and rubbed against her. When your best friend reams you out and your own cat is taking her side, it gives one pause.

"Kelly, there's a couple things you need to know."

I told her about the text Sam sent moments before his death. Then I launched into a somewhat abbreviated account of my recent collaborations with Tite. Her eyes opened wide like the aperture of a camera as she processed the information.

"I'd say your right brain is trying to throw your rational, logical left brain under the bus."

"I guess. And what's really confusing is Al and I can be nuts about each other one minute, then before you know it we're making each other crazy."

Kelly nodded. "You've been independent all your adult life, Susan. Can he accommodate that?"

"It seems to be a stumbling block."

"Can you accept that he may have very deep feelings for you?"

I pushed the eggs around on my plate. "It's a struggle."

She reached across the table and covered my hand with hers. "What's your heart telling you?"

I put my right hand over my heart and held my left up to my ear like a phone. "Hi, thump-thump. Wassup today?"

"Very funny. You've muzzled your heart for so long, it's way out of practice."

"So how do I figure it out?"

She rubbed the bridge of her nose the way experts do immediately before addressing inferior beings. "You find a quiet place and go there alone. Think of all the things about Tite that bother you or make you crazy. Write them down. That's the easy part. Then next to each thing that bothers you, write down exactly why it annoys you. The first list is about him; the second list is about you. Be brutally honest, especially with the second list. You have to go beyond the superficial."

"People *do* that?" I recoiled.

"Then put the list aside." She continued as though I hadn't interrupted. "Focus on Al—what he looks like, how he moves, who he really is at the core. Maybe you'll be able to hear that heart of yours."

I shook my head glumly. "What does all that get me?"

"Insight," she responded. "The first part is the analysis piece. The second part helps you understand your feelings."

I shoved my plate across the table. "Jumping into an alligator pit sounds like more fun."

We cleared the table. Kelly had to leave to pick up Travis from preschool, but she had a minute to help load the dishwasher.

"Susan, your life in the last few weeks reminds me of that carnival game where the heads pop up randomly out of holes, and you're supposed to smash them with this big hammer before they disappear."

I remembered that game. I loved it as a kid, always scored better than any of my peers. I smiled in acknowledgement.

She straightened up and waited for my eyes to meet hers. "The problem is you're not the one with the hammer. You're one of the heads that's going to get smashed."

CHAPTER THIRTY-SEVEN

"Where are you?" Monica bellowed into the phone.

"Here, in my office, down the hall."

"The news is calling you 'an intended murder victim.' Is that right? Should you be here?"

"No, I should be on a warm beach with a Piña Colada."

"I'm for that. Meanwhile what should I tell all these TV and radio people?"

"Tell 'em no comment. Find me if a client sneaks through, okay?"

"You and every other lawyer in the office. Mrs. Kendall wants to come in around four."

"Tell her that's fine."

Mail and phone calls consumed the day. I was on everyone's list: late on discovery requests, missed deadlines on a dozen cases. Maybe I should give my malpractice insurance company a heads-up.

"You're a celebrity." Betty sat down on the other side of my desk promptly at four. "Tell me about it."

I gave her a sanitized version, omitting the pool adventure and explaining how the Haskins' murder had really gone down.

"How will this affect Ellen Righetti?" she asked.

"Hopefully she'll be released within a week. I've got to file some paperwork."

"Sam would be so proud of you," she said warmly.

"Yeah. He'd also say that's one down and one to go. But I took a wrong turn trying to find his killer, and now I'm back to square one." I sighed.

"But you've freed Ellen. Sam would say you've evened the scales."

I rubbed my thumb across the chiseled letters of the stone from Sam, too dispirited to respond.

"Maybe this'll help," she said, hoisting up a pastel-colored boutique shopping bag and placing it on the desk. "I compared bonus payments from his last years at the firm with our checking account deposits. None of the bonuses came home after January, three years ago. That's about when I took over the checking account."

Anthony Cullerton was killed in September two and a half years ago; Cullerton's first check arrived in October. Did the amounts match?

"Betty, does the date September fourteenth mean anything to you?"

"Our anniversary is September fifteenth. Why?"

"It's probably nothing. I'm wondering if Sam was in town on September fourteenth two and a half years ago."

"Sometimes we went away for the weekend to celebrate. I can rummage through old calendars and see what I can find," she said doubtfully.

"That'd be a big help."

She nodded, nonplussed that I wasn't telling her the significance of the date.

"Has Tite talked to you yet?"

"No." She shook her head. "I expected him to come calling long before this."

"Me too," I said, relieved that the details of Sam's financial life were still unknown to the police.

Betty wrapped her arms around the shopping bag.

"I'll give you this *only* if you promise to review it and let me know what you come up with. Then we'll tell Lieutenant Tite together," she said firmly.

"What do you take me for?"

Her smile vanished. "I'm spooked, Susan. Sam and Benton were both pillars of the community. It seems like they didn't know each other, but they were connected by the Righetti case." She raised her hands, clapped the palms together in a prayer-like pose. "What else was Sam involved with that I don't know about?"

"Betty, you told me before that whatever Sam did with the money, he did it for a good reason. I believe that, and I know you do too," I said in an effort to reassure her. But I felt like when I give a final argument, convincing everyone but myself.

***

Sam received quarterly bonuses in the last three years, twelve in total. When I compared the bonus payments and the amounts the firm paid Sam after he became a judge to the deposits into the brokerage account, they matched perfectly and totaled almost $240,000.

I put in a call to Kevin and told him the bonus totals. "Does that sound right to you?"

"Yep, that's right on. The partners call it the golden age. We took on two really big clients about three years ago, a bank and an insurance company. Remember we expanded and added three associate attorneys? There were only three partners then, Sam was one of 'em, and they made out. Now we have more partners, so the pie gets split a lot more ways. But Sam was a founding partner; they had a special clause in their partnership agreement, so he was still getting a large share of the firm's profits after he went on the bench. Funny thing is, before we picked up those two clients, bonuses were just token amounts for everyone, even founding partners."

"Luck of the draw," I muttered.

"What d'ya mean?"

Sam had a money tree just when he needed it to pay off Cullerton. Also, Betty never missed the bonuses because there hadn't been any before she started taking care of the family finances.

"Just that Sam was fortunate," I answered lamely.

"No, he deserved it. No one here begrudges him a penny. He volunteered on boards, did pro bono legal work for charities, really built up the firm. When the gravy train rolled, no one deserved the ride more than Sam."

"Spare me the Horatio Alger."

"Sounds like you've turned in your membership card in the Sam fan club," Kevin observed.

"Just tired. And I'm swamped here."

I refused his offer to help out, and we hung up. I played catch-up till long after darkness pushed the daylight aside.

The phone rang on the after-hours number that only a chosen few know.

"Marshfield Law."

"How are you?"

Tite had never before opened a phone call with a social pleasantry.

"Dandy, thanks. You?"

"Grand." He sounded relieved. "Remember Judge Kendall's file on Ellen Righetti seemed a bit thin?"

"Yeah."

"Guess what we found in Benton's locked desk?"

"You're kidding!"

"Four volumes of trial transcripts and Sam's file on Brenda Haskins."

"The originals?" I squealed. "How did Benton get hold of that stuff?"

"We found a key with it. You told me where Sam's file was kept down in the firm's basement, so I matched the key we found to the storeroom key. Bingo."

"How did he get it?"

"The deductive mind at work. I started with the firm. Turns out Benton was a tax client of Theodore Iverson. Iverson specifically remembered a conversation they had about old files. Benton seemed concerned about security and storage in case he lost his records. So Iverson, wanting to impress him, not only tells him, but *shows* him the whole set-up, including the index book. All this happened right around the time Sam went on the bench."

"But the key?"

"Iverson swears he didn't give it to him and there's no reason to suspect he'd jeopardize the firm's security. My guess is Benton took it without the firm's knowledge, had it duplicated and returned it ASAP. Tyler said it wouldn't be unusual for a client to drop by the office two or three times a week at tax time to sign stuff and drop off documents, so Benton would have plenty of opportunity to 'borrow' the key. From what Benton told you that night, it seems he had a locksmith in his pocket."

"What does all this mean?" My synapses weren't firing tonight.

"Benton knew Sam was zeroing in on him as Gordon Haskins' killer and the doc had to take him out."

"Benton's no hero, but he didn't kill Sam," I said stubbornly.

"I trust your instincts, Susan, but I've got to follow the yellow brick road, and it's leading right to Benton."

I doodled the words "money trail" on a note pad in the ensuing silence.

"What's going on with Gillespie?"

"You're full of questions tonight, Counselor."

"Tsk, tsk. I promised to stay away from her so you could grill her to your heart's content."

"So kind of you," he said dryly.

"Her mother swore she was too sick to go to work that morning. She signed in at a neighborhood medical clinic at ten a.m."

"So for her to be Sam's killer she would have had to have taken an early morning train to Joliet, snuck into the courthouse and been back in Chicago by ten?"

"With a terrible case of the flu, confirmed by her clinic."

"Not likely."

"You haven't asked about the attorney, Bartley, the one on the jail list," Al pointed out. "It's not like you to leave any stone unturned."

"What about him?"

"Did you know he was Sam's nephew?"

"Everybody in the firm knows."

"He could have been in the library just like he says, but so far we haven't verified it."

"I see."

"There doesn't seem to be any reason he'd want Sam dead. It all points to Benton, Susan, except for his denial to you."

"But there's no physical evidence linking him to it. He got back to his office too fast that morning."

"You are a born defense attorney."

"Just stating the obvious. Those are two big holes in your case against Benton. Are you guys going to give Brenda a pass for the other night?"

"That's being reviewed by the state's attorneys' office." His tone became brisk. "But your answering machine tape will help."

"My tape?" I echoed blankly. "What about my tape?"

"It verified everything you told Ross. Good thing you have a timer on your machine. It showed you called just when you said."

"You took my tape?" I was incredulous.

The silence stretched for the length of a sunset.

"I thought you knew."

"How the hell would I know?"

"Ross left the warrant on top of your answering machine."

I hurried to where the answering machine perched at the end of my desk and flipped the cover open. Empty. A single piece of thin paper lay curled up on the floor, hidden under the desk. I had seen enough search warrants to recognize it immediately. I picked up the phone in a daze.

"You had my keys the other night. Is that how you got in?" I demanded.

"No. Ross applied for the warrant over the phone while I was taking you home. Then he called Iverson, the partner. He had a master key and let Ross in."

My mouth refused to form the words my brain instructed. Probably a good thing.

"Susan, I didn't know about this till after I left your place and went to the station."

"You're quite the hero."

"I swear I had nothing to do with that tape."

"What else did he take?"

"I saw the application for the warrant: it was just for the tape, nothing else."

I read the document. Tite was correct.

"It would have been too much trouble to come in today and ask me for the tape?" I said icily.

"The sooner we have the evidence in our hands, the better." Tite did not sound apologetic.

"Ross is an ass."

"You need a good night's sleep. Then you can really be your feisty old self."

I knew what I needed. I slammed the phone back into its cradle.

No matter how vigorously I swam, I couldn't lose the anger. So afterward I went to the gym, ran a couple of miles, jumped rope, then put on the gloves and sparred with the punching bag. My thoughts ricocheted from the $167,500 Sam wrote in checks on the Great Midwest account, to Ross's invasion of my office, to the memory of Benton and the syringe. I pummeled the bag till I couldn't hold my arms up any longer.

After I cleaned up, I went back to the office. An in-depth inspection satisfied me that nothing had been tampered with. My file cabinets are locked every night, and the only key is on my key ring. I sent an email to Theodore Iverson advising him of my extreme displeasure for allowing Ross into my office.

I pulled out a legal pad and listed everyone I knew who was remotely linked to Sam: family, legal community, courthouse workers, witnesses, clients, and friends. Digger Cullerton too. Under each name I set out all the facts I could muster to connect the person with the homicide or with a motive to get rid of him. I included myself for the mental exercise and Benton for the sake of argument. I doodled. I nibbled. I did some stretches.

Malone's name stood alone in the lower corner of the third page. My foray into his garbage had been disappointing and disgusting. His extraordinary reaction to the name of Cooper Hart could have been an alcohol-driven response to a stranger confronting him with his own wrong-doing, but my gut whispered that once his piece of the puzzle was in place, the rationale of Sam's murder would be clear.

Invading Benton's home hadn't been my most intelligent move, but it had forced his hand and achieved spectacular, if unanticipated results. It was time to push Malone's buttons. The first time I had been happy for the safety and protection offered by the Hospitality Suite and its patrons. This time I wanted him removed from all assistance, far away from a peacekeeping bartender. I needed the confrontation to be on my terms, and I needed to get ready.

CHAPTER THIRTY-EIGHT

If you want a handgun in a hurry, the sellers are on the East side, and they don't concern themselves with gun control laws. But the merchandise there isn't exactly brand-new-out-of-the-box, and I'd heard too many stories of exploding firearms and blown-off fingers to take a chance. If I wanted to buy from a legitimate gun dealer, I'd have to wait three days for a Firearm Owner's I.D. card. I didn't have three days.

I settled for Mace. According to the salesman, it was pepper spray, and a one-second burst would cause fifteen-to-thirty minutes of severe coughing, sneezing, and shortness of breath. The canister fit snugly in my closed fist, and the salesman showed me how to use the flip-top safety cap so I would have great difficulty spraying myself. I hoped he was right. It shot a ten-to fifteen-foot arc similar to a garden hose and my victim, should there ever be one, would suffer no permanent side effects. The best part was that I didn't need a special permit to purchase it.

I went home, ate, and loaded the fanny pack with the Mace, my cell phone, matches, and a new flashlight. If the cops had found my other one hiding under one of Benton's cars, they had not yet bothered to return it. I turned off the lights, put on some Eagles and tried to get lost in the easy rock 'n roll.

At eleven, I drove to Malone's. The house was in total darkness, the driveway empty. I parked at the end of his block, walked through the alley behind his house and took up a station in the shadow of the garage diagonal from his. I had a good view of his garage, yard, and the rear of his house. I alternately tensed and relaxed small muscle groups to stay awake. An elderly gentleman walked by in his pajamas and a bathrobe. He was having such a pleasant conversation with himself he didn't notice me.

The temperature dropped as the night advanced. To keep my mind from dwelling on the cold, I tried to think of ways to force Malone to reveal the truth about the Cooper Hart case. The cop's life was a mess. Was there anything left that he valued? His freedom, certainly. Had he discovered Sam's problem in South Lombard and blackmailed him to keep it quiet? Was that incident somehow connected to Cooper Hart's death? Was the Hart-Malone-Sam connection merely a coincidence?

I pressed the illumination dial on my watch, convinced an hour had passed, but it had been only twenty minutes. The cold seeped through my jacket, and I longed for the driver's seat of the Acura, heat on full blast.

Light suddenly flooded Malone's backyard. A neighbor's dog shattered the stillness with raucous barking. I melted deeper into the shadows.

Malone trudged out of the house and entered the garage through a side door. Seconds later the bay door rose, an engine turned over, and the old Silverado chugged out. If he went left, I'd be spotlit like a vase in a china cabinet. I gathered myself for a frantic dash up the alley.

Thankfully, he turned to the right. The car paused and the overhead door descended. I strained to make out his license plate as he drove away. CEN 446. Only one taillight was working: the other was decommissioned as a result of the smash-up.

The house was probably empty; I debated whether to search it or follow Malone. His destination was likely a bar, but were any still open at this hour?

I made a snap decision, sprinted back to my car, and roared through the alley after him. I gambled that he had turned right. A single taillight glowed about five blocks ahead. If it wasn't Malone, I was on to plan B, whatever that was.

The speedometer jumped to fifty as I gained on my quarry. He stopped at a red light. I braked a block behind him and crept up to his rear bumper. CEN 446. Bingo!

He turned left onto a main thoroughfare. I fell in a hundred yards behind, allowing the few cars that were out at this time of night to get between us. The road angled out toward the mall and the interstate, past the fast food chains and all-night gas stations. I stayed a quarter mile back. Before long the streetlights disappeared, and we were in the country. A solitary vehicle passed us going the other way but other than that we owned the road.

Malone slowed for a right-hand turn and I was almost on his bumper before I knew it. I cruised by, then did a quick U-turn. He had disappeared down a nameless county road identified only by a six-digit number. Malone's taillight had disappeared, but I couldn't be more than two minutes behind him.

I drove about a mile when a vehicle approached from the opposite direction. It came on hesitantly, as if the driver was searching for something. As we drew closer, I saw that the car bore the now-familiar license plate. I grabbed a baseball cap from the passenger seat and jammed it on my head. The road was too narrow for both cars, so I swung as far to the right as I dared when we drew even and kept my eyes straight ahead. After we passed each other, I took my foot off the gas and divided my attention between the road ahead and the rear-view mirror. Malone made a left turn. I noted the spot, did another U turn and accelerated back to within a few car lengths of where I had last seen his truck. There was no shoulder, so I nudged the passenger side tires off the road and killed the engine. I checked the contents of the fanny pack, exited the car and locked it.

Kelly's warning about running out of friends drifted through my head. But I was positive Malone had the answer I needed, and this was the time to get it. One, I had the element of surprise on my side. Two, Malone was not nearly as clever or demonic as Benton, and I was confident he was not leading me into a trap.

I covered the ten yards between my car and the narrow gap where the Silverado had vanished, with muted, cautious steps. My flashlight revealed a dirt and gravel trail, too primitive to be called a driveway.

I hovered at the juncture of the road and the trail, listening intently. The silence was eerie. No humming traffic, no buzzing electricity. An owl hooted, seemingly so close he could pick off my baseball cap. A gentle breeze stirred through the branches of soon-to-blossom trees.

I made my way crab-like down the path, settling softly into each step as if I was crossing a sea of grapes and couldn't crush a single one. After a hundred yards, the trail emptied into a clearing. A dilapidated aluminum house trailer sat dejectedly in the middle, bathed in a sallow glow cast by the crescent moon. Malone's Silverado and a pick-up truck were parked nose to nose. I hesitated. If Malone was meeting a drinking buddy or hooking up with some paramour, the less I knew about it the better.

High above, stars winked like watchful silver eyes, amused by the antics of us mortals. I picked my way slowly and carefully around the entire perimeter of the clearing. The trailer was dark and quiet, except for a block of light that escaped from a solitary window on the opposite side. I tensed, eyes probing every inch of the plot of land and the rectangular box. But for the vehicles and the ray of light, the mobile home could have been devoid of human activity for the last six months. Staying low, I scurried across the clearing and snuggled up against the cold metal. Rising up on tiptoe, I peeked through the window into a room that took up roughly half the dwelling. A battle-scarred table and a sagging, filthy sofa made my first apartment seem like a palace. The light emanated from a lamp with a single exposed bulb, no lampshade. This room was separated from the rest of the trailer by a wall with a cutout space in the middle. I tried to see through the space into the front end but couldn't get the right angle. I crouched back down and, with my light off, slouched toward the front of the trailer, hoping for another window. My right foot caught on something and I went sprawling with a deafening clatter.

I landed awkwardly, face down in weeds and long grass. I untangled my legs and crouched on elbows and the balls of my feet, every muscle taut, ready to flee. The silence was hushed, expectant.

Nothing happened. Remarkably, I still clutched the flashlight. I switched it back on and discovered a metal bucket on its side a few yards away. Alternately cursing my stupidity and silently rejoicing that my clumsiness hadn't roused the cavalry, I rose and spotted a second window at eye height in the darkened part of the trailer. I stayed buried in the weeds for a good five minutes, then tucked the flashlight back in the fanny pack and crept toward the window, straining for the slightest abnormal sound. I straightened up and peered in. The interior here was dark, barely illuminated from the other room. I was focused so totally on trying to see this part of the trailer that all other senses were blocked out. That's when a gloved hand clamped over my mouth as tight as bark on a tree.

"Don't struggle, don't scream," a whispered voice commanded. "Nod your head if you understand."

Up, down, hyperventilating.

"We're going in the house."

My legs were jelly. I was half-pushed, half-dragged around the corner to the entrance of the mobile home. My captor pulled me up the wooden steps, kicked the door open and propelled me inside. A loud click and one bare light bulb dangling on a wire from the ceiling illuminated a nightmarish scene. A rusted out sink and a wall oven with no door hinted that this room had once been a kitchen. Larry Malone was spread-eagled on the floor, his considerable belly pointing skyward. He was either dead or out cold.

"C'mon." I was prodded around Malone to a table with two hard-back chairs. The hand still tattooed itself across my mouth.

"Sit," the voice hissed. I did so and a dot of cold metal pressed into my right temple.

"I'm taking my hand away. You make a sound, you're dead. Understand?"

Nod.

"Put your hands behind the chair."

I did as instructed. The hand slowly peeled itself from my mouth, and the dot of metal disappeared. I heard a ripping sound and my arms were yanked together behind me. My wrists were cemented together with thick, sticky tape. He peeled another strip off and wound it over the first. Somehow the fingers of my right hand remained free. The fanny pack hung in the small of my back, out of sight under my long jacket. My assailant seemed unaware of it.

"Is he dead?" I gasped.

Cold steel started at the bottom of my ear and traced my jaw to my chin. I shivered involuntarily.

"Why don't you show yourself?"

A hand rested on my shoulder. It held a gun, the barrel of which lightly touched my neck. "I don't want to kill you," the voice said hoarsely.

Malone's limbs twitched. His head lolled as if barely a thread connected it to his body.

"Shit." My assailant stepped out from behind me and hurried to the sergeant. It was the same figure who only a few weeks ago had stepped through the evidence tape and greeted me on the fourth floor of the courthouse. A sharp intake of breath, then I heard someone sigh as if her heart was broken.

Tite glanced in my direction, his mouth a thin line. I thought I saw a hint of remorse, but the lighting was bad.

He grasped Malone's shirt collar with one hand and his belt with the other and hoisted him up like a sack of potting soil into the chair across from me. Malone's head slammed on the table and he started to slip to the floor. Tite jammed the chair in tightly, keeping Malone from sliding off. Then, without a backward glance, he hurried out the door.

"Malone!" I hissed, desperately working to loosen the tape. "Malone, wake up!"

The sergeant groaned but remained motionless. I banged my knee hard against the underside of the table, hoping to jolt him into consciousness. He moaned louder.

The top of the chair reached my shoulder blades. I stood and slid my arms up and over it. With no small effort I located the zipper of the fanny pack with my right hand and pulled it open.

A car door slammed. My fingers rummaged blindly through the fanny pack. Knife, phone, Mace! I grabbed the cylinder and slid back into the chair just as Tite appeared in the door. Behind my back, out of his sight, I popped the flip-top safety cap open and manipulated the dispenser so it would spray away from me.

The handle of a gun protruded from Tite's waistband. A silver and black cannon nestled in his gloved hand. He surveyed the room.

"What are you going to do?" I barely recognized my own voice.

He shook his head. "It was supposed to be just one more casualty. Now it's gotta be two. Why couldn't you have gone back to the courtroom? Why did you have to be so persistent, Susan?"

The Mace would shoot in a straight line, but in the time it would take to stand up, turn my back and press the dispenser, I'd have three holes in me. I had to keep him talking and hope he'd put the gun down.

"Why are you doing this?" The close-to-tears tremor in my voice wasn't artifice.

Regret swept across his face like wind skimming a calm lake. "You still don't get it?"

Suddenly, as if the movie just ended and the credits started rolling, I understood. "You and Malone were in it together," I exclaimed, a sense of exultation flashing through me in spite of the circumstances. "You probably steered cases to him, then you split the payoffs from the blackmails. Now that he's been caught you're afraid he'll make a deal and take you down."

Tite nodded. "Very good. Larry's so depressed about his life going to hell, no one will be surprised by his suicide."

"Suicide?" My gut did a flip turn.

"This is Malone's extra gun." Tite raised the weapon in his hand. "He keeps it in his car. I called him from a pay phone and told him to meet me here."

The synapses were burning. "Were you blackmailing Sam about Anthony Cullerton?"

"Who?" Tite looked at me blankly.

"Was Sam paying you off?"

"He was one of our accounts receivable," Tite answered laconically. "But he wanted to pull the plug."

I felt like I was awakening from a weeks-long sleep, slowly starting to focus. "Sam was on to your scheme, so you had to take him out before he blew the whistle."

"I knew you were a genius from the minute I first saw you."

He leaned over, grabbed Malone's limp right hand and put the big gun in it. I shrank back in horror as he slipped the safety off and placed

Malone's index finger on the trigger. With one hand he yanked Malone by the hair into an upright position. With the other hand he brought Malone's gun hand up so the barrel was two inches from his temple.

A car horn blasted the night, seeming to come from right outside the door. The braying sound continued, incessantly. Tite's face twisted in alarm, and he turned toward the entrance, the gun momentarily forgotten and pointing toward the floor. A discordant clang ensued, like pots and pans banging together. I sprang to my feet, spun around, and aimed the spray at Tite, then jammed my thumb down on the nozzle. The one-second burst made a reassuring hiss.

"Goddamn!" He could barely get the word out he was coughing so violently. I whirled around to see him doubled over, sneezing and gasping. I held my breath, gave him a wide berth and sprinted to the open door.

"Marshfield!" he choked out. "Don't move."

I bolted through the doorway, leaped down the steps, spun around the corner of the trailer and plastered myself against the back wall. Tite sounded like he was coughing up his intestines. He would expect me to run back to my car, but what would that accomplish? I should phone 911 but I needed a quiet place where I could get the phone out and manipulate the buttons behind my back. Mostly I needed to free my arms. The forest beyond the small clearing was a black morass: no help there.

In a few minutes, the hacking lessened, and Tite burst through the front door.

"Marshfield!" he shouted in a tone that left no doubt he was the hunter, and I was the hapless prey. I continued around the trailer to the opposite front corner and peered around the edge with one eye. Tite pounded down the path toward the road, a swath of brilliant white light slashing from side to side in front of him. A minute later, a raucous clatter split the night, followed by an expletive from the lieutenant.

I darted behind Malone's vehicle to get a better view of Al's movements. His searchlight cut to the left, then bobbed down the road to the right, in the direction of my car.

Malone's bashed-in quarter panel had a few sharp, rusty edges. I selected the meanest blade-like plane, turned my back to it and started sawing at the tape that bound my wrists, trying not to sever a major artery. My arms ached within a minute from the unnatural angle and effort. I increased the pressure, oblivious to infection or pain, certain that Tite would kill Malone and me unless I could get free. One layer of tape split and the bond loosened a fraction.

The bobbing light that was Tite's lantern reappeared through the trees headed in my direction in a jerky rhythm. I redoubled my efforts, the second layer split and I was free. Tite's light bounced from side to side now as if he was running. Something, probably the voice of reason, told me to dash into the woods and call the cops. But what would happen to Malone? I rubbed my arms and legs vigorously to restore circulation and ducked back into the cabin. Malone was holding his head. The Mace had dissipated.

"Malone!" I ran to him.

He looked at me in confused stupefaction. "Where's Al?"

"Tite wants to kill you before you can rat him out. He got your gun from your truck. He was going to make it look like a suicide."

Malone shook his head in disbelief.

"Listen!" I said desperately. "I maced Al and escaped. He's out there looking for me now, but he'll be back soon. We gotta stop him!"

Malone looked at a spot on the floor which grew larger as we stared. Together we traced the source to my forearm, which was dripping blood. The sight seemed to revitalize him.

"Ma…a…rsh…field." Tite's singsong call wafted through the night air, making my hair stand on end. "You're here…I know you're here." His tone had the sweet allure of a snake oil salesman.

Malone's face puckered as he struggled for understanding. Without another word, he bent over and lifted his pant leg, revealing an ankle holster. He unsnapped it and handed me a small gun.

"Hide!" he grunted, and gestured to the second room. I bounded through the doorway into the other room, positioning myself out of sight but with a view of most of the kitchen.

"Larry." Al's voice was silky smooth, quiet.

"Al, what's going on?" It was not a greeting but a plaintive question.

"Last thing I remember you had your arm around me, then I passed out."

"Yeah, you had me worried." Al came into view now, right hand extended to Malone, left in his pocket. He started to ease his left hand out. Something metallic glinted in the light.

"Stop, Tite! Don't move your hands." I swung into the space between the two rooms, instinctively adopting the shooter's stance from the movies, my gun aimed at the middle of Tite's chest.

Tite swung his head in my direction. Without warning Malone stood quickly, grabbed Tite's left hand and arm and slammed it into his upraised knee. The metallic object clattered to the floor.

"Stunner?" Malone looked wide-eyed at Al.

Tite's right fist came from nowhere and walloped Malone's jaw with a sickening crack. He dropped like a sack of wet cement. Tite stood over him, fist clenched, then turned deliberately toward me. As he reached into his jacket under his left arm, I remembered his shoulder holster.

I aimed above his head and squeezed the trigger. The shot pinged off the wall behind Tite and he flinched.

"Take your jacket off. Keep the gun in the holster," I commanded in a surprisingly commanding voice.

His eyes calculated every possible scenario.

"That's the first time you've ever shot a weapon," he pointed out pleasantly. "You won't shoot another human being."

His arm stayed inside his jacket.

"Maybe not. But I'd shoot you, Tite."

He smirked. His arm slowly slid out from under his coat. When the barrel of his gun came into view I swung the little .22 from Tite's chest to the bulb that hung over the kitchen table, steadied my right wrist with my left hand and shot off another round. The bulb shattered with a popping sound and darkness smothered the trailer. I dodged into the other room, which was also dark, and dropped to all fours.

"Suuu...san." I could feel Tite's presence fill the arc between the rooms. I took small, regular breaths and envisioned myself on a faraway beach so his ESP wouldn't detect my presence.

"It wasn't supposed to end like this," he said softly.

What *was* it supposed to end like? I replied silently. Tite strode to the middle of the room from where he dominated the entire space. As my eyes grew accustomed to the dark, I watched him pivot in a small circle, straining to hear the faintest movement.

"I haven't got time for hide and seek!" he announced harshly. He turned on his heel and marched back toward the kitchen, then stopped abruptly, listening for telltale rustling on my part. I caught myself half-rising and froze.

"You got no place to hide, Marshfield. And no pepper spray. I found it outside."

Tite swept out of the trailer, slamming the door behind him. He'd be back. Maybe I could shoot him in the arm or leg. But the little .22 would barely slow him down unless I hit him in the head or chest. I didn't know if I could do that.

A car door clapped shut. I raced blindly into the kitchen, kicking something and sending it skidding across the floor. The stunner! I grabbed it on the run and crouched low next to the door. When Tite entered, I'd jam the stunner into his leg, paralyze him, then call the cops. Fear gave way to a naive hope.

Shuddering silence.

Where was Tite? What was he doing? The seconds leapfrogged into minutes.

Malone made a sound not unlike a lobster about to be boiled alive.

"Malone, are you okay?"

A moan, then Malone struggled to a sitting position.

"Tite's outside!"

"What say?"

I brought him current.

"You still got my little gun?"

I was fishing in my jacket pocket when the door exploded open and a small, heavy object whizzed past me on the floor, hit a table leg and spun crazily away.

"Oh, God! Grenade!" Malone yelled. "Get outta here! Twenty-second fuse!" He scrambled to his feet and lurched toward the door.

"No!" I pushed him back. "That's what Tite wants—he's waiting for us. The window—let's get out that way!"

Malone's forehead furrowed. He nodded and we sprinted to the other room. He yanked at the window and it screeched open. He turned, gestured for me to go first and shoved me through.

"Run like hell," he whispered hoarsely.

I tumbled out, sprawled on the ground and took off for the woods. How far do you have to run to get away from a grenade blast? At the edge of the clearing, I took a quick look back to see Malone rise slowly from the ground and lurch in my direction.

I ran about ten yards through the woods, oblivious to the branches and brambles tearing at my clothes. An explosion like a sonic boom lit up the scene like a major league ballpark at night, and the ground shook underneath me. I dove behind a tree and wrapped my arms around my head, not knowing if there would be more explosions. After a minute, I peeked out to locate Malone. The roof of the trailer was leaning at a crazy angle and flames were licking up from inside.

"Malone!" I yelled.

"Over here!" The voice drifted weakly from my right.

I thrashed though the underbrush in the direction of the sound. The fire provided some ambient light, but I couldn't see clearly and didn't want to turn on the flashlight in the event Tite was still lurking about. Finally I made my way back to within a few feet of the clearing. Malone was flat on his back, staring at a spot a few feet into the woods. The unnaturalness of the scene brought me to an abrupt halt.

"Susan, help!" The call didn't issue from Malone but from the woods where he was staring.

I reached into my pocket for Malone's .22.

"Help!" The voice, which I recognized now as Tite's, held a new urgency.

"Al, listen to me!" Malone begged. "The girl's outta here. She's smart. She'll get back to Ross and tell him everything. You gotta make her look crazy. When they find my body here, they'll know she's right and they won't stop till they find you. Let me go, I won't rat you out, ever. When I show up like usual and everything's hunky-dory, they'll think she's gone 'round the bend and they'll commit her."

Tite was silent. The flames from the trailer flickered behind him like a scene from hell.

"Nice try, Lar," the disembodied voice floated from the brush. "But I can't spend the rest of my life wondering when you're going to up the ante on me. Nope, it's over, partner."

Bushes parted like a center stage curtain and Tite appeared, gun trained on Malone. He was less than ten feet from me. "How you die doesn't matter anymore. Marshfield fucked everything up." He sighted his weapon down at Malone.

"Tite!" I barked his name, dodged behind a tree and went down on one knee. Tite's gun swung to the space I had just vacated and thundered twice. The bullets whistled through the foliage where I had been standing seconds before.

"Susan?" Tite cried with a strange catch in his voice.

Malone made a clumsy dive for Tite's legs. Al swung his weapon back toward the sergeant. In that second I drew a bead on his chest and squeezed the trigger, twice. "Don't let me kill him," I begged silently

Tite's face, illuminated by the raging fire, was a sculpture of astonishment. His eyes searched for me as his legs gave way and he fell to the ground, blood seeping from his fingers as they clutched his chest. My own life force seemed to drain away, and I looked curiously at myself to see where I had been shot.

Malone crawled over to Tite, grabbed his gun and backed away, saying something I couldn't comprehend. I found myself kneeling beside Al.

"You...are a...piece of...work," he said weakly.

I shook my head in denial.

"Sam..." His body went into spasm.

"Al!" I took his hand and pressed it into mine. His facial muscles thawed a degree.

"Sam wanted...to do right...at the end." He struggled for breath, a rattling, choking effort.

"Didn't let him." The eyes disappeared into themselves like water draining down a sink. The hand in mine turned to clay and his body fused into the soft ground.

Something touched my shoulder. "You gotta phone?"

Al's face was a death mask. I touched his cheek, then wiped my hand, wet with his blood, on my jacket.

"Sorry, Marshfield." Malone was gruffly sympathetic. "We need to get help out here."

I fumbled in the fanny pack and gave Malone the phone. "You... you call."

I staggered around the edge of the clearing, half seared by the fire, half numb with the night chill. I needed to get far away from the lifeless figure on the forest floor, that mass that used to be a human being and was now a slowly cooling cluster of molecules. My stomach couldn't hold itself together and I brought up whatever was in there. I stayed on my hands and knees for a long time.

I rolled over. The moon had departed but one star was particularly luminous in the black sky. I lay on my back, staring at the pinpoint of light.

CHAPTER THIRTY-NINE

Every law bone in my body screamed "Shut up!" when the police started their questions. But a dead body, a suspended cop, an exploded house trailer, and a lawyer intimately involved in a second homicide seemed to raise a lot of issues.

Fortunately, the trailer was out of the city's jurisdiction, and the county cops were a shade warmer and fuzzier than their city counterparts. Malone was taken away in the cops' divide-and-conquer routine. I related my story to the officer in charge, Walters, against a now-familiar backdrop of sirens and flashing lights. He was alternately incredulous and spellbound. When I told him about the clanging noise that distracted Tite, Walters disclosed that a current teenage pastime was flinging aluminum cans onto the road in the wee hours and that in fact a few hundred cans were scattered on the blacktop near the driveway. I told him that if he ever identified the kids who pitched the cans I'd give them a generous reward.

When Chief Ross from Joliet made a guest appearance, Walters treated him with courtesy but not much more. I watched with interest as the county cop and the homicide chief spoke intently, presumably regarding Tite's dereliction of duty. Ross was disbelieving at first, but as the details fell into place, his face hardened into a concrete slab.

The authorities wouldn't let me drive alone, so I was chauffeured home in an unmarked car while a uniform followed driving the Acura. My driver was pleasant and didn't ask questions.

I now knew the "who" of Sam's murder but the "why" was still out there. I tried putting the emotionally-charged events of the night into a timeline, hoping to see something that had eluded me, but the effort was like trying to stop ten runaway trains at once. Mostly I tried not to think about my final confrontation with Tite.

I had one last chance for an answer: one person left who knew the real story. I called him about an hour after I got home. Malone wasn't anxious to meet me, but relented when I reminded him that I had saved his life, twice. We arranged to get together at a coffee shop when it opened in a half-hour. It didn't occur to him to ask how I obtained his home number.

***

Malone was waiting at The Good Bean when I arrived. We sat at a table near the door. We both wanted to get this over quickly.

"How'd you know about the trailer?"

I explained how I'd followed him from his house.

"Were you still bird-dogging me about the Hart case? Why you got a hard-on about that?"

I shook my head at the physical impossibility of his question. "You were my last chance in the ninth, Larry. Every other lead into Sam's murder was a strikeout. If you hadn't gone to meet Al last night I'd still be freezin' in your alley."

Malone grinned at the thought, then turned serious. "Al told me how he gamed you. I thought he was playin' with fire, but he didn't see it that way. He was really pissed when I told him what happened at the Hospitality Suite."

I took a slow sip of coffee. The outwitter had clearly put one over on the outwitted. But who was I kidding? Al and I had some improbable chemistry going on, but neither of us had been honest with the other. Our agendas were totally opposite: mine to find Sam's killer, his to hide.

"Marshfield." Malone's growl reminded me that we weren't here to psychoanalyze my relationship with Al. "What did you wanna talk about?"

I leaned toward him, eagerness trumping exhaustion. "What was Sam paying for, Larry? What did you and Al have on him?"

Malone scratched at whiskers that sprouted from his cheeks like thistles. "You owe me," I warned.

He reached for a cracked billfold, pulled out a five-dollar bill and slid it across the table to me.

"You be my lawyer. Then I can talk, and you gotta keep it secret."

He was way ahead of me on that one. "You bet. Privileged." This little subterfuge was minor compared to some of the things I'd done in the last week, and I was beyond caring. I stuffed the five in my pocket.

"Last night, Al said Sam was one of your 'accounts receivables.' What did he mean? How did that happen?"

Malone's face bunched up, his eyes scanned the coffee shop. He drew his chair close to mine and leaned forward, elbows on thighs, fingers interlocked.

"Okay. It starts with Cooper Hart. The kid was a straight arrow, Eagle Scout, the real deal. He died when someone fed him Mexican Brown and microdots, three times as much as any human being could handle."

I groaned inwardly. Mexican heroin and LSD, a lethal combination.

"Hart went missing with two friends during a party. When he came back, he started weirding out, just acting crazy. Couple minutes later he was dead."

"I got a lead on one of the guys he disappeared with, turned out to be someone I knew, told me what went down. The guy's long gone from here now."

I looked at Malone expectantly.

"The *third* guy..." He pointed his index fingers at me like they were twin guns. "Was Sam's son Harry. He fed Cooper the drugs...killed his best friend."

I felt Sam's presence at the small table. I looked at my friend, bewildered. His eyes slid away, then came back and met mine with an expression that managed to encompass both sorrow and hope.

"Al thought we hit the jackpot." Malone's words floated above me like cumulus clouds in a summer sky. "Problem was, Harry was just a college kid, barely survivin' on a part-time job. Sam was a big-shot, had a lot to lose if his kid got indicted for DIH."

Drug-induced homicide.

"Tite reeled him in," Larry continued. "I handled the lowlifes, but I wasn't going to mess with a lawyer. Sam was Al's only customer."

I shook my head, not wanting to believe but knowing Malone's story was irrefutable. Sam faded away.

"How much did he pay you?"

"Twenty-five hundred a month. Al and I split everything down the middle."

"How long?"

"About three years, till your friend decided he didn't want to play anymore."

"You remember what month Sam started paying you?"

Malone scratched his head with a grimy hand. "I s'pose this is important?"

"No, I'm wasting my time and yours."

"Okay, okay. Don't get huffy. Lessee, Hart kicked in spring, we wised up to the Kendall kid pretty soon. So probably June three years ago."

Sam had written the first check on the First Midwest account the last day of May three years ago.

"How'd Al get into Sam's chambers?"

"He went to the courthouse the day before when it was open. He waited till Sam left for the day, then picked the lock to his office and made himself at home. We had cell phones so if anything went wrong he could call but it all went according to Hoyle. I can imagine the expression on the judge's face when he walked into his chambers the next morning and saw Al."

Malone grinned like Jack Nicholson in *The Shining*. The fact that I had saved this moron from certain death was singularly depressing.

"I don't think Al in his wildest dreams planned to murder your judge. He was gonna push the same old buttons and Sam would cave, same as always. It just didn't go down that way."

The apparition of Sam being savagely beaten surfaced again. This time the attacker had a face. I rubbed my eyes to make it go away.

"What I can't figure is why Al told you *anything* about the cases.

Why didn't he just feed you some b.s. so you'd go far, far away?" Malone shook his head in wonder. "What a fuck-up."

"He liked playing with fire," I answered. "The closer to the flame, the better."

Hmmm.

"Now that I think about it, Al kinda lost his edge when you started poking around," Malone said. He rubbed his mouth with the back of his hand and I could see his brain trying mightily to fit the pieces together. "Hey, were you…" He leered, then checked himself. I gave him a look that dared him to continue.

"Um, that about do it, Marshfield?"

"As far as you and me, yup, we're done." I removed the five-dollar bill from my pocket and slid it back to him across the table. "You're fired as a client, Malone. I hope someday I can forget I ever met you." I stood. "And don't worry, this conversation's privileged."

I turned on my heel and walked out into a still-dark morning.

CHAPTER FORTY

The fire at the trailer and Tite's death were major news, but the rest of the story remained a mystery to the general population. Unfortunately, my presence at the scene fell into the "news" category, but my role wasn't disclosed. Reporters jammed the phone lines and camped out in the lobby of my office building; after two days of their clamoring, I was desperate to be somewhere else.

The state had agreed to release Ellen Righetti without further hearings, but it would take a couple weeks for the paperwork to make its way through channels. I decided our former client needed a visit. Betty called as I was making the arrangements. We hadn't spoken since the day she gave me her records, which seemed like a lifetime ago. I owed her an explanation so I invited her along for the ride downstate.

"Hello, Susan." Sam's widow slid into the passenger seat. "Your invitation couldn't have come at a better time."

"How so?"

"The police interviewed Harry about Cooper's death." Betty's hands massaged each other like two high school sophomores on their third date.

I sighed. The only way the cops would know about Harry was through Malone. The sergeant must have cut a deal. I wondered if it included his keeping quiet about the blackmail scheme so the police would save face. Sometimes the very folks who are paid to administer justice tie her up and lock her away.

"The statute of limitations hasn't run yet. Harry could still be prosecuted."

"They might have witness problems." Malone had said that the only person who knew that Harry gave Cooper the drugs was long gone. Hopefully, he'd stay that way. Malone's testimony, if it ever came to that, would not be allowed because it was hearsay, totally based on what the third party had told him.

"They didn't arrest Harry, but they will if they decide to bring charges. Harry told me the whole story after the cops finished with him. He's been beating himself up over this since it happened. I suspect he's actually relieved now that it's not his own dirty little secret anymore."

"He didn't confess, did he?"

"Of course not. He didn't live in his father's house all those years for nothing."

We hummed down Interstate 55 in a melancholy silence. Miles of bare farmland stretched away on both sides of the road, waiting for seed.

"Has Ross spoken to you?" I asked.

"He spoke to me after they interviewed Harry." She fingered the scarf that looped around her neck. "He told me that Tite blackmailed Sam until he refused to pay anymore."

Her silence was eloquent. I could forget about trying to break the news gently.

"We can't hold one mistake against him," I said softly.

"My son made one mistake. My husband made another one and repeated it, month after month, for three years." There was a sting in her voice I had never heard before. "How the hell…"

I glanced at my passenger. Betty was slumped against the window, her face as pale and fragile as the dead leaves you rake up in spring after they've decayed all winter. "This hurts to the bottom of my soul."

I knew a restaurant at the next exit. I pulled off the interstate, drove into the lot and turned off the engine. "When you trust someone and then they betray your trust really deeply, you wonder if you can ever take that leap again."

She stared straight out the windshield. "You wonder about a lot of things."

"How about some coffee?" I asked.

She was a statute in the passenger seat. With the engine turned off, the car turned chilly in a hurry. "Okay."

The restaurant was empty in the late morning. It was the kind of place that either hadn't changed since the seventies or someone had spent a fortune re-creating that look. We took a window booth and gave our order to the waitress.

"I have something for you," Betty said, digging an envelope from her purse and pushing it over to me. "Two and a half years ago, Sam and I spent a long weekend in New York." Her lips tightened into a pencil-thin line. "We were celebrating our anniversary."

I pulled out a half dozen four-by-six color photographs. The first was of Sam and Betty at the base of the Statue of Liberty. The second memorialized Sam at Yankee Stadium. The third pictured both of them atop the Empire State building. A different date was imprinted on the face of each picture: 9/14/12, 9/15/12, 9/16/12.

Ironclad. Except I knew the date could be changed at the touch of a button.

The waitress brought our orders.

"You're sure this was two-and-a-half years ago, not three-and-a-half or one-and-a-half?"

"Oh, yes. For some stupid reason, I kept the airline itinerary and some other souvenirs with the photos. It was two thousand-twelve."

She took a grateful sip of coffee while regarding me over the rim of the cup. "Give it up, Susan. Why is September fourteen, two thousand-twelve so important?"

If Sam was in New York on that date he could not have been the hit and run driver who took Anthony Cullerton's life. I let that percolate, then recounted to Betty what Mr. Cullerton had told me about his grandson and Sam's money orders.

"I checked what Cullerton told me against your records. The timing and amount of Sam's withdrawals from the Great Midwest account coincide perfectly with the payments to Tite after Cooper's death, then the withdrawals doubled in October when Mr. Cullerton started receiving money from Sam. Cullerton never told me how much the payments were."

I leaned toward her, elbows on the table, and continued. "Sam was balancing the scales. He was giving money to someone he felt deserved it to offset what he paid Tite for blackmail."

Betty's fingers wrapped around her coffee cup. "I thought I knew him as well as you can know another person. How could he keep all this from me?"

The question hung in the air. She took a big breath that caught in her throat.

"Sam loved you and Harry and Gina," I said slowly. "Sometimes when love is that strong it makes people do things that seem… unfathomable. Like you said, he was trying to protect all of you, in his own way."

She stirred her coffee with a tarnished spoon. "That's what we want to think, dear. Maybe he was really protecting himself."

We again fell into the palpable silence that was becoming a hallmark of this excursion. By the time I remembered my chocolate ice cream, it had turned to a brown puddle in the bowl.

"Maybe it's time we allowed Sam to be a human being like the rest of us," I said.

She rotated her coffee mug in a small, endless circle on the table, not making eye contact. "I need to think about that."

Betty wasn't allowed to accompany me into the penitentiary. She wanted some time alone anyway, so I dropped her off at a park on the outskirts of Collinsville where the prison was located.

If it's possible for someone in a shapeless orange jumpsuit to look radiant, Ellen Righetti accomplished the task. She had received the news of her impending release and was working on her resume, seeking a position helping ex-cons. She was quick to grasp my telling of events and Benton's complex machinations. I'd never before offered a job to a client but I sensed in her the quickness of mind and diligence that could smooth out the bumps in my office. She seemed thrilled with the offer and thanked me, beaming widely.

∗∗∗

The city park where I left Betty was five square blocks, flat and grassy with a couple of playgrounds, a baseball field, and tennis courts. I parked and spotted my friend near the center of the park and walked over. She was standing by a community garden: a hodgepodge of plots in different stages of care and growth, surrounded by solid wooden benches. It was a chilly day and the sun spent most of its time hiding behind rolling grey clouds. Occasionally the clouds broke and the world was bathed in a rosy hue. When Betty greeted me there was a trace of brightness in her eyes that hadn't been there earlier.

"I'm thinking you have one deliriously happy client," she said.

I nodded.

"You should put out a press release about Ellen Righetti. Maybe that would put a stop to this 'Solicitor of Death' business."

I flinched at her reference to the media's sobriquet for me since they discovered my presence at the scene of two recent homicides.

"Yeah, not good for business."

"Any truth to it?" Her eyebrows rose in a question.

"I'm not ready to talk about what happened at the trailer, Betty. Maybe, in a while."

She looked at me like she was searching for something but couldn't find it. She slipped her arm through mine and we made our way back to the car. We settled in for the long ride back to Joliet, most of which was spent in a silence that was comfortable but profuse with thought. I dropped her at her house. The front door opened as she approached and Harry welcomed his mother with a hug.

I drove around aimlessly. "*Alone Again, Naturally*" wouldn't stop playing in my head. Gilbert O'Sullivan, 1972. I couldn't remember the words so I just hummed the melody.

THE END

Val Bruech

Valerie grew up in Chicago where she rode her bike to the library to check out mysteries. After law school, the opportunity to practice criminal defense gave her first-hand experience with wrongful verdicts, pathological liars and unsolved homicides. All of these themes are woven together in her novel, Judicious Murder. In the course of representing the unjustly accused for more than twenty years in Oregon and Illinois, she learned that the true story is usually the one buried the deepest and most difficult to uncover.

When she's not writing she's biking around Portland, Or., hiking in the Columbia River Gorge or swimming. Fur, the feline in Judicious Murder, is modeled after Izzy, a shelter rescue cat. Izzy had a red "x" on her cage which meant it was to be her last day on the planet. That was sixteen years ago. She and Val have lived happily together since.

Valerie's been published in Oregon Coast Magazine and took first place in the Portland Japanese Garden writing contest. She's a member of Willamette Writers where she served as secretary for two years.